Why Is My Bra Still On?

Kristen Wasyliszyn

Cusp Literary Provisions

Cover Artist: Valeriya Simantovskaya

Cover Designer: David Provolo

Developmental Editor: Amy Tipton

Content, Line, and Copy Editor: Julia Rylen

Marketing Strategist: Alena Dobriakova

This book is dedicated to my wonderful blood and hand-picked families—you are all as brilliant as you are kind. To the quiet do-gooders, the wonky art kids, the differently beautiful, and the hard-working folks riding the 21A in Saint Paul, Minnesota.
And to my husband, Shawn, for without you, I'd be without you—and that would be unbearable.

Chapter One

Opal

I feel like flipping this table, tossing the exotic fruit, flowered drinks, and fragile stemware—all meaningless now.

But.

I set it. I set the table and need to calm the fuck down so I can charm my friends into killing me.

Opal Slepecki tried harnessing her anger with one of those cleansing breaths people always droned on about. When that didn't work, she put her head between her ankles and settled with the kind of stretch they taught her at Indignation Suppression, a class she was "strongly urged to explore" after a misunderstanding involving bourbon and a bicycle.

The stretch helped.

She scurried to the kitchen junk drawer for stationery reserved for apologies and an occasional thank you, and wrote three notes she never imagined writing, slipped them into the pocket of her rumpled dress, and waited for her three friends to arrive.

At least the table was ready.

The spread rested in the middle of a table in the middle of a gazebo in the middle of Minnesota. The structure, wooden and screened against mosquitos, sat off the home's expansive deck. No pool room or seldom-used formal dining area would do. This sort of undertaking had to be delivered somewhere safe and familiar, where they had spilled drinks and secrets over the decades.

The entry door opened at the front of the house and a voice called out. "You in the gazeb?"

Footsteps echoed through the entryway and onto the back deck. Her golden retriever took off.

Here we go.

Luna, prompt as usual, breezed in, wearing a belted kaftan with a slit so high it encouraged a peep at her tanned butt—*planned, no doubt*—and unwrapped a plate of cranberry coconut macaroons. She placed them on the table with the other pretties. Her eyes had always reminded Opal of a kid's drawing of a sunrise—perpetually optimistic.

Opal stood to hug her.

"Hey, hun, how's it going?" Luna asked and did a double take. "Whoa, haven't seen that dress in a minute."

"I freaking love these things." Opal picked at a toasted edge of a cookie before popping it into her mouth.

Luna lifted her shoulder to her chin and batted her long eyelashes at the compliment. The treats she brought took hours to make; Opal had made this particular recipe a grand total of *once* after Luna had shared it.

Too many components for me. Never enough for Luna.

"You should ditch the neck modeling thing and open a patisserie," Opal said.

Luna's eyelids dipped a fraction.

"Why? Is my neck getting crepey?" she asked, her hand nearly touching her throat as if in a magazine ad.

"No."

Luna sighed and fussed with the items on the table, straightening and eyeballing. "Whew."

"You have at least two weeks before we talk about year-round scarves," Opal said with a teasing smile.

Luna shook her head. "Helpful."

"Haaay!"

Opal and Luna turned to the sound of heels clicking against the wooden floor. Urse strode in and tossed her tailored blazer over a chair as if it housed moths.

"What a day. God, I'm glad to be here. I need a drink." Urse unhooked her bra beneath her camisole, shimmied it out of the arm hole, and chucked it at Luna, who recoiled.

"Ew! It's still warm!"

Opal laughed, her heartbeat steadied by their banter.

Urse turned to Opal, "You okay?"

"Yeah, why?"

She drew a line in the air outlining her outfit. "That dress is a cry for help."

"It just needs belief, plus it's the only one I have with pockets," she shrugged.

Urse glanced at the plate of macaroons and wrinkled her nose.

"Dig in," Opal said.

"Coconut? You know I don't trust anything that doesn't get wet after chewing. I'll take a glass of something though." She picked up a piece of passion fruit and grinned at Luna.

After two tries with Opal's silver tongs, Urse tossed them to the side of the bucket and scooped the clear balls of ice with her hands before pouring Macallan over them.

"Ope, I like your ice cubes," Urse said.

"My ice cubes like you, too."

Two twitchy black squirrels spiraled up the large oaks in pursuit of one another. Autumn was taking hold, putting a slight chill in the air.

"They aren't cubes, they're *rounds*." Luna's lips offered with her splitting-hair smile.

"Be that as it may, Luna and I are so very"—Opal clutched her chest—"thirsty."

"Oh, geez, sorry. This day has made me lose my manners. Can I fix you two a drink made with love?" Urse feigned a pious look.

"That'd be great," Luna said. "I've got a photo shoot tomorrow, so make it weak, pretty please. My chin and neck have to look fresh."

Ruby glided in noiselessly, clad in black, and half-hugged everyone. Her willowy form squatted to greet Opal's dog, her stacks of gold bracelets nearly camouflaged by fur as she rubbed under the dog's collar.

Urse handed Ruby a drink with a nice *round*.

"How's life in Rubyland?" Luna asked.

"Good." Ruby pulled her chair out without making a sound.

"Spicy as usual," Opal said.

Smiling, Ruby tilted her head and pulled her charcoal hair over her shoulder. "Okay, fine. Very good."

"Go on," Luna said.

Distracted, Ruby mumbled, "Cool ice balls." She continued, "I do have some good news. The potential buyers for my holding company have officially secured funding." Nodding, she lifted her glass, taking a sip.

Opal and Luna clapped; Urse snapped her fingers.

Maybe I should tell them later. I don't want to ruin her moment.

An odd quiet followed the ruckus.

"What?" Opal realized she hadn't heard what was going on after the clapping. She turned to the group who stared at her.

"Okay, what's up? We've had millions of happy hours but only one on a Tuesday that I can remember," Urse said. A pencil poked through her toasted brown hair as if she worked at a clipboard manufacturing plant. All business.

"It's definitely odd." Luna fiddled with her silver hoop earring.

Opal hesitated; her stomach felt like pancakes being flipped prematurely.

"Okay. There's no easy way to say it. No. Easy. Way." She blurted, "I'm pregnant."

Luna's jaw dropped, and Ruby and Urse appeared frozen.

Maybe winging it wasn't the best idea.

"Kidding! Kid...ding. It's not that bad. I only have pancreatic cancer."

Grimaces spread through the gazebo. Weeping willows made a whooshing sound.

Opal hoped it would have landed funnier as delivering the news in raw form seemed harsh.

"Okay. Fuck—what?" Urse stammered. "You are in your fif-."

"Turns out my pancreas is gold-star jacked up," Opal confessed. If she made eye contact, it would break her.

Luna stood, with her long arms out, and moved toward Opal. Her kaftan caught on a chair; she turned, unhooked it, and tried again.

God, I hate this. I'm not the hugged, I am the hugger.

Opal, who only noticed their vast height difference when embracing, could feel her friend shake.

Slight frames don't provide comfort. This moment calls for strong, soft arms, and I'm the only one here who has them.

As expected, Urse jumped into solution mode. She didn't get on the cover of business magazines without tenacity. "How bad is it? We'll grab the best doctors. Who do we know?"

Opal shook her head.

Ruby pulled the neck of her black cashmere sweater over her nose and blotted tears, quiet as could be.

"I'm already in the 'pick your epitaph' stage." Opal eyed the wooden floor. It was so quiet she could hear the floorboards creak under her feet.

"Have you gotten a second opinion?" Urse pushed.

No, Urse. No second opinions. I just fucking googled it.

"I've exhausted all avenues." Opal tucked hair behind her ear and continued, "I know this is a lot to put on all of you."

Speaking quickly, Urse offered, "I'm okay. We can call in some favors and get the best care in the—"

"Come sit by me, Urse," Luna whispered, patting the empty seat next to her.

She did and held Luna's offered hand.

Ruby fished her eyeglasses out of her oversized bag. The thick, black rims she wore when trying to hide.

"I want to die at home, not in a Swiss hotel where the guests leave in body bags," Opal said. "My fellah is finishing up his work contract and will be back soon, anyway." She caught Luna's eyes bugging at Urse; she ignored the snotty look and their theories on the whereabouts of her husband. "I need your help with my euthanasia or is it 'youth in Asia'? I've heard it both ways," she smiled.

Several moments passed. The sounds of crows and cattails were amplified now.

"Please. By the time I'm ready mentally, I probably won't be physically."

Opal turned to Ruby for steadiness, but she didn't look up. Instead, her head drooped like a late season peony.

"I don't like it," Luna chimed in. An emerald green scarf with rolled edges held her black hair from her face, accentuating her lucrative jawline.

Urse cleared her throat. "First of all, your husband is de—"

Luna jerked Urse's hand before the word landed. From across the table, Ruby flinched.

"Opal." Urse spoke through tight lips with her fingers spread on the table. "I've known you for over forty years. If you think I'm going to fucking murder you, you're crazy." Opal had heard that tone before—mostly to late-night bartenders.

"You aren't hearing me, Urse. Let's hit pause and grab a drink."

"No one here will kill you, Opal. Not to mention it's illegal in Minnesota—as in everyone goes to el jailo."

"Well, I won't." Opal smirked and flicked her glass, a clean *ting*. "Here's to not having this conversation again."

They raised their glasses without clinking and drank an obligatory sip. Ruby, ironically dressed for a funeral, left the gazebo to vomit in the yard.

Well, she's always been a thrower-upper.

The memory of a guy who called Ruby "the most beautiful woman he'd ever seen" *while* she threw up tugged at Opal. She smiled and slipped into the house, returning with a wet towel. "You need time?"

Ruby nodded. She dabbed her high cheekbones and covered her mouth with the towel, shaking her head with watery eyes.

Press them as if they'll do it. Assumptive close. Get them the notes.

Opal palmed Ruby one of the folded papers from her dress pocket. She stuffed it in her bag and bolted through the house for her car.

As Opal stepped back into the gazebo, Luna asked, "Ruby take off?"

"Oh, you know her. She needed to escape and hide—"

"Fucking tragic Ruby," Urse interrupted, clearly irritated.

"Now is not the time." Luna pinched Urse under her arm. Urse jerked away and winced.

"Listen," Opal continued as her retriever leaned against her leg. "I've been stressed about telling you for a while. Any chance we can wrap this up so I can lay down? I'll call later about my...fuck, I don't know what to call it."

Slow and steady. If I show fear, they'll panic and I'll have to take care of them.

"You're the only ones that love me enough to help," Opal said. "I know I can count on you."

I don't have the energy to make them feel better right now.

Opal inched them toward her front door. She removed the second note from her pocket and gave it to Urse. "Read later, okay?" Urse began unfolding it until Opal grabbed her hands. "I said, *later*. Jezus, Urse."

Urse rolled her eyes. "You're being nutso, but, whatever."

Luna took her note and kissed Opal on her cheek. "You know me, I don't make trouble." She tucked it in her phone case.

Each friend had in their possession the name of the item they needed to kill her.

Inch, inch, inch them out.

Urse's Mercedes stood still as Luna's car stopped—then started—*wait, you go—no, I'll go*—out the long, tree-lined asphalt driveway.

Now, for the other two things I have to do before my exit: find my replacement and tell at least one person what I did.

I hope there's enough time.

Chapter Two

Urse

"Call Ruby, merge Luna," Urse demanded of her car.

Opal's copper mailbox, framed by autumn leaves, disappeared from Urse's rearview mirror. "What the fuck was that?"

She would have peeled out if the neighborhood wasn't so uptight with its plaid cut lawns and blooming cold weather flowers. A far cry from the dirt patch they called a lawn at the trailer park growing up.

Luna chimed in. "Did Opal say anything to either of you?"

"I'm literally queasy about it, as I'm sure you saw," Ruby said.

"Meet me at Jack O'Brien's," Urse said.

Fifteen minutes later, Urse pulled into the lot, parking with a stripe under the middle of her car. Luna's eyes lingered on her parking job and shook her head, then turned to Ruby who shrugged her shoulders.

"I know, but it's an empty lot."

After pushing the bar door open, Urse lifted three fingers to the hostess. Grabbing menus, she mirrored the women's energy and wordlessly directed them to a high-top at the bar.

"Opal's lost it. There's no way she's dying. She's chubby, for Chrissake." Urse said. She straddled the barstool leaning in.

Ruby grimaced. A bespectacled man in a leather apron approached their table. They leaned back from their huddle as if it provided better acoustics.

"Ladies, my name is Dana. I'll be helping you out tonight."

Urse turned toward him slowly. "Oh, you are going to help us, huh?"

Dana wiped his hands on his thighs.

"Well, Dana is it?" Urse didn't wait for him to answer. "Do you know where I can get toxic mushrooms?"

She slapped Opal's note on the table. It read: "Poisonous mushrooms please." Urse cocked her head to the side and fake smiled with her arms up in question.

"Urse. Enough." Luna shook her head. "I apologize for my ill-mannered friend, she's had a...challenging day."

Dana's bushy eyebrows furrowed and he looked around before saying, "I mean, not that, but I can get you Adderall."

Ruby stared at Luna.

Luna flipped her coaster over seven times and said, "I'll take a whiskey sour."

"Make it two." Ruby whispered. Reaching into her bag she pulled out her note and inched it toward the center of the table. It read: "Heroin please" in Opal's handwriting with an off-kilter smiley face.

Urse stared over the bar to the greenish pond outside. A mallard stretched its wings in a mating ritual. She pinched the bridge of her nose and shut her eyes. Her knee bounced, hitting the table from time to time.

"I'll take the Adderall."

Luna and Ruby finally laughed.

The small table barely had space for elbows. So, they huddled.

Luna's normally taut jaw slacked as she leaned toward Ruby.

"I don't get it. How could this even happen? She eats well," Ruby said, pushing her glasses up until they were a headband.

Urse squished her lips to the side. "A little too well, probably."

Luna smacked the side of her arm. "What is wrong with you? Seriously. And at a time like this."

Urse rolled her eyes. "Don't you two get it? She's not really sick, it's just a—I don't know what to call it—a psychotic break or something. For fuck's sake, she's only in her early fifties."

Dana clumsily set Luna's drink in front of her then placed Ruby's on her coaster. He frowned and said, "Oh, excuse me," and swapped the drinks, gawking at Ruby.

"Thanks," Ruby said.

Luna looked puzzled. "Didn't we order the same thing?"

"Yes," Ruby answered.

"Mental giant." Urse mumbled, turning. "Hey, lover. Where's my drink?"

Dana shuffled to the table and whispered, "Sorry, I thought you wanted 'shrooms."

Despite herself, Ruby laughed.

"Here, take mine. If I start I may not stop." Luna slid it toward her.

"Perfect," he said and scooted away.

The smell of popcorn filled the air as old game shows littered the TVs hanging from each corner of the bar.

"I don't know what to do with myself," Ruby said, staring into her drink.

Urse squeezed her shoulder. "Let's just play along with whatever Opal wants until we can get our bearings. No upsetting our little nutjob, okay?" she said.

Tears rolled down Luna's cheeks. "I don't like it. What if she *is* sick?"

"You already mentioned that. Fucking hell. She isn't sick, okay?" Urse snapped.

Luna nodded. Ruby handed her a napkin.

"I better go. I have a 7 a.m. photoshoot tomorrow and need to put on a happy chin."

The women hugged longer, tighter, and warmer than in the past.

"Wait, what's on your note?" Urse asked.

Luna tightened the scarf by separating her ponytail. "I'm not comfortable talking about it."

"For fuck's sake, Luna." Urse gritted her teeth. "As if my shady husband isn't enough, you're going to play games, too?"

Hoisting her bag over her small shoulder, Luna said, "My prerogative."

Luna and Ruby settled the bill and headed out, but Urse stuck around for one more drink and the Adderall.

On the way home, Ruby pulled over by Pleasant Lake, turned off her ignition and searched for the single razor blade stashed in the middle console.

Chapter Three

Opal

"How are you, pretty girl? We survived that stressful gazebo unhappy hour yesterday, huh?"

A sun patch forced Opal's golden retriever's eyes squinty. She kissed Carol's snout, blowing heat into her fur. A signature kiss in case the dog lost her eyesight in old age.

To think, soon I may be too sick to remember her.

Their house was vast but homey. Windows stretched the length of most walls; the only clutter was trapped dog fluff in seldom noticed corners of the mid-century modern home. The soapstone counters were free of toasters, ding dongs, or salt and pepper shakers.

"You. I worry about you, my love." Opal gulped hard as she scratched Carol's neck. "Who gets you when I'm gone?" The dog tipped her wet nose up to breathe as Opal hugged her. She leaned back to look into Carol's amber eyes. "We have three choices. Urse would forget to feed you from time to time, but your life would be exciting. Luna would be lovingly regimented—I know you enjoy a good routine. Or Ruby—she doesn't know it, but she needs you." Carol inched over to spread out the scratches. "I guess you go to the most loyal."

I can't believe I'm letting you down.

Opal could feel her blood pressure rise as she stood, the familiar heat in her palms and cheeks both signs to *slow the frustration.* "The girls better not ignore my asks or they'll have another thing coming."

Tiny bits of dirt stuck to Opal's bare feet as she shuffled to the spacious kitchen to make her usual oat milk latte. She stopped to rub the bottom of one foot against her calf and turned on her espresso machine. The fancy, all-in-one, five-star-rated motherfucking glorified coffee maker that she paid too much for made a funny sound and stopped brewing. She hit the side of the machine.

Dammit, I just can't. Nothing is ever fucking easy. Nothing.

She hit it harder then slammed her mug against it, smashing porcelain over the counter and floor.

Piece of shit.

The rage ebbed up from its hiding place. She jerked the cupboard open and began smashing dishes against the kitchen wall. The violence of breaking glass was nowhere near satisfying, so she threw harder. The backsplash would be better; the plates broke easier against the imported tile.

That sound.

Now that *was satisfying.*

Catching Carol cowering under the dining room table, she stopped. Ashamed, she drooped and whispered, "I'm sorry." After hugging Carol, she guided the dog into a spare bedroom so her paws wouldn't get cut on the broken bits.

Damn. I wasn't even this mad on the day I found out.

On the ironically sunny day of her cancer diagnosis, Opal had a haircut appointment. She'd parked her doctor's "on a push, two to six months" prognosis in the rear of her mind and kept her time with her stylist, Taylor, as if nothing earth-shattering had just happened.

As Opal sank into the oversized salon chair, Taylor had fluffed up the black smock to cover her mini sweatshirt dress. Her space-age boots stuck out like mushrooms sprouting from a deck as Taylor tucked the smock into her collar.

Opal guessed Taylor was of Italian descent, with pale skin, blackish eyes, and a flair for the macabre. She spoke of tragedies nonchalantly, minimizing major life challenges much as Urse, Luna, and Ruby. Hell, she looked similar to Ruby, come to think of it.

She wondered if her group of friends would take Taylor in as her replacement or if the position called for more of a diplomat and less of one of them. Opal sighed, spit out her flavorless gum, and threw it into a trash bin ten feet away.

It wouldn't work.

It had taken the friends years to get the light right to tell their stories. They spoke of their assaults, the infractions large, small, or downplayed, and the ones that were exceptionally sticky. The stories spilled over warmed bloodstreams, over nice stemware and chipped cheese plates, or leaded crystal and chipped teeth. They spoke of the slaps, punches, and last words, the vengeances, and the *told-you-so's.*

And they didn't whine, or it would be worse. It could sometimes be worse.

The women's stories may not have made sense the first time they hit the air, but over time and trust, they deepened and unfolded, becoming less flattering—as the truth usually is. The story heard a million times morphs, stops and starts, spilling more truth over time until it's voiced in raw form. Eyes forced watery, whitecaps swell in stomachs; you go quiet before hearing or saying, "That is fucked up. I'm so, so sorry that happened to you."

Their history.

Then you see why she doesn't eat or eats too much or locks the door repeatedly or sleeps with a nightlight in front of a mirror or takes money or refuses money. You see why she is always defensive, why she can't let things go, why she lets everything go, why she can't say she's sorry, why she says she's sorry all the time. It all makes sense.

You see.

You see and you love her for how the truly rotten of a thing she has to live with makes her who she is, and yet, she chirps anyway. You recognize her because you have a bit of rot as well, and this time, it's presented as cancer.

Opal, Luna, Urse, and Ruby found chirping easier together. A four-piece puzzle.

They leveraged their strengths into small and large fortunes over the years. They made money while they had the looks and marbles, and understood even the prettiest of pomegranate seeds turn rusty pink, eventually.

Taylor, the stylist, was a dark red pomegranate seed; she needed more life to lament—though Opal didn't wish it on anyone.

Opal had tilted her head at the pretty stylist, imagining the woman sitting in her spot in the gazebo. The right replacement, but wrong timing. With all they had going on, her friends needed a solid brick of a woman; no flinchers.

Taylor combed through her tangles as Opal rubbed her nose from the cloying hair product scent.

"Weird question. Do you know any capable private nurses? You know our type of person. My friend is going through rough health stuff and could use some help," Opal asked.

Taylor stopped detangling to think.

"There's this lady I like—she's been my client for years. She's hilarious. They call her 'The Closer' at work. Cracks me up. You'd like Tess. I'll ask her first. You know all those hippo laws."

Hippo? Oh HIPAA.

"Cool, cool. Thanks."

Taylor started combing again. "Speaking of people we know, do you know any professional snoopers?"

"Snoopers? Oh, yeah, I have a private investigator friend, Snookie Bubotz. I'll share her contact info." Opal didn't ask why the twenty-something woman needed it, as she should be in her prime stalking age.

Taylor used her blow dryer to get the hair off Opal's smock and gave her a handheld mirror to inspect the back of her cut even though her hair no longer mattered.

"You are one talented lady."

Opal settled up, leaving Taylor a five-thousand-dollar tip with a note on the shiny credit card paper that said:

It's not a mistake. You deserve it, always remember that.

p.s. Our wee secret. It'll be null and void if you mention it.

It was time to give away as much money as she could.

She'd numbly driven home.

After a day of living with the rough date of her death, Tess, the nurse Taylor referred, had called.

"Taylor, our stylist, mentioned you know someone needing health care services?"

Opal slathered butter on her English muffin. "Sure do. I don't suppose you're free for a coffee?" She pinched her cell to her shoulder while putting the lid on the butter dish.

"Sure. I'm open in an hour, if that works?"

Opal liked how fast Tess moved.

"Do you know House Spy Coffee on Snelling?"

"Love it, yes."

"I'll be the one with pancreatic cancer."

"Oh, vinegar eels. I'm sorry to hear that. I'll be the one without it," Tess said.

They both laughed, even though Opal had no idea what vinegar eels were.

Opal applied a daytime lipstick, changed into a pair of wide-legged jeans, a Galaga T-shirt, Redwing boots, and headed out.

House Spy smelled of charred coffee and chemically sweetened muffins and looked clean enough to pass an impromptu health inspection with straight A's. As Opal stood in line to order, the bell above the door rang, and a tall, slender brunette sporting a chin-length bob, straight short bangs, and ample hips entered. She had a pointy chin like Urse, dark eyes framed by long eyelashes like Ruby, and a youthful face like Luna.

As cute as a dog waiting for a school bus.

The hair on the back of her neck rose.

"Tess?"

Tess smiled, lips together, and shook her hand. The one-hand-over-the-other shake. Bold. "Nice to meet you."

"What's your poison?" Opal asked.

"Latte, oat milk." Tess smiled enough to reveal a crooked front tooth, making her seem friendly.

Opal ordered the coffees as Tess scouted for open seats. A young man wearing a bucket hat and skinny jeans vacated a table with his laptop leaving a dirty napkin.

"Here you go, sir, you forgot this," Tess smiled at him sweetly and dropped it into his open computer bag.

His face reddened. "Thanks."

In that moment, Opal realized Tess was the one—her replacement. Smirking, she said, "How long have you gone to Taylor?"

"Seems like forever. I will never quit her." Tess smiled and subtly licked the rim of her mug before drinking—a lipstick trick so few knew about. She was likable. "Opal, I'm sorry to hear about your health challenges."

Opal never knew how to respond to obligatory comments, so she answered in kind and sipped her latte. "Thank you, I appreciate that."

After two hours of comfortable conversation, four coffees, and a shared scone, Opal said, "It's a shame we just met. I feel like we would've had an award-winning friendship. You'll help me through my cancer, though, right?"

Tess smiled and tilted her head. "I feel the same way. Old soul stuff, I guess—and yes, I will help you."

As they headed toward the parking lot, Opal noticed Tess's vintage Mercedes, parked away from door ding possibilities. "Wow, what a gorgeous car."

"It makes me feel like my hard work means something."

Making sure not to smudge the window, Opal cupped her eyes and peeped in. "Elegant, like you," she said.

"Aw, shucks. Thanks. Weird story. Shortly after I left Duluth and an awful social working slash candy-striping internship, I decided to treat myself right. Would you believe I bought it from a teenager back in the late eighties? A teenager." Tess shook her head at the memory.

"Holy cats, I'm from Duluth, too."

"Figures, right?"

Opal had thought finding her replacement would have been harder. Tess had fallen right into her diseased lap.

Carol nudged her arm, shaking Opal from the past. "I know what you're thinking. I better get overnight shipping on the new espresso machine."

Chapter Four

Ruby

Sitting in her caramel-colored chair with black trim, Ruby Redstone tugged a plush blanket to her waist. She made a cozy nest for her favorite navy coffee mug—designed with what looked like prison time marks—and waited for her laptop to fire up. *Minnesota Business A.M.* played on low from the other room as downtown Minneapolis slowly came to life.

I'll worry about the heroin note later.

The stacks of jingly bracelets Ruby seldom removed clicked against her computer as she searched. After typing "pancreatic cancer," she knew Opal's news was grim.

Pain described as sharp stabbing sensations in the abdomen with nerve pressure around the liver and gallbladder if enlarged; bowel pressure with acute discomfort and incontinence...

She x'd out of the site quickly, as if the symptoms would stick if the tab were left open.

Ruby became still, a game she and her sister, Ann, started as kids. When trouble percolated at the Redstone house growing up, you had a better chance of safety if everything was still. It gave chaos no lighter fluid. Ricochets seldom bounced off of quiet.

She had tried to stay at the gazebo to be supportive of Opal, but couldn't. The need to be *still* had overtaken her.

Only Ann and Opal understood.

God, I miss Ann.

Her sister's research studies landed her in Antarctica and physical mail only arrived if weather conditions allowed, which was seldom. Ruby didn't think it was fair to fire off a note with the news of Opal's cancer.

Might as well wait until she gets back in a few months.

Ruby sipped her coffee and worked on her quiet puzzle. *One across: a large bird. Easy one.* Her gold pen completed the word: *E, M, U.* The capital letters filled the squares without veering outside the lines. *Two across: sugar regulator.* She covered her mouth as if slapped. *Pancreas.*

She folded the *Times* and surveyed her living room to escape the word. The bubbly fish tank housing fifty dollars' worth of goldfish, the eclectic decorations, and original art were safety trinkets, their value in their permanence. The same keepsakes year in and year out kept her grounded; her possessions absorbed the icky truth of her wrist cutting without judgment. Thanks to Nighttime Mom, growing up, trinkets were thrown, smashed, or lost in the fray.

Nighttime Mom had appeared after five drinks or five p.m. until Daytime Mom woke after sleeping the dark off, washed, cleaned, and compensated for her other side, softening the name calling, face slaps, and butter for baked goods. Daytime Mom's apologies were cookies.

Ruby always left them to stale in the jar.

Opal had eaten Daytime Mom's cookies—once. On that horrible but memorable day, Ruby and Opal had met as little kids. She remembered feeling uneasy when Daytime Mom had invited Opal for a playdate after they had met at a funeral. The invitation had stuck out as suspicious, as she and her sister, Ann, had never been allowed to have friends over.

"Mom overheard some ladies talking trash about her at the funeral, like, 'who even knows what's going on in that house. No one has ever visited the Redstone's, then, *boom.*" Ann had flashed her small hands for effect, her friendship bracelets making a large, pastel blur. "A playdate with this

Opal. My guess is she's probably a real dinkus."

"She seemed okay when I talked to her," Ruby answered.

"You would say that." Ann rolled her eyes. "In any case, your weird new friend is coming at four. Ma said to clean your filthy room."

Ruby glanced around her meticulous room, straightened the edge of her purple crazy quilt a fraction of an inch, and headed downstairs to wait.

Daytime Mom sat smoking at the Formica kitchen table, staring out the window to the lush backyard. "Apple season is around the bend. When I see that tree, I see two hundred apple pies and twenty-five crisps. It never ends, Ruby, I'll tell you that much." Feelings tangled when Daytime Mom talked like that, a mixture of sad and nervous. But Ruby knew enough not to trust her, or she would need a turtleneck to cover scars on her jugular.

"Listen, that girl Opal from the funeral is coming over today. You know how I feel about company. Normally, I wouldn't have offered but she seemed like a nice girl—plus her parents are dead. I whipped up a batch of snickerdoodles for you two," Daytime Mom said, blowing smoke rings up and to the side of her mouth. Ruby admired the color of Daytime Mom's real hair; the afternoon sun filtering through the kitchen windows only shined on her. Her elbows and angles were exactly where they should be—no sign of eating any of her own baking. You don't get to look like Cher at a distance if you did.

The doorbell rang.

Ann yelled, "Door!" though she was the closest.

"Go ahead, Rube." Daytime Mom tapped her cigarette in an amber-colored ashtray.

Ruby opened the door to Opal, wearing orange and brown plaid flared pants and a long-sleeved matching T-shirt. She waved goodbye to the rusted car that brought her and said, "Hi, Ruby."

"Hi, want to see my room?"

"Yeah."

Opal removed her well-worn laced leather clogs at the door and shyly followed Ruby upstairs. On the seventh stair, Ruby stopped abruptly, remembering the cookies. Opal face planted into her behind. They both laughed.

"My face just met your butt." Opal put her hands over her mouth to stifle her loudness. Ann turned to see the commotion and rolled her eyes.

"Do you like snickerdoodles?" Ruby asked.

"Do bears s-h-i-t in the woods?" Opal whispered.

"I like all desserts except lemon."

Opal nodded. "Exactly. Vanilla is boring, too, but never trust people who pick lemon."

They nodded in meaningful agreement.

After escorting Opal to her room, Ruby fetched a plate of cookies and watermelon. She closed the door behind her and they began their friendship through comparisons of likes, dislikes, and wishes. They hardly noticed the time when the Redstone's phone rang at seven o'clock. Opal was supposed to have been collected at five-thirty.

Ruby made the *shh* sign and pressed her ear to the floor vent to eavesdrop on the call. Opal followed suit.

"Oh, well, I understand. Yes, of course, we would be happy to watch your Opal. She is a darling. Uh-huh, no problem. See you then," Nighttime Mom said and hung up.

"Jezus Christ. I'm not a daycare center. Butch, make me another drink."

Footsteps sounded on the stairs.

Ruby jumped up, grabbed a book, and settled on her bed. Opal copied her.

The bedroom door creaked open. "Opal, dear, your grandmother is running behind. Something about the Eucharist offering running late. Make yourself at home." She swirled ice in her tumbler as she disappeared down the hallway.

"Is she mad at me?" Opal asked.

"No. Why?"

Downstairs, the grandfather clock gonged.

"I'm sorry my grandma's late."

Ruby's parents' voices spilled through the floor vent louder and ruder.

"What? Oh no, it's fine." Her face was hot; she began her sign language tic.

Nighttime Mom tore into her dad for the same nonsense from the prior night. "A Slo Poke sucker? She gave you a Slo Poke? Jezus H. Christ, if that's not blatant, I'm not sure what is. That bitch is going to have a size nine up her ass. Who does she think she is? Fucking whore. Go ahead, cheat on me with her. See what happens."

Ruby could hear Nighttime Mom stumble down the hallway. "And another thing, Ruby, if you and your cunt friend are eavesdropping, I'll cut off your fucking airway."

Opal's eyes widened, she covered her mouth and held herself as if cold. "Can I call my grandma?"

"Not yet. She'll calm down in a few minutes, then we can go down and call," Ruby whispered.

Opal raised her chin and nodded, rocking back and forth. They waited ten minutes before checking on Nighttime Mom.

"Stay behind me," Ruby said.

Opal nodded, mouth open.

The girls inched downstairs. There was no trace of Ann or her dad as they continued down the hallway.

Glancing into the open bathroom, Opal said, "I think your mom is dead."

Nighttime Mom had crashed out on the toilet. Her green polyester pants and white cotton undies circled her calves, an Eva Gabor wig tilted to the side where her head met the wall. The wig was as close to frivolity as their household allowed. "Get Gabor in here," Daytime Mom would joke on her good days.

"She's a light sleeper." Ruby shrugged. "My dad always says, 'She has breadcrumbs in one hand and a hammer in the other.' Come on, let's wait for your grandma upstairs. I bet it won't be long."

They retreated to her room and the encyclopedia set. Ruby laid on her back, knees tented with the book on her thighs. The sign language alphabet diagrams on the inside of each book provided her endless hours of comfort. Ruby handed one to Opal, who didn't take it.

"Ruby, I don't think your mom is supposed to be like that."

She put down the book and crossed her arms. "Like what?"

"Like being mean to you," Opal whispered, looking around.

"It's only for a few hours. In the mornings, she's nice."

"You are my friend." Opal lifted an index finger with chipped pink polish. "No one can talk to my friends like that, got it?" Her voice may have wobbled but she looked Ruby straight in the eye.

Ruby's hands were moving fast: *A, B, C...* Opal cupped them, as one would a grasshopper. She kept signing, but Opal's hands edged closer until movement stopped. They faced one another until a car horn beeped outside.

"My grandma's here."

"Thank you for saying I'm your friend."

Opal took off a magenta and lime green friendship bracelet and handed it to her new friend. Ruby's first. She smiled.

"You are. I have a lot of friends but sometimes they turn on me and call me 'Angry Opal O'Leary' which is dumb 'cause my last name isn't O'Leary. And, well, my face was in your butt so we have to be friends, remember?"

They giggled.

Opal surprised Ruby with a hug then ran down the stairs two at a time, slipped into her clogs, and left without looking back.

Ruby watched a dented car with mismatched hubcaps take her friend home, and headed to her lilac-painted bedroom in case anyone woke up from the bathroom.

Alone in her room, Ruby admired the new purple crazy quilt Daytime Mom sewed to match her handmade rug that "tied the room together." Sure, Daytime Mom did nice things. But according to her Swatch watch, sober mom was gone for the remainder of the night.

She wondered if Opal was right and guessed her new friend wouldn't be back. She winced, replaying Nighttime Mom's language in her head. Maybe other moms didn't swear.

Ruby went to Ann's room and jumped hard onto the bed, knowing her sister was hiding under it.

"Hey!" Ann laughed.

"Opal said Mom was mean." Ruby hung off the side of the bed, her soy sauce colored hair touching the floor, and peeked at Ann.

"Oh, she's Walter Cronkite with all the facts? Sheesh, it's nighttime. She's good in the day."

"I guess. Mom still in the bathroom?"

"Yep, and I already peed and brushed." Ann wrinkled her nose and nodded, satisfied.

Ruby sighed. She knew better than to eat watermelon since Nighttime Mom hogged the bathroom.

The only bathroom.

"'Night, Ann."

"You, too."

Ruby had gone to her bedroom, peed in her "Try Harder, Charlie Brown" garbage bin with two liners, dipped into her collection of gas station Handi Wipes, cleaned up, and went to bed.

Dammit.

Ruby's coffee spilled on the edge of the crossword puzzle and her leg, interrupting the dusty memories. She stood, setting the mug on the end table.

She moved her fancy bracelets to reveal the friendship bracelet, barely threads and only slightly magenta after decades of erosion, and walked to the most luxurious item in her home, slipped into the deep folds of the drapes, and stood still.

Though she had been dead for decades, Nighttime Mom's voice popped up. *"Oh dear, what are you going to do without Opal? Heroin for a parentless girl. Isn't that a doozy."*

Chapter Five

Urse

The day after Opal's trash news, Urse opened the cabinet housing a dozen mugs, pushed the "Urse Rhymes with Terse" coffee cup aside, and grabbed the one reading "ugh" in lower case letters.

Yeah, feels right.

She emptied two stevia packets from last month's Jaipur quartz convention into the cup, filled it with coffee, then settled into her sofa. The convention offered enough freebies to keep her stocked in spices and sugar packets for a year. *All tax-free.*

Her cell chimed and flashed a picture of Opal at a charity gala. If Urse looked closely, she could tell Opal had her middle finger out just a little around her wine glass as her mischievous smile faced the camera. Urse picked up the call.

"Mornin'."

"Morning. Listen, I need you to get cracking on a few things for me," Opal said.

Urse fiddled with the belt of her silk bathrobe kimono as Opal bossed her over the phone. She lit a joint and took a deep toke.

"So, about my cancer—the subject I want to talk about the least. Wait, what's that sound? Urse, are you *smoking*?"

She exhaled. "It's chill."

"It's 9 a.m."

"If not now, when? Opal, c'mon."

"Fine, I'll buy you a trucker hat that says, 'wake and bake' and you can pair it with one of your fancy boardroom outfits and really keep 'em guessing."

"Okay, okay, get me the hat. I'm listening."

"Buy a cool dress for our last party, have some of that bitter-ass coffee you like, and for Chrissake, eat something. Oh, and I need some of those poisonous mushrooms you know about. After that, call that hot brother of yours. Johnny should know I'm sick; do *not* tell him you are helping me die. Make sure he doesn't blab. And for fuck's sake, if you're wearing that weird kimono, go shower."

Of course, the note. Poisonous mushrooms. She's slick as my second husband's hair.

Urse sighed. "Slow down, quick talker. Your mission is batshit. Not sure how many times I need to say it, I'm not killing anyone. Well, maybe my granite vendor from Ontario, but definitely not you."

"Two."

"Two *what*?" Urse asked.

"How many times you've said it, both of which were annoying and insensitive."

Urse inhaled a noisy toke into the phone. "Not how I see it. If anything, you're the one being a fuck."

"You French your mom with that mouth?"

Urse laughed despite herself.

"Opal, just because you think you're sick doesn't mean you are." Her voice softened. "Let us not forget the kidney stones, the diverticulitis, and the breast cancer scare, all of which you thought would end you." Urse smelled her coffee, wrinkled her nose, and set the cup on a glass side table.

"This is different, Urse. Honestly, if you ever loved me a day in your life, you will help me. Get the fucking mushrooms."

It was so quiet, she heard birds chirping from Opal's yard in the background.

"Please," Opal added.

Urse touched *end* on her cell.

Nuh, nuh, no. I'll play along, but she's fine. Probably a mix up at the cancer lab. Happens all the time.

Opening her laptop, Urse curled her long legs under her "weird kimono" with its thread-worn butt area and shopped for a dress for their next gazebo meeting. A dress fit for a fake death.

Urse shook her head like an Etch A Sketch, erasing the thought.

Size: 6.

Click.

Color: black.

Click.

PayPal.

Click.

She had no say in anything regarding Opal's bullshit *kill me* occasion. She turned the word in her head like a Rubik's Cube. *Occasion. O-cay-shun* which wasn't OKAY at all.

It is a puzzle, this whole grubby affair. I mean, where the hell am I going to find the poisonous mushrooms Opal's asking for, anyway?

The only ones she knew of grew on the banks of the Mississippi.

Of course. Funny what stories friends choose to remember. The mushroom request came from that screwed up night my stupid brother talked too much.

Urse's memory flooded back to the night—the early days of the friends' get-togethers when they didn't need money to boost their looks. It had been an autumn movie night. Luna had hosted. She had spent a month making a brick fire ring in her front yard on a small ridge overlooking Lake Como in St. Paul. The invitations had read: "Unveiling of my Nuvaring" on the top, followed by: "Fresh apple cider, whiskey, and blankets will be provided. Movie starts at seven o'clock. No outsiders. They can watch from afar." Luna had smuggled the ring in from the Netherlands from a photo shoot and had acted awfully big that month.

Urse tipped her head back in a laugh. *How did we miss Luna being an exhibitionist for so many years? We missed a lot of things back then, I suppose.*

The night her brother blabbed, Luna had called in a tizzy. "I was preparing for movie night, opened my canvas screen, and would you believe the whole damn thing was eaten by moths or something? Do you happen to have one?"

"No, but I think Johnny does."

"Oh, thank God. I knew I should always have two in case something like this happens."

"Yeah, but then you'd have two moth-eaten screens," Urse offered.

"I'll call him right now." Luna's Southern accent was barely audible.

"Wait, is Snookie able to make it?" Urse said hopefully.

"Nope. She's missing again."

"Ah, rats. Next time," Urse said. "See you in a few."

The lawn chairs were positioned in a semicircle around the fire ring overlooking the lake. Luna had raked the first batch of fallen leaves so the area appeared tidy. The gold light from inside the house paired with the flames, providing a softness any lighting expert would find agreeable. After the women's first apple cider whiskeys and gossip, a car rolled into Luna's arborvitae-lined driveway.

"What's my brother doing here? He's not invited," Urse said, recognizing the green Volvo.

Luna sighed. "I know. He said he would only bring the movie screen if he was allowed to attend."

Ruby turned toward the car, the corner of her mouth upturned.

"Oh, it gets better, he"—Luna made air quotes—"*demands* to sit next to Ruby."

The women turned to Ruby whose face turned scarlet.

"Ew." Urse guzzled her second drink and lit up a joint.

"Nothing 'ew' about him, unless he wanted to sit next to you, Urse," Opal said. Her Grandpa Henry's fur hat with flaps tipped to the side, too big—although her shorts were too small. "And take it inside with the weed, there's too many people around." She picked up a few random sticks and chucked them into the fire.

Evening walkers strolled by, along the lake.

"Your ass is so tight you could shit nickels." In a huff, Urse stomped to the house to smoke and pop an upper.

"Thanks for noticing," Opal snarked as Urse was about to open the door. "What was that about? Was it me or is she being a twat?"

"I can still hear you, Opal. You're deafening."

Opal grimaced and ducked. "Sorry." Turning to Ruby, she shook her head and mouthed, "Not. At. All," and Ruby stifled a laugh with her fluffy scarf.

"Naw, she likes it when it's just the four of us," Luna said. "And she's..." Her hand went to her mouth miming drinking.

Urse let the screen door slam shut. Inside, she poured another drink and moved a few spoons into the knife organizer and hurried back so she wouldn't miss anything. She managed to get to her seat without tripping. A win.

"Let's switch the conversation to something fun, Ruby," Opal said.

Ruby scooched in her chair.

"Yes, you, Miss Real Estate Mogul, hiding. Turns out you aren't invisible. Let's facilitate what's inevitable. I'm going to need you to get a leg over Johnny, okay? Just to see what happens," Opal kidded.

"You really should," Johnny appeared out of nowhere carrying a large tote with the movie screen and a bouquet of blue asters with pussy willows. His broad shoulders and smile afforded him the benefits of every doubt.

Opal covered her mouth with her mittens and lifted her legs from the lawn chair as the women laughed. Ruby pulled her flannel blanket over her face.

Johnny handed the bouquet to Luna. "For hosting."

Luna smiled and dipped her nose to smell.

"What's on the big screen tonight, hens?" Johnny asked. His sunny blonde hair matched his thick cable sweater.

"Christ, you look like a dumb fisherman in a soap commercial," Urse said.

Luna frowned at Urse then said, "*Moonstruck.*"

The women applauded.

"As long as you're here," Luna said, "what about making a fire in the new state-of-the-art fire ring I made with my own two hands?" More cheers. Luna cradled the flowers and curtsied.

"Do you have two sticks I can rub together?" Johnny asked.

Urse whipped a Zippo at him. It bounced off his hand and onto the ground.

"Nice catch," Urse said with a smirk.

Sitting flush with the ground, the fire ring fit inside two five-foot logs. The sides were made of steel surrounded by zigzagged pavers. Luna had placed tea candles around the fireplace for added ambiance.

It didn't take Johnny long to get a well-established fire going.

"Luna, how did you know how to make this? It looks professional," Opal asked.

"Picked up some weird skills at my grandma's fire walking show, I guess." Luna pinwheeled her arms theatrically and grass greens and sea blues tinted the fire with a *poof*.

They clapped and hooted.

"What's making it so colorful?" Opal asked and moved closer to the heat.

Luna poked a log with a craggy stick, rolling it to its unburned side. "Fire salts. My grandma used them when she walked on hot coals."

"Wha—?" Opal started.

"That's for another day," Luna interrupted. "I want to hear what Urse was like as a kid."

All eyes moved to Johnny.

"I need another drink," Urse mumbled.

There were things from her past that would make slugs shiver, things Urse didn't want anyone knowing. She didn't care for others' versions of her seeping into her cultivated friendships.

Johnny smiled mysteriously. "Well, there was that one time when Urse poisoned one of our mom's boyfriends."

And there it was.

The women sat up straighter and leaned in, the fire salts lighting their smooth faces in magnificent ways. The booze fought the weed for control, one making Urse weepy, the other giggly.

"What?" Johnny cupped his hand to his ear. "Ruby, you want me to pull up a seat? Aw, shucks, thought you'd never ask." He pulled a lawn chair close to Ruby but far enough away to not be exclusionary.

"Go on," Opal said. Shivering, she tied the flaps of her grandfather's fur hat under her chin.

"Well, long ago and far away—well, about fifteen minutes, anyhow—in a humble single wide, your heroine, one 'Ursula Escobar,' decided she did not care much for our mom's boyfriend. Mind you, he gave me the creeps, too, with his 'special girl,' and 'special boy' talk and filthy jokes. I mean, we couldn't have been more than five or six, and he certainly didn't tell them when Ma was around." He rubbed his blonde chin scruff.

Luna refreshed drinks, provided magazines to even out lawn chair legs, and offered a choice of peanut butter or oatmeal apple cookies from a metal tray with an autumn scene pressed into it. Ruby declined politely.

Johnny said, "God, I love your baking," and pinched one of each. "Well, it just so happens the summer our dad ditched us, Urse and I found a dead body in the Mississippi, practically in our backyard. Anyway, our trailer park newsletter said the guy died from eating poisonous mushrooms and probably fell into the river accidentally. That incident inspired young Urse to dabble in the art of poisoning. Don't worry, friends and…future lovers." He turned to Ruby and grinned. "She made a dirty old man sick, nothing fatal."

Drinks and cookies slid off of Luna's serving tray, her mouth open. "Urse, you said your dad died in a pontoon accident."

Urse lifted her shoulders and put her palms out, neck swinging side to side. "I lie sometimes," she slurred.

"Urse?" Johnny's eyebrows flattened. "Sorry, Sis. I thought they knew about dad. You okay?"

Her head bobbed. "It's all good, I promise. I'll be a better friend tomorrow."

The fire crackled. Awkwardness squirmed in the air. Urse began to sob.

"No more drinks for my sister. Might be time to go." He stood and moved toward Urse. "I'm sorry. I didn't know you hadn't told them that story. Come on, let's get you home."

Urse nodded. "I'm sorry, too." She rested her head on his arm.

"Ladies, I better get my sloppy sister home. I doubt she ate anything today. Unfortunately, I won't be able to make out with Ruby just yet." Johnny saluted.

Urse had also been sorry. She had the bad luck to have a child molester pick her before she poisoned him.

The painful memory hadn't surfaced for years—and wouldn't again if she could help it. She eyed Opal's note.

The poisonous mushrooms are on the banks of the Mississippi. But if Opal doesn't get her shit together, she's liable to hurt herself. I need to prove she wants attention or is having a mental break—not dying.

Chapter Six

Luna

Luna placed four eggs in a cup of lukewarm water, lined up the dry ingredients alphabetically, and set the wet precisely seven inches from the dry. As she measured the baking soda, the expiration date on the box caught her eye. She chucked it into the garbage and went to her pantry to take another from the neat row of identical products.

Her Roma ancestors baked when trouble went down, as did she. Historical trauma was sifted and folded, then baked in and eaten by loved ones. Had hurt not been shared by many, one may likely have died from it. Worrying about the wild gazebo happy hour would have to wait. When life turned confusing, measuring, timing, and exacting suited her personality.

At first, she was shy about being nude in front of her grandmother's cookbook and recipe for olive oil cake, but once the batter was mixed for seven minutes, her modesty evaporated.

Luna smiled, thinking of the fiery woman who had loved her so deeply she was unaware a person could be unloved. Grandma Ada's firewalking could get all of New Orleans' jaws jacking with a single shake of her well-proportioned hips. The only thing gray about her were her eyes; she looked so young, everyone assumed her to be Luna's mother. Let alone all the bikini-wearing showgirl stuff she did at her performances.

Her grandmother had given her seven things: unconditional love, good bones, superstitions, cooking, profiling, a journal, and her special tarot cards.

Luna's everyday deck paled in comparison to their more intricately carved cousin. She kept them next to her leather journal. The journal held her life's plan—but not the recording of the past that could get someone thrown in prison. Instead, it was filled with hopes and plans for when her schizophrenic mother would get better and come home.

One could always control fantasies, if nothing else.

The cards knew she needed structure.

As directed by her grandmother, they were kept hidden and came out only for trying times.

Now was such an occasion.

With the cake pans in the pre-heated oven, Luna focused on the cards.

I've missed you, dear destiny-telling friends. You'd never ask me to kill you, would you? No, of course not. Bless ya hearts.

She flipped three cards. *Treachery, death, and creation.* Odd combination.

And now.

Two dozen hungry brown recluse. Even plotting her own demise Opal has to be edgy—and Lord help everyone if she gets pissed. What is she up to?

Opal. From the first time they met, she'd been mischievous. Luna smiled wistfully, thinking of when they first became friends in college, back before she trusted Opal fully. Opal's insistence on fun and inability to keep still. Her reluctance to speak of her past. Even Luna's career had started from Opal dragging her to a casting call for "an attractive woman with dimples."

"Oh, come on. We've got to aim high. If we get our teeth kicked in by life, so be it," Opal had told her.

Sure enough, they'd cast Luna for a dental ad though her face had none of the dimples required on the spec sheet. The commercial had become a pop culture sensation. Its nonsensical, obnoxious jingle, *"Chompers, chompers, chompers turned my teeth into champers, champers, champers"* played incessantly until the camera landed on Luna's full smile and a random hand model's thumbs-up. Little did anyone know Luna's life work would be a jawline, neck, and ear model.

With her pretty neck and stiff jawline, Luna could also categorize a person's traits with an accuracy that would make an FBI profiler blush. It was only after she met Opal that she realized her attention to detail and ability to read people was unique. Her flamboyant grandmother had taught her the art of observation as a way to earn money; charm, it turned out, was merely a byproduct.

"How about that guy? Read *him*. The good-looking one. Do it! Do it!" Opal had chanted at a grungy bar while they celebrated the filming of Luna's first commercial.

Luna took a big breath and narrowed her eyes. "If you insist. He has an uneven haircut—probably can't afford an expensive one. He's put together—everything's new and in place but his polo is too small in the shoulder on one side. It's a second from the factory. I bet the label is crossed out with factory ink."

Opal half-smiled. "I'm going to need character traits before I talk to him."

"He's a good guy. He doesn't have much money but just bought his buddies a drink. He backed up politely when the server went by. His friends didn't even notice the server. He has a beat-up watch, not stylish. He's proud of it. It probably means something to him. Maybe an heirloom."

"You crazy Dutch bastard, you!" Opal winked and walked toward him.

Luna laughed, accidentally spitting some of her drink on the floor. Already violently female, Opal popped her hips out and sauntered toward her target, strawberry blonde hair bobbing.

Well, she has moxie. I'll give her that, with her Dale of Norway sweater, fishnets, and brass knuckle accessories.

Alone with her Bacardi diet, Luna began tidying up the bar, wiping up used cocktail napkins with fresh ones, and throwing red half-straws in the garbage near the beverage pickup area. As she waited for Opal to return, drinks from two separate admirers appeared.

Luna looked up from the gifted drinks to sneak glances at the guy she'd read. He leaned down to Opal's ear and she threw her head back in laughter, looked up, and motioned Luna to join them.

Balancing the drinks in one hand and fluffing her hair with the other, she approached the pair and handed Opal one of the drinks.

"Luna, this is my cousin, Arthur. He bought his polo at the outlet mall and is wearing my Grandpa Henry's old watch."

"Oh, come on. He's your cousin?" Luna flirted with Arthur from under her thick eyelashes, her favorite Lady Di move.

Arthur stood up straighter. "I am—and thank you for saying I'm a good guy."

The memory of first meeting her husband made Luna's heart ache; she put her head in her hands and sobbed. The cry felt unnecessarily decadent.

Focus. Closing her eyes she touched her middle fingers to her thumbs and breathed from her qi to a settled state.

The scent of the orange in the cake filled the kitchen; her eyes popped open. She pulled the pans from the oven.

If I get caught helping Opal kill herself, it might open the door for bigger worries. If the police looked into my past, there would be added problems. I can't take the risk. I'll get the spiders, then bail.

A row of clear quartz attached to fishing line hung from the kitchen's curtain rod, casting splashy light onto the cakes, making them look marbled. Luna imagined her grandmother sending her good energy through the reflections; she'd decorated her own home much like her grandmother's in New Orleans. Her five-bedroom house in St. Paul was covered in vibrant shades of crimson, copper, and green with polished surfaces, and it smelled pleasantly of melted brown sugar.

And while she loved the home at first glance, she bought it for its big panes and the opportunities that came through them. Luna usually walked nude in front of the window right before Arthur pulled into the driveway each night. She kept up the practice after he left, but hadn't felt sexy since Opal's cancer news.

I wish the cards could tell me where to find the deadly spiders. Those damn hairy creatures. You can't plan for them, let alone the horrible memory of them. I can't believe Opal remembered the day of my freak out. It must be thirty years ago now.

The distant time flooded back: the scent of old popcorn, candy-sweet perfume, and dank basement.

Back then, the friends had made Luna drive everywhere so they could witness her Honda's odometer rolling over to 200,000 miles. The day her car turned the big two hundo, they had been coming from ice skating.

"Afternoon. Do we need to stop and get antifreeze? We are so close!" Opal said, squeezing into the backseat with her skates and sheepskin canteen, braids poking out from her fur hat.

"I filled it before I left. Thanks for thinking ahead, though," Luna answered.

"And make sure to tap your brakes. It's icy out," Opal said.

Once Urse and Ruby also piled into the car, Luna said, "I made you all lavender shortbread. Urse, check the glovebox."

Urse slid her red mitten off. "Brr! This car is saving its energy by not heating up." She pulled on the latch. "It's stuck."

Luna reached over and smashed the top of the dash. The door popped open to reveal four bags of cookies. The yarn of their mittens muffled their delighted claps.

Once at the ice rink, the girls piled into the heating shack which smelled of feet, radiator-dried wool, and hot cocoa. Ski pants, long johns, and single gloves littered the floor like a messy kid's room. The long benches that covered cubby holes for street shoes were mostly occupied, so there was no room to put their skates on.

Urse sauntered up to a group of teenage boys. "Hey guys, do you mind sharing your seat with us?"

"Yeah, yeah. Slide over, guys." One of them puffed his chest out and lowered his voice. "I'm Pete, sort of the leader around here."

"I can see that. Thanks. You can buy us hot cocoa later." Urse winked and ushered him away from the open bench.

The teens huddled. Pete said, "Okay, meet us back here in an hour."

"We'll play it by ear." Urse smiled and waved.

Opal, Luna, and Ruby all flirted their goodbyes.

"You'd think one of us would have shame," Luna said.

Urse handed Luna the first ice skates she'd ever held. Funnel cakes, sure; ice sports, well, only the cards could've known.

"Okay, first off, you'll need to loosen up the laces."

As Luna's fingers touched the laces, a dozen hairy spiders shot out of the skate as if hydraulically. Terrified, she jumped on the bench and screamed, "Nooo! Get them away, get them the hell away!"

Urse laughed at first but stopped when she saw Luna's tears. "Lune, it's okay. It's just a few spiders. They're harmless."

Moms stopped lacing their children's skates to stare; a few guided their kids out of the heating shack.

Luna covered her ears and squeezed her eyes shut.

"Luna, I'm going to take the skates outside, okay?" Opal said gently.

Ruby slid in next to Luna and leaned on her leg.

Her breath calmed. She opened her eyes to a room full of people staring at her. Ruby offered her hand and she stepped down.

Vanilla Ice's "Ice Ice Baby" played over the rink stereo system.

The custodian for the heating shack burst through the windowed door. "Okay, let's go." He hiked his thumb over his shoulder toward the exit. "I don't know what kind of drugs you girls are on, but this isn't the place!

Gather your things. Come on, let's go." Filler feathers escaped from the tears in his quilted, belted snow onesie.

Urse rushed him. She looked down on him by an inch, her face dangerously close to his. "Drugs? How dare you? To think a guy wearing a dirty, brown, ripped snowmobile suit with nothing under it should be telling us we shouldn't be near kids?"

"Wha—" He sputtered, eyes wide as he backed away.

"Keep your dirty paws to yourself. We are leaving, perv." Urse gathered her belongings and addressed the crowd. "And remember, kids, no one gets to touch your swimsuit area!"

"Yeah, yeah." Opal nodded like an excited horse.

The friends gathered their skates and headed for Luna's Honda where they skooched down, laughing. Urse tried to unroll the passenger window, but it was frozen. She opened the door and yelled, "Pete, we could use those four hot cocoas."

"What was that about?" Opal asked Luna once settled.

"I don't even know. I hadn't thought about spiders for years. Maybe it had something to do with when I worked at my grandma's fire walking show."

Luna stared out the window and continued. "I must've been five or six. It was a pretty big production back in the day—you can ask anyone from New Orleans and they'll know my grandma. Anyway, she did palm readings, tarot cards, and walked on coals practically naked. She had men from around the world come to watch her. Some women, too, I suppose. It was my job to choose an audience member from the show for a private reading. I'd look for rich folks, you know—no plastic shoes and boring, well-seamed clothes—that sort of thing. Well, one night, my grandma began reading this guy's palm when—just as things were getting good—dozens of brown recluse spiders jumped out at us. In my head, they came from the crystal ball, but my grandmother said we probably stepped on a nest. I'll never forget—"

Knock, knock, knock on the Honda's window.

They jumped.

"We've got your hot cocoa." Pete had two in his hands. Another teen with acne and a runny nose had the rest. Three other teenage boys in layers of sweats stood staring.

Urse opened the door, poured a bit of hot cocoa out, leaned over to the blemish-faced kid, and kissed him on the cheek.

Pete looked as if his wallet had been stolen.

"Thanks, men, now go hit up some girls your age." Urse patted Pete on the shoulder and slid back into the car.

"Go on, Luna." She passed the hot cocoa to Opal who filled the cups up with the peppermint schnapps from her canteen and handed them out.

Luna nodded. "The man the spiders attacked was Abner Hokanson. I'll never forget it. His face swelled to the size of a watermelon. Apparently, he was allergic. He started seizing. Sweat, spittle. He had a boyfriend that screamed, 'No, don't go' over and over—the whole ball of wax. Then it all stopped. He died right there. I was hysterical. My grandmother held me tightly and kept saying, 'Count to seven, Luna. Everything will be okay if you just let the magic number calm you down'."

She dabbed her tears with the end of her scarf, smudging her mascara. "I killed him. I chose him—I chose Abner Hokanson specifically because of the handcrafted English shoes he wore."

"Oh, Luna, it wasn't your fault. It was in his cards as you say," Urse said.

Ruby reached over the seat and squeezed her shoulder.

The hot cocoa steamed up the windows, making a muggy winter cocoon.

Knock, knock, knock.

"Don't push it, boys. Vamoose!" Urse yelled, and reached over and pressed the horn. It didn't work.

"I didn't mean to ruin skating. That's never happened before. It's embarrassing," Luna said.

"Who said it's ruined? Skating sucks anyway," Opal said. "I have to practically fold my feet in half because skates are so narrow. As my grandpa would always say, 'When given lemons, make orange juice and keep 'em guessing.' Come on."

Opal got out of the car and began making snowballs with the perfect wet, sticky snow. Luna lined them up in straight rows.

Once they'd made one hundred, Ruby said, "Stand back." She put her arm out as if keeping fans off a red carpet.

"Okay, once I start throwing, there will be a pause to rearm. Open the car doors as a shield and let them rip," Opal said.

They mocked seriousness. The first round smashed into the shack's custodian. The second, Pete, who caught on quickly and fought back with intentional throws.

With their frozen ammo exhausted, they'd jumped into the Honda. *Tunk, tunk!* The snowballs had pelted the roof and windows, making wet thuds just as the odometer flipped to 200,000 miles.

I don't get it. Does she want me to face my spider fears?

Of course.

The cards.

Death, treachery, and creation, death, treachery...

Chapter Seven

Opal

Three short sunsets after her diagnosis, Opal had known what she needed to do. She would ask one random resident at her volunteer job at the nursing home for their take on her diagnosis. *Hopefully a wiseass sage.* It was too important of a question to not get a stranger's opinion.

She had volunteered at the lowest-of-the-low-income facility for five years and still, it felt adventurous. Yet, it had taken Opal years before she realized the residents reminded her of her long-gone grandparents with their funny stories and insightful advice.

Under the canopy of the nursing home entrance, a bunting chirped noisily from its nest. Opal kept her eyes down as she passed a Kleenex-dabbing crier.

The smell of bananas, old afghans, and urine greeted her at the counter serving as a check-in. "Howdy, Margie. How's that grandson of yours doing?"

The chubby receptionist's face brightened, making the woman appear twenty years younger. "He won his spelling bee over at Highland Elementary." She swiped through her phone for a picture and held it up to Opal. The boy stood with a denim shirt and khakis wearing a sash that read, "#1 Bee."

"I'll *beeee* damned. That's great."

Margie laughed. "Oh, I see what you did there."

A scrub-clad nurse pushed a cart with a noisy wheel down the hall.

"Any characters in need of my charm today, Margie?"

Eyebrows raised, she scrolled through her computer while forming an *O* with her lips. "Mr. Johnston. Room 10. Backstory, he's not shy about being a dick. No family, no arms, and one step from hospice."

Opal rubbed her hands together. "My kind of guy," she said. "He won't get handsy."

Margie's shoulders raised, covering a giggle.

On the way to room 10, Opal stopped to find a dried apple of a woman with fluffy gray hair leaning off her wheelchair with a sock in her hand. "Is it okay if I put your sock back on?" she asked.

The old woman nodded. Opal stretched the fabric over gnarly, overlapping toes and past swollen ankles to the woman's shin.

"Good as new," Opal said.

She wondered if they were all just time markers. Human place holders, as she would soon be. Her Grandpa Henry used to say, "Time flies like an arrow, fruit flies like a banana." And right now, she and the others in the home were the tip of said arrow.

Only her husband knew of her volunteering. While it was warm and smelly and settled, it felt old and wise and grounded. The folks in the state-run nursing facility understood her old-timey sayings and sense of humor in a way no one else could. They could play cribbage and gin rummy and took her at face value. Many never had money but worked themselves to brittle bones. They understood the taste of government cheese and overtime, bus schedules and working sick. Opal had eaten that same cheese after her parents died. Her teeny shoes weren't replaced until a toe scrunched. Kids made fun of her clothes and the embarrassing car her grandparents drove, and, without the accident, she would have been here, too. The only difference between the nursing home residents and her was the settlement held in a trust until she had turned twenty-five.

"Mr. Johnston?" Opal asked, standing at the entryway of room 10.

The armless man was propped up on a hospital bed with a shiny polyester blanket. He glanced up from the magazine on his lap. *Poor guy must have been staring at the cover all day.*

"Christ, now what?"

"I'm Opal. I volunteer here. Thought you may like some company."

He shifted. "No."

"I'll take that as a *yes*."

The room had an empty bed made with threadbare sheets. The pillow that rested on it read, "Home is where the fart is" embroidered in blue stitching. Unlike other residents' rooms, Mr. Johnston had no photographs other than of himself in a military uniform: a handsome, confident-looking man with hand-painted soft enhancements of his hair and buttons. *Old-timey Photoshop.*

She scraped a 1980s orange plastic chair across the floor and positioned herself closer than the Midwest deemed polite.

He inched away. "Why are you sitting so close?" His yellowed teeth had smears of what looked like instant potatoes stuck between them.

Opal tipped her head back and inhaled a big breath. "I'm about to tell you something no one knows. And while I know it's a little weird, your opinion is going to guide me whether you like it or not."

"Who are you again?" He licked his dry lips, nearly touching his nose hair. The noise of doors closing in the background filled the air.

She had a soft spot for the angry or mean. Once you won them over, they were yours forever. Or in Mr. Johnston's case, probably a few weeks. "Doesn't matter, seeing as though neither of us has a lot of time left. I'm going to dive right in. Ready?"

Opal pretended to be a ventriloquist and spoke from the side of her mouth. "I sure am, Opal. Please, go on."

Continuing in her normal voice, she said, "Glad you asked. I'm dying and I want my friends to kill me before the pain gets too bad."

"That's the best news I've heard all day."

Opal burst out laughing.

"You haven't thrown me out, so you're intrigued. Want your pillow fluffed?" She moved toward him, not waiting for an answer. He leaned forward. She punched the pillow a few times and returned it.

"What do you want me to do about it?" he asked.

"Well. I want to know if I'm doing the right thing or if I should ride it out."

A few moments passed. Mr. Johnston turned his filmy, cataract eyes to the window overlooking the parking lot and spoke. "The greatest act of love is killing someone in pain."

Opal hadn't seen that coming; she nodded as tears surfaced.

The silence housed authenticity.

"What do you call a man with no arms and legs in the ocean?" Opal asked.

"Bob," he answered. "There's only two people in the world with the guts to tell me that stupid joke. My ex-wife and you, and I snuffed her out."

His eyes bugged out and they shared a laugh.

She stood and kissed his cheek. He jerked back at first but softened when it landed.

On the drive home, Opal's achy shoulders and back were lighter, her vision sharper.

She kicked her shoes off and threw her keys on the dusty, antique ratan table in her home's entryway. *Maybe it's time to call the housekeeper back.*

Opal wrote, "Op loves Ol" in the dust.

It had been hard keeping up with the big house since Oliver left six months ago. They used to clean the house after sex on Saturday mornings, as they were sweaty anyway. Sex, sweet everythings, fair trade coffee, and cranberry pancakes. Rituals they fell into and needed. At the beginning of their marriage, they decided to look into one another's eyes for three minutes straight, without speaking, at least once a week. At the beginning they were giggly, but after a few years, the feeling morphed into something deeper. Three minutes of seeing. Three minutes of *I miss you so much* and *can't wait for our next stare.*

The day she had found Oliver in their bathroom was blurry, in moment and memory. Sure, she had tried to find the source of the blood, and a path to fix him, but he was stiff. The mottled veins on his muscular forearms had looked like the marble veins on the bathroom floor—all veins, nonetheless.

She called the authorities.

"What city and state, please?"

Opal tried again: 911. "Please, my husband's hurt—" She begged them to come in a calm voice so they'd arrive quicker on account of her being composed and concise.

She stayed with Oliver for forty-five minutes before the knock at the door. She stroked his salt and pepper hair and talked to him as if it were a normal day.

When the paramedics showed up, they phoned the coroner.

Just a hiccup. We have things to do, my love.

Blurry, blur, blur.

"Officially, it's called segment elevation myocardial infarction." The county worker, in a rumpled shirt, put his used plastic gloves in his charcoal pant pocket and lowered his head. Opal liked him for trying not to be as mechanical as his job dictated. How could he have known their love ranked among history's greatest? He couldn't know Oliver's eyes welled up when a kid hit a home run. He sure as hell didn't know Oliver was responsible for newsworthy anonymous donations and soft face kisses after rough sex. If he knew, he'd pause, thinking this myocardial infarction should've landed elsewhere.

Blur.

From what she was told, she had attended a funeral; she certainly didn't remember. That was one theory. Another was that Oliver would come back soon and everything was fine.

He would never leave me. He is overseas on business, fixing a client's computer system. He'll know what to do about my cancer. I hope he gets back soon. I best plan anyway in case his contract goes longer than expected.

Opal shook her head.

No. Keep moving.

Chapter Eight

Ruby

As she did most Sundays, Ruby geared up for official alone time. Tucking her long hair into a Kromer hat against the chilly Minnesota fall day, she made her way to the roof of her condo building and headed to the ancient Adirondack chair she'd hauled up the stairwell a few years back. This morning, she rested her travel mug on the chipped paint of its flat arm and plunked down quickly. The roof provided perspective; she was no one and nothing on the roof—despite being someone in the business world.

The *just jump* voice was more aggressive the closer she was to the edge.

I'm safer in the chair.

The city felt softer on Sundays, as if hungover and slower to rise.

The rooftop, the place providing answers with its calm and solitude, wouldn't be able to fix her current predicament. Ruby hadn't budgeted for the fear surrounding Opal's situation; the stages of grief came at once, and not in a healthy order. A martini shaker of emotions poured into the appropriate glass and still remained undrinkable. And now, when she thought it couldn't get worse, her terminally ill friend requested a lethal dose of heroin.

It's so out of our league. Weed, sure. Even an occasional dried mushroom. But H?

She exhaled uncomfortably. Using the letter for the word made her feel like an old person using another generation's slang to appear trendy.

"Play sweet French music," she said into her phone. The soft music, muffled from inside her pocket, soothed her, as if she could hide between the notes, skinny and safe—until Opal's voice popped into her head.

"I know it's a lot to ask, but I don't have much time," she'd said. "Obviously I'd never consider anything so insane unless..." Opal's voice had trailed off. "All those heroin people can't be wrong, right? And it'll look like an accident."

Ruby shook her head. She had seen Opal weed-high a handful of times through the years, mind you, but *heroin?*

The risk.

It's like my death itch. The out of nowhere prompt to swerve into a semi, the *floor it, close your eyes* pull toward darkness, terrified Ruby. It came and left within an eye blink, unannounced, yet moved her when everything else felt beige. Since she had read an article that the French called it *L'appel du vide*—the call to the void—she felt a kinship with anyone in a beret.

How fucked up am I that risk and death are my only thrills?

Soon Opal will be forever safe. Lucky.

Lately, sliding her razor blade against her wrists hadn't taken her away from the sadness. Normally, the sharp scratch focused all the world's suffering into one red line on her existing scar—and she controlled it. The ugly noise of the world evaporated and the cuts took over, in an expected way; it settled her chaotic mind.

I wish it were me, not Opal.

The words rolled around in her head before it dawned on her.

I could do it before Opal does. I should.

A sense of warmth washed over her as it sank in. Ruby would help Opal, then check out first. Sticking around after Opal left would be futile, anyway.

Nighttime Mom's voice popped into Ruby's head when she was sad—never when she laughed. *"Hey, dummy, you're pretty, not smart. Fig-*

ures heroin would be in your life and you'll let Ann down. Good job," was today's offering from dead Nighttime Mom.

The wind snuck under her jacket, so Ruby headed back to her condo needing more coffee for today's outing. Rummaging through her junk drawer, she pushed aside a Costco rebate, toothpicks, and linen napkins to find the wide-lined yellow legal pad she favored. Among the mess was a glint: her favorite pen: the shiny, gold one Johnny had let her borrow once.

Ideas she wrote in her high, tight printing, bracelets clicking with each letter.

Strip Clubs

Biker Bars

Gyms

She doodled pictures of each item in the margin, shading with an experienced hand.

Glancing at the microwave clock, she jumped up. Luna would be there in a few hours.

Better get moving.

The hot shower warmed her core. Normally, her Sunday routine was to wash off the old ideas before the new week. Sadly, this Opal thing wasn't circling the drain. She squeezed her eyes shut.

Do not say that or any other stupid euphemism around Opal. I have to help and be mindful of her feelings.

Picking up tips from the show "Intervention," she sported a black hoodie, Vans, and a puffer jacket. She twisted her hair into a middle bun, and pulled out two long strands to frame the front of her face. She could pass for a twenty-something with this getup.

Her phone tinged.

Luna: *Here*

Ruby: *Be right out*

She grabbed her bag and headed outside. *Where is she?*

Beep beep.

Ruby turned toward the horn. Luna was waving from a Ford Focus she'd never seen before. Inside, Luna was dressed in her own black hoodie, jean jacket, and grubby jeans.

"It's a rental," Luna said before Ruby asked.

"Good thinking. Wait, did you use *the* fake driver's license?"

"Indeed," Luna flashed her a V sign. "I swear that old joke is never old." Each one of the group had a fake driver's license bearing the name *Connie V. Lingus* from when Opal worked at the Department of Motor Vehicles for three months in the early 1990s.

"Ha ha. Do you remember that time when Opal invited all her new civil service friends to meet us?" Ruby asked.

Luna imitated Opal's cadence. "I would like to make a toast to my comrades in arms. I have a newfound respect for all of you."

"I bet she still 'has a guy'"—Ruby smiled, raising her fingers into air quotes—"at the DMV."

Their bittersweet memory distracted them momentarily.

"Miss Rube, you're killing me with that purse. I don't think druggies have them."

"I'll stash it under the seat."

"You nervous? I'm surprised you're doing it with all your business stuff. It's so risky." Luna fumbled with the radio.

"I mean, yeah, I'm shaky thrilled. I mean *scared*—I'm shaky scared," Ruby said. "You?"

"We are in a Ford Focus. What could go wrong?"

The radio knob came off in her hand.

"Thinking our story is this: we heard heroin softens laugh lines."

"Um—" Ruby started nervously.

Luna laughed.

"You're a jerk." Ruby pushed the side of her arm and watched as Luna adjusted the rearview mirror and tapped it seven times. The rental felt and sounded tinny, every bump realized like their college cars.

"I guess we ask someone standing around. If that doesn't work, we head to a biker bar," Ruby said.

"Now I'm nervous. I think we need a code word for 'let's get out of here'."

"How about 'psst'?" Ruby stared out the car's side window.

"That's good. Realistic." Luna smirked.

As the litter turned from pinecones to used condoms, they started looking.

"Here—pull over." Ruby pointed to a spot in front of a Salvation Army thrift store where a group of people stood smoking.

"Let's go in, pretend we're shopping, and hit them up on the way out," Ruby said. "And when I say *we*, I mean *you* do the talking." She smoothed her hair.

"Duh, but jump in if I get stuck. You know I don't like improv." Luna pulled her hoodie over her head and put the rental car keys in between her fingers in case she needed to get stabby.

The women perused the aisles of the thrift store, lifting pottery and glassware for valuable markings as Urse had taught them. The store smelled faintly of old lady perfume, Fabuloso, and dusty candles.

Luna google-lensed a wooden statue then set it back down. She used her fingertips to wave at a pudgy baby in a shopping cart. Customers milled around open carts of new items brought out from the back, prompting Ruby to dig along with them. *Ha, peer pressure.*

Ruby tipped her head toward the door. Luna nodded.

They walked out of the shop. The group of three men and one woman stopped talking as they approached.

"Hey," Luna said.

An anemic guy in his thirties with black hair and sideburns up-chinned her. His build, thin as an onion skin and normally unthreatening, took on trickiness within the group. The other two men might have been brothers with their wiry frames and puffed chests. They loomed around six feet and each wore hats burglars would wear.

We could flirt our way in.

The woman, on the other hand, looked *street*. Emotionless and wearing a slouchy cropped top, a buckled leather jacket, and skinny jeans storing diabetic-sized proportions.

Ruby mirrored her suspicion. *I bet she has a Nighttime Mom, too.*

"Can I bum a smoke?" Luna asked.

Ruby wished she'd thought of the smoke angle.

The side-burned anemic produced a cigarette with dirt filling the cracks of his hands.

"Thanks." Luna's eye contact lingered on him.

Ruby crossed her arms. *Does that read as defensive?* She uncrossed them and started her sign language ABCs. She kept her hands behind her back so no one would see. The fast, comfortable movements soothed her; the control of the letters, knowing the forms and what came next. They needed *her* to exist.

Luna dipped her head and cupped her hand around the guy's lighter for her cigarette. She took a deep drag as if she'd smoked her whole life. Ruby stared at her. Luna lifted a shoulder with a *"what?"* look.

"Lady, what are you doing behind your back?" one of the brothers asked Ruby.

Busted.

Ruby brought her hands around, still rapidly moving in sync. The group softened as they *oohed and aahed*.

"Nervous habit since I was little."

The woman narrowed her eyes and studied Ruby. "You're so fast," she said.

"Lots of practice."

"Weird question," Luna piped up. "Do you know where we can get some party favors?"

Oh, God. Party favors.

Ruby's hands sped up.

"Like balloons?" the guy asked.

Luna's voice lowered, "Naw, like *party-party*." Her eyes widened, she ashed her cigarette and tapped the crook of her arm.

"Oh, *party-party*," the man nodded with the others in the group. He leaned down, looked at the pavement and said, "I'll need time. Go back into the store, hit up the shitter. No matter what happens, stay in the bathroom for at least twenty minutes then we'll meet you outside."

Luna nodded. "Thanks for the smoke and stuff." She winked at him.

Ruby and Luna walked past aisles of quality or otherwise used items to the store's bathroom.

"Easier than I thought," Ruby whispered.

"Right? I thought so, too. I mean, what is this world coming to?" Luna said flatly as her shoulders lifted to her ears. Ruby could imagine her as a girl, burdened with heavy superstitions and carefree confidence. Well, up until the *Big Trouble*, anyway.

"We aren't in the clear yet," Ruby said.

"Yeah, we still have to pay."

"Oh, no. I don't have any money on me. It's all in the car."

"I've got a few hundred on me. How much do you think it is?"

Ruby assumed around a hundred but wasn't sure. She would've googled it but didn't want it on her search history, especially with the sale of her business coming up.

"That should be good, right? How long have we been here?" Ruby asked as she organized her bracelets from light to dark.

Luna eyed her phone. "Seventeen minutes."

"Good enough."

Ruby washed her hands, waved the motion towel dispenser, and wiped up. She wrapped the paper towel around the door handle and said, "After you, madam."

Luna lifted her chin high. It read as fake confidence.

Outside, the thrift store staff were huddled around the Focus's smashed driver side window.

"Aww, lawdy," Luna said.

Ruby closed her eyes. *My purse.*

"Your purse."

"Anyone have a broom?" Ruby asked the staff, her confidence disintegrating.

"Want us to call the cops?" a matronly woman with a *Grace, Asst. Manager* name tag offered.

"No, that's okay, we know better."

Ruby liked to watch Luna and the women talk. None of them seemed to need to select words; they spilled from their well-lined mouths in the correct order effortlessly with nuanced meaning. They pushed and pulled and landed on top quickly and confident in their space as they maneuvered through the world.

I have to win people over in the quiet. People see what they want me to be; my only job is to not get in their way. They project me into their existence.

"Go ahead and take a broom and dustpan from the shelf," Grace said.

Ruby smiled a thank you.

Glass crunched. When she opened the car door, there was a brick on the front seat. On the side without holes, it read "LOSERS" in cigarette ash.

Maybe getting Opal's heroin wouldn't be as easy as she thought.

Chapter Nine

Urse

Figuring Opal's news had enough time to settle, Urse called her brother from her chrome and wheat-colored office decorated by a needy friend of Opal's.

From across the room, the fireplace cast light on the company's accolades displayed on the mantle. The International Association of Industrial Minerals and Providers award had been pushed forward. The historically male association had nominated Johnny—only. Urse and Johnny did a quick ownership shift, giving her an extra percent majority share. Forcing them to etch her name into the plaque was worth every struggle. Those types of wins fueled her.

Tapping their company intercom, she called Johnny's office. "Hey, weirdo. What are you up to?"

"Not much. Going over my modeling contract for Milan," he joked. "You?"

"I've got to talk to you about something. Meet me at my car."

Urse pulled three raw sugar packets from her bag and emptied them into her tea bottle. She nabbed her cashmere coat and bag from a hook that, when not in use, laid flush with the wall.

Johnny was waiting in the hallway. He bowed slightly and said, "After you, kind stranger," and put his hand out.

Urse rolled her eyes and they walked down the showy office stairs.

They had purchased the commercial building a decade ago to support

The Crystalporium's growth, after the once tiny crystal shop had morphed into a procurement business for all things aggregate. The brother and sister team had fought, thrived, and earned their way to the top of the heap. Now, years later, their building was in itself a big deal, an example of how specialty-sourced rocks could elevate architecture. Johnny had procured a four-ton chunk of a quartz mined from the Ouachita Mountains for the lobby wall. It turned out so well, it made the cover of *Wishlist Architectural Designs* and had Minnesota's wealthiest petitioning for one of twelve open venue availabilities per year.

Now, in Urse's murdered out Mercedes, she turned the music off and said, "I've got some garbage news. Opal thinks she has pancreatic cancer and is dying."

Johnny's head jerked back. Blue eyes bulged.

They had known Opal since they lived in a single wide with their mom, Wanda. When they ate pie crust cookies and hit up the dump to clean and paint chairs to sell.

"How can you *think*? Don't you *know*?" he asked, visibly shaken.

"Well, she says she knows, but looks fine. She's probably mixed up."

Johnny studied his sister.

"Why would Zee lie?" he asked.

I haven't heard "Zee" for years. He's scared.

"She's not lying—there's probably a simple explanation, like a mix-up or something. Get this, she wants us to get poisonous mushrooms, in case..."

"Urse. I'm sorry. You know I love that one—she's like our sister. Wait, mushrooms? I don't get it. I need a minute here. She wants to eat—" He leaned back on the headrest and closed his eyes. "Oh, shit, she wants to off herself."

"She doesn't know what she wants. She's fine. Let's just appease her and it'll work out in the end. Let's go." She flipped her car visor down, releasing a free oil change coupon. "Do you remember what the poisonous mushrooms by the trailer looked like?"

He pinched the bridge of his nose and said, "Yeah," and clicked his seatbelt for the fifteen-minute drive.

"Good. I'll get them to say I did. I want to appear open-minded while I shoot holes in her sanity."

Once at the Mississippi shoreline, Urse removed her shoes and looked for treasures while Johnny ventured up the wooded terrain out of sight. She walked *heel-toe, heel-toe* like she was trying to pass a drunk driver test. Her bare feet took her back to when they were kids scouring for pretty rocks.

After half an hour, he came out with a smooth, whitish, sloped mushroom in his open palm, the other hand behind his back.

"Meet our dangerous friend, *Amanita phalloides.*"

"Johnny! Shouldn't you be wearing gloves?"

He shrugged. "Old wives' tale."

The water made her melancholy. "This river knew us when we were little," Urse mumbled.

Johnny nodded. "It's always made me nervous. Come on, let's go."

They headed back to the office, each drowning in their own sad thoughts.

"It'll be in my top desk drawer in case you decide you don't want to give it to her," Johnny said.

Urse nodded and gave him a hug, and when he pulled back, it dawned on her. *He looks like Dad. My God, Johnny's the same age as Dad when he left. Our dad. I wonder if he is still alive? If he would be proud of all we had accomplished with The Crystalporium. Would he even understand the P&L-prompted offers from the biggest private equity firms in the states?*

If. If wishes were horses, beggars would ride.

Dad rode alright. Right out of their lives.

The night he took off, she and Johnny had finished their after-dinner chores—he swept, and she cleared dishes—and left for their bedrooms.

The trailer walls, constructed of thin paneling, had allowed for easy listening.

Her mom had said, "What's your timeline for getting a job that actually pays?"

Urse heard this played out argument for years.

She knew it by heart; next, Dad will say, "Give me a break, Wanda."

"Jesus, Wanda. Can you give it a break for one goddamn night?" her dad said.

"When am *I* going to get a break?" her mom asked calmly.

Urse peeked out of her room to watch. This fight seemed different. Quieter than usual.

Her dad approached her mom's back as she washed the dishes. "Come on, Wanda, please? Enough." He tried putting his arms around her waist.

She pushed him back with her butt, hands still in the water. "A *paycheck* is sweet talk, not sweet talk."

He closed his eyes and pinched the bridge of his nose. "Christ, Wanda," he said. "I swear you were born with rigor mortis." He walked to the wall-mounted bull key holder, grabbed the truck keys, and left.

That was the last time they saw the family truck or their dad.

By the time grass grew where the truck once parked, Urse figured her dad might not ever come back.

And now, Opal thinks she's leaving me. Fat chance. Plus, something's off. Opal's been repeating herself a lot lately. If anything, she's still wrecked after Oliver's death. Hell, I haven't even mentioned what I saw in Opal's bedroom to Johnny. I mean come on. Crazyville.

After Oliver's funeral, the women had met at Opal's to unwind.

Since Ruby was using the main bathroom, Urse had made her way to the one attached to Opal's bedroom. It was her favorite bathroom in Opal's house because of the wall of varying shades of blue crystals purchased from The Crystalporium. As she walked in, out of the corner of her eye, she had caught a form in bed. Urse had jumped, one arm out straight, one arm on her chest. Once she had caught her breath, she realized the "body" was several gravity blankets, formed into the shape and size of Oliver sleeping in bed.

What the fuck?

Returning, she cornered Luna. "You are not going to believe what I just saw." She glanced around to make sure Opal couldn't hear. "She's got a freaking formation of blankets in the shape of her dead husband in her bed," Urse whispered.

Luna got close to Urse's ear. "I wasn't going to mention it but I found a Post-it note in the fridge that said, 'Oliver, we are out of blueberries'."

Opal entered the room and Luna backed up. "How are you holding up, Ope?"

Her voice sounded robotic. "Oh, he's away on business. He'll be back soon."

Urse dropped her plate of berries and shot Luna a look.

The memory of the funeral turned vivid now that Opal's eccentricities looked more like mental illness.

We can't kill a crazy person.

Chapter Ten

Luna

Opal's cancer news and asks for weird instruments of death weren't as detailed as Luna would have liked. No *if-this-then-that* or suggested timelines. No flipping direction, whatsoever. And with Urse swearing that Opal is crazy and Ruby checked out—as usual—well, the burden was on Luna and there wasn't enough time to make an informed decision.

So, I won't kill her.

Luna tapped the soft-boiled egg resting in a silver holder seven times with her butter knife. *One more or less tap and something terrible will happen.* She scooped the warm egg out of its shell, making sure to end on seven bites. The egg was cooked perfectly.

Now, on to solutions for the Opal situation.

Obviously, the only sane thing to do was a group tarot card reading.

Cards—a strange word considering they were made of wood, resembling drink coasters with whittled pictures of cups, wheels, and swords.

"Hide them," her firewalking grandmother had said on the day she left for college in Minnesota. "I think they like to be alone until big moments. No need to waste their energy on the adoration of strangers. Use them only for you, and those you love."

Leaving her grandmother and New Orleans were two of the hardest things Luna had ever done. Her grandmother tried to make it easier by mentioning the cards had *wanted* her to go. It had also helped that Luna had plotted the big move with military-like precision.

Luna had anticipated everything in Minnesota, with the exception of the electric colors of the trees and the grandness of the Mississippi. She remembered paddling her hand in its water, feeling it clean and tide away her past. She had heard the river started from a rock and you could step over it. *Maybe I imagined that and I'm thinking of that Indigo Girls' song.*

Once at her dorm in Minnesota, she had fit her key into the door and wrinkled her nose. Her first home away from her grandmother and New Orleans consisted of graying beige indoor-outdoor carpet, two beds, and two brass lamps on kid-sized desks.

There was no way to sleep in the mess. The cleaning, puzzle piecing, and decorating kept her up until 3 a.m. She strung white Christmas lights. She wrapped an impressive assortment of Romani scarves—in deep cranberry, fuchsia, and green—around the curtain rod. She placed numerous pillows, assorted by color. Her mother's Luna moth coffee mug, now residing on her desk, provided the only stability her mother ever offered.

She slept.

Someone knocked at the door.

Luna lifted her head from the pillow, getting her bearings, and glanced at her alarm clock: 8 a.m.

A sing-songy, "Hell-oo."

So chipper.

"One sec." She threw on a pair of jeans and ponytailed her hair.

Luna opened the door to a disarming beauty.

"Morning!" A cloud-white-toothed smile. "You must be Luna."

"Urse? Let me help you with your stuff."

Luna sneakily rubbed the handle of the Yves Saint Laurent bag for clues when Urse handed it over. Taught to authenticate a bag from her days as a reader for Grandma Ada's firewalking show, she went to work. Seams: even and double stitched—but not the correct thread color for that year. Leather: stiff like the real deal—decent. Hardware: wrong zipper.

Fake.

"Thank you." Urse eyed up the room. "Wow. It's all organized without missing a detail, huh?"

Luna didn't know if it was a compliment until her new roommate spun around the room and added, "I like your style."

She struggled, absorbing Urse's symmetry. Intimidating. Atypical, for certain.

Guys probably adored her.

Next, Luna scanned her outfit. Curious. Bally shoes—reason enough to pick her for a special reading. Expensive tastes, though she came from humble means. Her shoe had black sharpie ink covering a small worn patch at the toe, and her jacket seam, hemmed by hand.

Over the next few days, the two got to know one another. *You like egg foo yung? Ha ha, I do, too! What? Crystals? My brother and I own a small shop called The Crystalporium. Yes! Get out of here! Tarot cards? Are you serious? You've got to be kidding! What—me, too? STOP! Seriously? Too weird! Yep, love—naw, hate them. Yep, you too?* And on into the night. Urse brought the vodka college kids could afford and Luna brought goblets.

The more drinks they consumed the more honest they became. Urse detailed her dad's fatal pontoon accident, leaving behind her and her brother, Johnny. Luna shared that her mother had schizophrenia, and described the firewalking show on the bayou.

Luna closed her eyes at the first memory of meeting Urse. Now, some thirty-odd years later, the frivolity that defined them hid behind worry.

Urse was about to pick her up to spy on her third husband.

Luna's doorbell chimed. Urse appeared on the other side of the peephole of the heavy, oversized door in a low-cut black sweater, mini with black tights, pointy leather boots, and a camel hair jacket nearly dragging on the floor.

"Smells good in here," Urse said as she crossed the threshold.

"Uh, I thought we were going to spy on your husband?" Luna said, glancing down at her see-through pajama bottoms and hoodie.

"We are. I need to look better than I feel," Urse said. "Go change so we don't look out of place."

Um.

"Urse, we are heading to Home Depot."

"Right. Well, in case shit goes sideways, it'll be better if we match outfits," Urse said.

Luna shook her head. "Okay, okay. Give me five. There's some fresh toffee bars on the counter. Help yourself."

"Thanks, I'll be outside. I just need a quick pinchy to get me through this," Urse said.

Imagining exactly what they needed to do at Home Depot made Luna's stomach jittery. She threw a trench over a short knit dress and slid into white tenners she bought on her last work trip to France.

I hope I can keep my kicks white if we need to run.

She met Urse outside.

"Thanks for doing this with me, Lune. I know the timing sucks with what Opal is going through but I have to find out if Fitz—"

She wagged her finger, "Don't you dare. We don't know if the receipts mean anything. I'm here for support in case anything gets ugly, okay?" Luna said.

"Over fifty-nine thousand dollars of receipts from Home Depot in the last six months *is* ugly, considering I just shucked out a few mill for our *newly-constructed house.*"

Fitz struck Luna as more of a fine pastry chef than a man who could wield a nail gun, but she needed facts before judgment. Urse had shared times, dates, and amounts of the suspect transactions on a spreadsheet—all provided by Urse's accountant—along with a cell that read, "Is he taking out additional cash at the checkout?" "Is he fixing someone else's house?"

Luna had taken it upon herself to laminate, highlight, and bind the information into a dossier titled, "In the Pudding."

"What's this?" Urse opened the folder.

The first page was a recipe for Luna's chocolate pudding that Urse liked; the other sheets were perfectly organized data in case Urse needed to burn another wedding dress.

She leaned against Luna. "When does this get easier?"

"When you pick a husband that doesn't enjoy baby talk in bed," Luna said. "Come on, let's hope for the best."

As Luna suspected, their outfits garnered more attention than necessary. Whistles poured in. They slunk to the service desk, as conspicuous as a pantless clown on stilts.

"May I speak to Amy B, please?" Urse asked.

Luna did a quick read of Amy B, a down-for-revenge type of gal by how *call to duty* she seemed. Her ponytail was slick, probably made with wet hair; maybe a single mom with no time to fuss. She had bland blue eyes with dark circles like that of an old poodle and an untanned area where a wedding band would normally reside. Her nails were clean but unpolished, much like herself. Luna would have passed her over for a firewalking reading.

"Come with me." Amy B moved from behind the counter and ushered them into the back security room. "Out," she barked at the security guard who appeared asleep.

He left without a word. The room smelled like the inside of a dirty microwave, though the counter surrounding the security cameras was tidy.

"Okay. I've done a little homework on your husband. I matched the times on the receipts with the security tapes." Amy B softened. "I'm sorry you have to deal with whatever he's up to, but he does go to the restroom every time he's here."

"Okay, but—"

"And another man leaves shortly after him," Amy B paused. "Every, single, time." She clicked the security remote that pointed to the device. The grainy footage showed Fitz walking past the "No Merchandise in Restrooms" sign as he tucked his shirt in. She fast forwarded the video. "That's the guy," she said, pausing it.

"That motherfucker," Urse said, rubbing her eyes. "He loves himself so much his prozzie even looks like him."

Luna pinched the bridge of her nose. *I feel trouble comin' on.*

"Amy B, I thank you for your help on this matter and trust you will keep this to yourself." Urse handed her an envelope. "I gave you a bit extra for your discretion, and if you ever need a job, hit me up. I own The Crystalporium."

The woman smiled and stuffed the envelope into her back pocket. "I hope everything gets easier now that you know. You may want to duck out. According to his routine, they should be here any minute."

"Of course. Can I use this room to collect myself for a minute?" Urse asked.

Ut-oh, Urse never needs to "collect herself." There's no way my sneaks are staying white.

Amy B nodded and left.

Urse was on lookout at the security guard's chair, her face wan. Luna let out a, "Lord, I didn't see that a comin'," her accent slipping out.

"Mister I-Know-You've-Been-Hurt-Before wasn't smart enough to elude my prenup, so there's that."

"Let's go home," Luna said.

"I need to use the bathroom first." Urse shot up from the chair and ran out the door. Luna glanced at the security feed in time to see Fitz enter the building near the plumbing section.

Oh no.

Luna chased after Urse whispering, "Come on, let's go home. We have the information you need."

"I just want to say hi to my husband."

Urse didn't do well with ambiguity, so Luna reluctantly followed her into the men's bathroom. Urse opened the middle stall. After lining the seat with toilet paper, she climbed up and offered Luna a hand. "Give me your phone."

Luna turned over the cell. "God, this place is disgusting," she said, pretending to retch.

"Out of the mouths of, I assume, babes." Urse pointed to the stall wall which read: *Life is a cheap joke, I fucked your mom.*

"If I had a nickel," Luna joked.

The door opened. Someone rattled their handle; the women froze, and the stranger went to another stall.

Urse mouthed, "It's Fitz. I can smell him."

Luna nodded.

Ting ting.

Shortly after Fitz's phone chimed, someone entered his stall.

"I've missed you," Fitz said.

They heard belt buckles moving.

"You've missed *this,* is all."

"You locked the door, right?" Fitz asked.

"Jezus F, it's not like Moneybags is going to catch us."

Luna winced as Urse closed her eyes.

Urse tapped video record on Luna's phone and angled it over the edge of the stall.

The voices continued. "Sorry. I'm paranoid. Listen, I've been waiting for this all. Damn. Day. Now, put that fist in me, and don't go easy," Fitz whimpered.

Something between embarrassment and numb crossed over Urse's face when she quietly stepped from the toilet to the space in front of Fitz's stall.

She fixed her eyes on Luna and returned her cell, motioning to keep rolling.

Urse backed up, and with all her might, kicked in the stall door.

Cah-RACK!

"What the fuck, dude?" the fister yelled.

"Moneybags wants you to know I never loved you, you fucking idiot."

The two men bumbled without saying anything. Luna could see through the crack of the stall that Fitz's nose was bleeding.

Good. I hope he's disfigured.

Urse moved to the sink and began roughly scouring her trembling hands, hitting the soap dispenser so hard the nozzle broke into the basin. Taking her by the wrists, Luna whispered in her ear, "Stiffen. Your. Back-bone."

With wet eyelashes, Urse nodded once, stood straighter, and departed the men's bathroom. Luna followed Urse's lead into the aisle of the store.

"Hand me that pipe," Urse said.

Luna moved in front of it. "Urse, no, we—"

Urse brushed past her, grabbed a pipe, and shoved it into the handle of the bathroom door. Luna smiled, relieved.

"One last thing," Urse said, turning down the aisle, her heels clicking against the store floor, jacket fluffing out as she strode. Luna sped up to match her pace.

Once at the front desk, Urse walked around to the intercom, flipped the *on* button, and said, "Attention shoppers. There is a man in the restroom that won't take no for an answer. Please take care of it for me."

Luna touched the tip of her nose and pointed to Urse who grinned.

We got through that, we can get through this Opal fiasco.

Chapter Eleven

Opal

Her stomach pain gnawed worse in the mornings.

Opal leaned forward from her side of the bed and hugged her belly, alleviating the discomfort momentarily. Grabbing a week-old glass of water from the nightstand table, she took a sip and steadied.

The pain screwed with her. It made her see what wasn't there, distorting damn near everything. Made her second-guess herself. Not about dying on her terms—the pain only solidified that. But maybe she was wrong forcing her friends to help. Maybe she was being selfish. Hadn't they already proved their loyalty through the decades? There was that night with the bicycle when their friendships had gelled. Or was their loyalty disguised as youthful entitlement? None of them had anything to lose financially back then. The stakes are wildly different now.

Now, they could lose their comfy, important lives helping me. Hell, if I had asked them to kill me on that crazy night, they probably would have done it right then and there.

The night Opal's anger splattered all over everyone's fancy dresses, she had realized there were only three people she trusted. Though she made friends like people made eggs, Urse, Ruby, and Luna had stuck with her when they shouldn't have.

The outburst had happened on Opal's thirty-fifth birthday, which, sadly, was also the day her grandfather, Henry, died. The stress from the loss had been so overwhelming, it prompted a big chancre on her top lip which peeped out past her overlined lipstick.

Another happy birthday call came in, this time from Luna. "I have reservations at The Haunt for steak and lobster, and a few surprises. We can get ready at Ruby's. I'm planning on wearing a mini-mini skirt and a silk button down. You?"

"You? A micro mini? You get that you're a pervert, don't you?"

"If I'm a perv, I don't *not* want to be one." Luna's laugh was high and giddy. "There's a town car coming for you at three. Be ready and don't overshare with the driver. The last time we waited a half an hour for you to finish up your thoughts on Sufism. We have celebrating to do."

Another year of being criticized for talking too much.

Opal decided on a vintage St. John strapless dress of black and metal sequins that was tight in the hips and baggier at the waist than a tailor would like, and toted a leather overnight bag. The stocky driver with smile lines arrived promptly.

Mindful of Luna's warning, Opal rode quietly in the back of the car until the driver asked, "Are you okay, miss?"

She met his concerned eyes in the rearview mirror while 70s music played from one speaker behind her. He handed her a tissue over his shoulder. She hadn't realized tears were rolling down her cheeks.

"My grandpa died today. I'd stay home but don't want to let my friends down. He's dead, dead, and dead."

And the only person who knew what she had done.

"I've never been more alone."

Telling a stranger always put things in perspective; no prejudices, no hugs. Outsiders shared their wisest thoughts when the luxury of plain speak presented itself in situations such as these.

"Oh, dear. I'm sorry. My Oma died a month ago. She told me if I grieved, I was an imbecile. Can you imagine?"

"Why wouldn't you?"

He aimed the rearview mirror at her.

"She said, 'You know me, I know you. We are in one another's blood and want happiness for one another. Silly death can't change that'."

"I love when people speak in headlines."

Opal watched as trees were swapped out by buildings.

When they arrived, Luna was standing on the sidewalk by Ruby's building.

"That's my friend."

"Your friend has a..." He paused. "...beautiful presence about her."

"Yeah, her skirt screams, 'angelic,'" Opal said with a chuckle. Leaning toward his ear, she whispered, "She's an exhibitionist, but let's keep that between you, me, and the pope."

His head turtled out, and twisted to speak. "Listen, be careful out there tonight. Pretty girls like you can attract the crazies, sometimes."

Luna opened her door and yelped, "Birthday Lady...uh, what's on your lip?"

The driver tooted his goodbye.

Opal covered her lips with her hand. "Stop noticing how disfigured I am."

After hoisting her overnight bag over her shoulder, she hooked arms with Luna and headed for the elevator. "Tonight is all about us drinking your abnormalities away. I did a quick tarot reading—you will have a beautiful year ahead."

As the women kicked off their shoes in Ruby's entryway, Urse snuck up behind Opal and lifted her off the ground, yelling, "Happy birthday!"

"My birthday wish is for you not to lift me," she said, kicking her feet midair.

Urse did a double take. "My God, that face thing needs its own zip code."

Ruby greeted them at the door with gin martinis in smoke-colored glasses. "Oh, honey, ouchie. Let's make it a *boozing* carbuncle." She lifted her glass at her own word play.

Luna slopped her martini, laughing.

"Ruby's first funny joke." Opal couldn't help but crack up.

As the women fixed their makeup, gossiped, and sipped liver-hating drinks, Luna presented each with hats the size of a hockey puck with fishing line ties for under the chin. She made Opal's with strips of black velvet and copper wire; Urse's with black yarn and feathers; Ruby's, with felt and leather.

"My heart is going to explode. These are so thoughtful."

Grandpa Henry would have loved her hat. Opal began to cry. It wasn't the hat itself. It was the time it took to make it. The care. The care her grandfather showed her was still around—it just looked different now.

She downed her drink in one fell swoop and shuffled to the bathroom.

A knock at the bathroom door. "You don't seem like yourself. You okay?" Luna asked.

"Sentimental, I guess. I just need concealer that someone doesn't want back."

The women had swanned into the steakhouse. Heads swiveled as the burly maître d escorted them to their table facing the tawdry crowd of patrons. Champagne and a platter of Malpeque oysters greeted them as they shoehorned into the corner booth.

The maître d helped Luna with her coat. "Champagne for your celebration," he said. "It's been too long. Our sales slump when you ladies aren't here."

The women had known him for years and called him "Bruce" though his name was Earl. Urse put him in a playful headlock as Luna kissed him on the cheek, leaving lipstick marks. Nearby tables began to hoot and clap.

"I see it's going to be a fun night." He fixed his gelled hair, straightened his blazer, and left smiling.

Ruby's eye wandered; that meant they were three drinks in. Best get something in their stomachs. Opal motioned to their server discreetly. "May we get some bread?"

"Certainly." Their fair-haired server dipped with a slight bow, her hands behind her back, jacket white as the end of a Q-tip.

"I'd like to make a toast." Urse clinked her champagne glass with her heavy silver knife.

The women raised their glasses. Opal covered her blemish with hers.

"May the fates grant you every happiness. You deserve what you have. Cheers." Urse's eyes watered, as they quieted in thought and drank.

Opal mouthed the words, "Thank you."

Their server returned with a bottle of champagne. "A guest at the bar wanted your table to have this."

"Which guest? Who opened it?" Luna asked. The women looked up to find a string of men at the bar lifting their drinks toward them.

"I was told not to mention." She leaned down and whispered, "I can tell you there's another bottle in the wings, so go nuts."

Luna stood and shouted to the bar, "Who sent us this champagne?"

All their hands went up with the exception of a man at the end of the bar eating broccoli.

"Send it back," Luna said as she straightened the salt, pepper, and napkins.

Their server grimaced. "What should I tell him?"

"Tell him, 'no thanks.'"

The confused women's postures lifted.

"What's up?" Opal asked.

"Wait 'til you see his eyes, then tell me what you think. He probably put something in the bottle," Luna said. She checked her lipstick in the reflection of her knife. "He reminds me of a dentist I once knew. A story for another day."

Ruby squeezed Luna's hand.

"Yeah, something's not right with that one," Opal said. "His eyes are dead."

Urse flipped her hair. "Dateable."

"Don't even joke. He looks like a guy with a seven-digit Social Security number." Opal wrinkled her nose.

The women's table became more serious as the perceived threat put them on high alert.

"I know the type. He's a walking Death card. I'd bet Urse's left ovary on it," Luna said to lighten the mood.

Ruby nodded. "He's a dangerous drunk. Trust me, I know."

Their server returned the bottle to Broccoli Man. He squinted at them, threw his lap napkin on his plate and headed their way.

"Oh no," Luna said. "He looks bristly."

"I'll take care of it," Opal said.

The apprehensive women were quiet as he approached their booth.

He loomed over their table and grumbled, "Ladies, is there a specific reason you wouldn't accept my generous gift?" Little beads of sweat appeared on his top lip.

"Thank you but we don't take drinks from strangers, and we've already had enough," Opal's words were tentative but loud, as he appeared edgy. Ruby moved their purses from the table to their seats.

"You don't look like a table that doesn't take things from men," he said, eyes menacing.

Opal couldn't help herself. "Fuck off, Jethro."

He jerked back, hand on his chest in mock shock. "Nice language," he said loud enough for people outside the booth to hear. He inched closer to Opal's face. His breath smelled like shrimp puffs left in an outhouse. "You sluts are so plastic, you're sticky." He stared at her then tipped a full water glass toward her and walked away, straightening his tie.

Opal jumped up, grabbed the tipped glass, and curled the end of the tablecloth so the water wouldn't spread. Then, in one fell swoop, she pulled her arm back and launched the glass, hitting him in the back of his head.

She grinned. Her perfect aim was apparently ageless.

Broccoli Man pressed the back of his head and whipped around. "I guess that face herpe makes you leader of the whores, you fucking orphan!"

Her smirk faded and she stiffened.

A collective hush overcame the busy restaurant as the bouncers approached the man, taking his elbow. "I'm leaving, gentlemen." He jerked his arm away.

The maître d approached their table.

"Bruce, how did he know I'm an orphan?" Opal laughed past her tears, anxious to rearrange her attitude and save face.

"I'll buy your dinner, but it's time to go. As much as I'd love you to stay, you can't throw glassware at people's heads no matter what they say."

"I disagree." Opal repositioned her tiny hat to cover her bad lip. Urse laughed at the sight. Ruby and Luna did the same in solidarity.

"Fine. But put our bread in a to-go box," Urse said. "And don't skimp on the butter."

Just then, Broccoli Man walked in front of the restaurant's window. The women shook their heads. Luna rubbed her index finger against the other as her grandmother did when expressing shame. Urse's well-manicured middle finger extended to meet him.

He pounded his fists on the window scaring the people eating at the booth below him.

"I've had it," Opal said. "Urse, you and Luna go out and distract him. Ruby, come with me."

The women bundled up their coats and grabbed their bags with purpose. Ruby palmed their server a tip and whispered, "Sorry."

The fair-haired server said, "Careful, though. That guy gave me the heebies, and your friend was right, the bottle was open in front of him before I delivered it."

Opal grabbed Ruby by the hand and calmly headed toward the door. Suddenly, she yanked her into the bustling kitchen. The smell of char, bread, and garlic surrounded them. Ruby grimaced in apology and kept her head down as their heels clicked against the quarry tile.

"Hey, ladies," a voice called out. "You shouldn't be in—"

"It's fine. We are health inspectors. Good news, you passed." Opal grabbed a fry off a plate as they whizzed by the kitchen workers. She pushed the door to the outside alley by the restaurant's dumpsters.

"How did you know about this door?" Ruby asked.

"Oh, I worked here for a few months in the 90s. They wouldn't tell me where they bought their steak, so I got hired and found out myself."

Ruby's eyes lit up. "You always have the tastiest steaks."

She grinned and tipped her face hat.

Normally Opal took three steps to Ruby's one, now she couldn't keep up. Broccoli Man was in the street talking to Urse.

"Hold these." Opal kicked her heels off.

"Ope, no. Be cool," Ruby begged.

She stuck her tongue out at Ruby and sprinted toward the man like that short Olympic gymnast before the pommel horse. Urse and the man seemed to be speaking calmly when Opal's sprint ended with a kick to his ass, shooting Broccoli Man to the sidewalk.

Opal heard Luna yell her name, then, "Cops!"

The officer approached them tentatively. Broccoli Man pushed himself from the sidewalk and brushed dirt from his suit. Pointing to him, the officer said, "You, say nothing." He had a deep voice and sturdy manner. His badge read *Officer Jeff*.

"Okay, ladies, what happened?"

Urse spoke quickly. "Well, hello there, good-looking. I'm glad you're here. This man threatened us." She coiled her long hair around her index finger.

The officer grinned at her. "Uh-huh. Have you four helpless ladies been drinking tonight?"

Urse shifted her weight to her back leg and inched the other out of her dress slit. "It's my friend's birthday." She leaned toward his ear and whispered in a voice loud enough for everyone to hear. "She's a Make-A-Wish recipient."

His cheeks puffed out. "Okay, stay here." He looked her up and down. "Quietly."

Urse smiled at him and held the tip of her pointer finger between her teeth.

Ruby mumbled, "I beg you, please, stay still."

"Evenin', officer," Opal said.

Behind her coat pocket, Ruby's hands were moving.

"Uh-huh. What happened? I saw the end of a kick," the officer said.

Opal's heartbeat quickened. "Well, this fucker is a complete psycho and had it coming."

Ruby slumped.

Opal jerked her head toward a nearby parked taxi. "Go home, Ruby. You have nothing to do with this."

"Nope." Ruby shook her head. "Not without you."

"Why are you wearing those hats on your faces?" the officer asked.

Opal ripped off her hat and said, "Because I'm clearly disgusting, my grandpa just died, and it's my fucking birthday. So maybe you give me a break and leave us the fuck alone to go solve actual crimes."

"That's it." He reached for his handcuffs when Ruby slapped them to the ground. "You've got to be kidding me," he said.

Opal made a break for a bike rack at the corner of Marquette and Sixth Street, running shoeless. In a flash, she shook the bikes, looking for one that was unlocked. Officer Jeff started after her when Urse tackled him to the sidewalk. He rolled over Urse with ease and handcuffed her instead.

"You're so strong, officer," Urse said.

"Am I being punked?"

"You're going to ask me out, you know."

"I know." Officer Jeff nodded. "I have to wrangle your idiot friends first."

Ruby screamed, "Officer!" and ran toward Broccoli Man, who had his hands around Luna's neck. He called for backup and tackled the man to the pavement, easily overpowering him.

With sweat running down his face, Broccoli Man said, "You clearly don't know who I am."

"And you don't know who we think we are, fuck-face," Urse said from the ground, handcuffed.

"You hurt, Luna?" Ruby asked.

"No. This better not leave a mark, I have a necklace shoot next week." Luna rubbed her neck and looked up as Opal accepted a bottle of bourbon from a homeless guy watching the bike rack.

Ruby shook her head. "She said her grandpa died."

"Oh no."

Opal swigged from the bottle and handed it back to the homeless man.

He looked at her lip. "Uh, keep it. Happy birthday."

"What's birthday girl's name?" Officer Jeff asked Urse.

"Opal."

"Opal, do us all a favor and get back here," he shouted.

"Never!" She jumped on a bike—wobbling a bit until her third pedal rotation—when the bike veered into the side of the squad car that Officer Jeff had called for backup. Opal flew over the handlebars and landed with her back on the hood of the car with a winter white boob out of her dress. She laid motionless until the city noise settled for the world to figure out what had happened. Peeping one eye open, she waved the tiniest of waves at Ruby, popped her boob back into her dress, and went back to playing dead.

"She's fine," the second officer said. "She just moved."

Three squad cars later, the women found themselves sharing a long bench in Hennepin County jail smelling of imitation Chanel No. 5 and bad crotch.

Ruby elbowed Opal. "I'm sorry about Grandpa Henry. He's the reason I know good men exist."

"I thought he was the only one I could count on, but—" Her voice cracked.

"You have us," Luna finished.

Opal rested her head on the side of Luna's arm. "I'm still drunk."

"No duh," Urse said.

Three hours and one phone call later, Opal whispered to the women, "Follow my lead. We don't know her."

"Who?" Urse asked.

The cell doors slid open. "Opal Slepecki, Ruby Redstone, Luna Bacur, and Ursula…"

"Present." Urse jumped up, clicked her heels, and saluted.

"You think you are so smart. The jig is up ladies," the bailiff smiled.

"The jig is up? Oh God, not the jig," Urse mocked.

On the other side of the bars stood a man that loomed like a large, Amish barn and a woman with a lanyard and a gold badge hanging from her ample chest. *Department of Revenue.*

Snookie Bubotz.

A casting agent couldn't have done better. Snookie's hair was pulled into a tight, low bun; her white button down, navy pants, and fitted blazer matched her serious, makeup-free face. The comfortable shoes almost made Opal laugh. Snookie Bubotz would never wear those ugly shoes unless in disguise.

"Nope, I'm staying here." Opal crossed her arms over her chest. "There's no way I'm leaving with this fascist."

The bailiff smirked.

"Nice to see you, too, Mrs. Slepecki. Looks like we've got you on a dumb-dumb charge Capone." Snookie laughed.

"Put the cuffs on them for transport," she told the guy with her.

Snookie did her magic on paperwork and had the women released to her charge. On the way out, Urse mouthed, "Olive juice," to Officer Jeff as the women tried to maintain their composure.

They funneled into the black Suburban with tinted windows and breathed a collective sigh of relief once they turned onto 35W heading north.

"Thanks, Snookie."

"You're welcome. I should let you know, your grandpa insisted on paying me a retainer years ago in case something like this came up."

Grandpa Henry had seldom approved of their shenanigans, but Opal had caught him turning away to smile when the stories were relayed. Even dead, he kept an eye on her.

"There are two kinds of people in this world. The best ones will fight for you even when they know they will get their asses kicked. The second type aren't worth a damn," he had once said.

Each one of her friends had fought for her, and while it was a shock to her independent system, she would never be the same.

She belonged.

They would get her the heroin, spiders, and poisonous mushrooms. Their history and secrets were more important than the risk of jail.

I hope.

Chapter Twelve

Ruby

While the excitement of the thrift store caper waned, Ruby couldn't wait to try again for the heroin. The adrenaline surge felt like four cups of coffee on a bright day, the same feeling she had when Johnny was within eyesight. As much as she didn't want to admit it, Opal's death had an element of excitement. The world was punishing her and it was, well, *fair*.

Ruby sprinkled goldfish meal into the water and clicked the tank, garnering a big-eyed fish's attention. Her cell rang, taking her away from the hypnotic goings-on of her aquarium.

"Fuck this." Urse's voice boomed without saying hello. "You know Opal's crazy, right? What is she trying to do, make us prove we'll do anything for her? She's sooo dramatic. Why can't she just say, 'Hey, girls. I need a little extra attention, wondering if we can all get together'?"

She pulled her head back in a silent laugh. "Urse."

"Ruby."

It was so silent, she could practically hear her goldfish eating.

"Dramatic? Didn't you just kick a door down and bloody your husband's nose a few days ago?"

"Well, now you are being theatrical. I had a *reason* for that. I didn't say to my friends, 'Hey, time to commit murder, cause I'm feeling a bit Van Gogh.' It's *murder*, Rube. You get that, right?"

No one had ever accused her of being theatrical, even when she was in the theater. "Urse—"

"Ruby."

She's such a snot. How is she Johnny's sister?

"Well, let's try to imagine how she's feeling."

"Am I the only one thinking clearly around here? Feelings? For fuck sake, Ruby, if we *beep* her and she's only crazy, then what? Ever think of that? I just *can't* with you—I gotta go."

Ruby chucked her phone onto the couch and watched it bounce to the floor. "Play a song about a friend being a jerk to their friend with cancer," she said to her home speaker system.

A robotic voice offered, "I don't know how to answer that."

Yeah, I bet you don't.

Urse is rude and obnoxious. One little slip up and she's on you, making you feel brittle. Well, guess what, Urse? I have a secret. Know that. I know a bit about your second skeezy ex-husband. I can inflict pain, too, if pushed. I may be quiet, but Nighttime Mom didn't raise no weakling. Go ahead, press me.

Why does everyone afford Urse and her big mouth so much grace? Opal certainly did, which bruised Ruby. As if Urse needed protection from hurt feelings. Maybe if we had told her about her rotten second husband's behavior right away instead of keeping it secret, things would've turned out differently.

Though it had been years ago now, Ruby recalled feeling scolded by Opal, as if the two of them hadn't been friends *longer*. They had gone out for sushi shortly after the incident.

"Opal, don't you think we should tell her?" Ruby had placed an edge of the wasabi mound onto her sashimi. "How could she marry that tool?"

"I don't know, it's a mystery. Probably trying to finish the Bad Dad, Bad Provider circle by marrying one. What good will it do if we tell her? It's the first time in decades she stopped ruminating on Andy. Let's give it time to settle. Rack it up to pre-wedding insanity. And Ruby, be nice to her, she's not as tough as she acts." Opal looked around impishly. "He's ugly-hot though, right?"

Ruby rested her chopsticks carefully on the white porcelain holder. "If you quote me saying *yes*, I'll call you a filthy liar."

"Something about that busted up schnoz I think—not to mention how confidently he wears an abundance of jewelry and hair products. It's seriously unreasonable. But I don't know."

"Super sperm, probably."

"Ew. Speaking of sperm, hand me that yum yum sauce," Opal appeared to be daydreaming.

Ruby passed her the silver dish. "Yeah, ew?"

"Fine, are you going to play hard ball and make me ask?"

"Yes, please," Ruby smiled and cupped her hands over her head as if winning a race.

Opal slouched. "Was the completely inappropriate pass Jeff made at you any good?"

Picturing Urse's second husband, Ruby squished her face together and nodded.

"I fucking knew it. Details—you owe me that."

"As gross as he is, he knew what he was doing. Remember when the lights went out for a minute before we were about to do our bridesmaid line up?"

"Yeah. I thought it was a trash omen."

"When the lights went out someone grabbed my arm and covered my mouth skirting me into the hallway closet of the church. I could smell it was him. He said, 'I love Urse but I wanted to try your lips out first."

Opal covered her mouth. "He didn't, that pig. Go on."

"He grabbed way, way, under my ass and planted one on me."

"Tongue?"

"Strong tongue."

"Unbelievable, this guy."

"It's garbage, though," Ruby said.

"Humanity at its worst. He probably whacks off to it—especially if Urse told him about ol' Walt Walt hitting on you, too?"

She imagined Urse's first husband, that goon Walter.

"I bet she mentioned it as a cautionary tale," Opal continued. "Oh, and do you remember the cake?"

"Lemon served with vanilla ice cream. We should have stopped the wedding right there."

Ruby shook her head.

The group couldn't take one more of Urse's lemon-extract-loving freaks. Pulling her out of the bottle was getting tougher with each heartbreak.

Chapter Thirteen

Urse

A purple and red cup holding an assortment of butter pats lined the front of Urse's open fridge. There were various cups of fancy descent, with individual-sized to-go items—mayo, mustard, and pizza pepper flakes—all brought home from restaurants and travel. Opal and Luna had poked fun at first, until she uttered the magic word: sustainability.

Oh, sure, after that, they all coughed up their to-go packets, hotel shampoos, and extra pens.

She took a grass-fed butter pat from the collection, smeared it over a half a piece of toast, and called Luna.

"Standby, I'll merge Ruby."

Urse began, "So, Opal got pretty bitchy when I said we all thought she was wacko."

"*We*?" Luna said. "Wrong pronoun, Urse."

"What we *all* talked about," Urse said.

"She's fragile," Ruby said.

"Whatever. Fine. In any case, I think she has dementia, not the Big C. Doesn't that make sense? She's always searching for words, forgetting shit, and is all-around loopy. It's like she's digging in her purse to find her purse."

Urse headed to the basement with her toast, kicked her slide off, and dipped her toe in the pool. *Warm.*

At the bottom of her pool were various crystals left over from The

Crystalporium. Oddly-sized chunks or colors that didn't sell made their way to the chlorinated water, serving as reminders not to rest on the money they provided. Income, people, and good fortune were known to screw people over and leave sometimes.

"Miss Rube and I had an adventure yesterday—" Luna began.

"To get the—" Urse paused, remembering every phone call was bugged. "—stuff?"

"Yeah. Long story short, we only managed to get Ruby's purse stolen and a smashed car window."

"See? It's not meant to be. I say, we don't help Opal with her instruments of d—"

"*Urse,*" Ruby cut in.

Luna piped up. "She's in the denial stage."

Bitch, I can hear you.

Urse stopped moving her feet. "Whatever—and good luck with what you have to get," she said and hung up.

She laid back on the pool's edge and stared at the wooden support beams. The chlorine smell calmed her.

Dammit.

Luna picked up the moment she hit redial. "Sorry. I'm edgy, I don't mean to take it out on you. It's like we don't have time to think."

"Naw, I should've been a better listener. I've been stressed out with her...ask," Luna said.

"You get Ruby's stolen purse sorted?" Her magenta toenails wiggled underwater.

"Yeah, it's fine. She can throw money at problems anyway."

"Good. Will you tell Rube I'm sorry? I'm too weepy to call," Urse confessed. She pressed a towel to her cheek to steady herself.

"You okay?"

She sniffed. "Yeah, only because I have you and Ruby. Talk tomorrow."

Urse hit *end* and called Johnny.

"Hey, do you think I'm in denial about Opal?"

"*Hi* to you, too." He paused. "I mean *yes*, but it's okay."

"But what if she's losing it like Ma that one summer?"

Johnny snorted. "The fun family adventure? Haven't thought about that in years. That was the first time we met Opal, wasn't it?"

The memory tugged, dragging her back to a time when Ma was acting out of character. For about a week, she had hounded Urse for advice on what was stylish. She had begun wearing tight jeans and would drop for pushups mid sentence; there had been blended green drinks and trips to the pharmacy for diet meds. When the pharmacist had asked who the pills were for, Ma beamed.

Urse knew it wasn't a compliment.

At the end of the summer, Ma announced, "Kids, we are going on a fun family adventure! We are going camping with some friends."

Um.

Urse and Johnny had never been anywhere, let alone a *fun family adventure*.

"We are heading up north past Duluth for a Rainbow Gathering," Ma added.

Da fook? Johnny and Urse sat, dumbfounded.

A week later, a blue van with three people and a sticky-looking kid pulled up to their trailer. The side door slid open, revealing a large cargo area. A plethora of blankets, apples, and toilet paper—slotted to roll around unsecured in the back of the van—greeted them.

In her Z Cavaricci jeans and a Mork from Ork T-shirt cinching her small waist, Ma looked younger than her circumstances and quite pretty. No one would have thought her source was the local Vincent de Paul thrift store a mere mile from their trailer.

Smiling, she leaned into the open van.

"Kids, I'd like you to meet my special friends: Irv on Steering Wheel, Val on Snacks, and Bill on Napping. I'll, of course, be on drums," she said to laughter.

Weird.

Urse and Johnny didn't laugh.

"And this little pip right here is our Moonbeam," she continued, motherly kissing the small, uneven-looking child on the top of the head.

"Let's hit the road," Irv said.

They loaded up their supplies when Johnny whispered in Urse's ear, "Shh, get in the van," in his best creep voice.

Urse rolled her eyes and hit him in the gut. "Gross. The universe just shuddered."

As they drove Highway 61 along the shore of Lake Superior, they watched their Ma cuddle, fuss, and kid with her new friends suspiciously.

When they pulled into the national park, they positioned the van among the other attendees of the festival and unloaded their camping gear. The atmosphere reeked of merriment, smiles, and dreaminess, and people were playing beach ball catch as they hauled their open bottles into the woods. Moms carried barefoot, shirtless kids; dads carried coolers and sleeping bags. Everyone followed everyone else, smiling. Music spilled out of nearly every group with bikini tops and cut off shorts as the standard wear.

Johnny wouldn't stop smiling.

"This *is* a fun adventure," he said, winking at an older girl wearing a white tube top and short shorts. The path to the festivity was paved with the scent of weed and patchouli, which smelled the same to Urse. Small booths offering food, games, and hair braiding lined the trail in the woods, none of which accepted money—only trades.

When Urse approached a hairy-chested food vendor, he asked, "What do you figure a fair trade could be?"

She shrugged.

"Well, here's a list of what I could use." He handed her a piece of green construction paper which read:

light bulbs

gas can with working nozzle

new music

a hug

"Oh, sorry, I don't have any of those," Urse said.

"Not even a hug? We all have those."

Had he been wearing a shirt, she would have traded a hug for a corn dog.

"Ah, that's okay. Here's one anyway." He held out a corn dog with a napkin wrapped around the stick. "Do something nice for someone while you're here, okay?"

"Thank you, I will." She raised the corn dog as if in cheers and pocketed an extra mustard packet for later.

"See right there? You gave me warm gratitude and it's appreciated."

Urse bit into the warm-on-the-outside, frozen-on-the-inside corn dog.

Johnny was on a blanket two booths down sharing a Walkman. Urse approached, corn dog in hand.

"Choice," Johnny said. "Let me have a bite. I'm starving." He stretched out his hand.

"Get your own. You have *no* idea what I had to trade for it," Urse deadpanned.

"God, you're gross. No one would take you for a trade anyway."

She handed it to him and waited for him to hit the frozen part. He scrunched his face and handed it back.

Urse smirked.

"So, should we talk about Ma?" He smooshed a mosquito against his ankle. "I don't know, but I don't like it."

"I think she's with Irv."

"Yeah. I think he has money. Did you happen to catch his key chain?"

Johnny wiped his palms together.

"No, Magnum P.I. Why?"

"There's a fucking Mercedes key on the shitty van ring, that's why. I think he's pretending to be some hippie or something."

"Why would anyone do that?" Urse asked.

"Because that's how you get a girl that likes you for you, not the bucka-roos." Johnny crushed another mosquito against his knee. Blood smeared.

"That makes no sense."

"Well, something's up with our special friend. I don't trust him." He erased the smear of blood with some spit on the end of his finger.

Johnny and Urse didn't trust men as a general rule.

"I gotta see a man about a corn dog and maybe some bug spray," Johnny said before taking off.

Urse caught up with Ma and her new friends. She studied her. Ma hadn't seemed so housekeepery with two ungrateful kids, a trailer, and husband that abandoned her. She seemed...*lighter.*

"Urse, why don't you run back to the van and get some toilet paper? It's the hot item to trade right now, you can get yourself something to eat," Ma said as Irv tossed the van keys. Urse caught them midair.

She headed to the dirt path back to the cargo van, passing the peace and love crowd. They seemed like the unpopular kids' moms and dads, but with confidence. She wished she had that moxie. Urse felt invisible at school; how Johnny could be so cocksure of himself mystified her. He put on no airs, embraced his station in life, and made cross-economic friends. He once told her, "These rich fuckers need us as character reference—know that, Boy George."

Once at the van, she searched for something to carry the toilet paper rolls in. Well, *currency.* The jingle *Hefty, Hefty, Hefty* popped into her head as she grabbed a garbage bag.

A voice called out, "Hey! Anyone home?"

She peeped out the front window to see who was speaking.

"Anyone?"

Urse's eyes landed on a tanned boy with reddish-blond hair, bulky muscles, and freckles like an English setter. He held a gray kitten.

"Hi?" Urse offered through the closed, locked van.

"I found this kitten and wondered if you had any food for it?"

She slid the van door open to reveal a blush-worthy guy her age. He smiled widely, revealing the whitest, straightest teeth ever seen.

"Hi, uh, yeah, I think I...what do cats eat?" Urse asked. All the ones she knew were feral.

"Cat food?" He laughed. "I think anything we eat should be okay. Adorable, right?" He cuddled the kitten to his face. "Want to hold her?"

"Sure." The fluffy gray mass cupped in her hands. "So soft." One of the kitten's hairs stuck to her eyelash.

"My name is Andrew, but my friends call me Andy."

"My name is Ursula, but my friends call me Urse." As if she had friends calling her anything.

"There's no food in the van, but I know where we can find some corn dogs."

"The breakfast of champions." He looked embarrassed as his face turned red.

Her laugh came out louder than she would have liked.

Urse, Andy, and the kitten made their way back to the gathering with a Hefty bag full of toilet paper. People of all ages stopped to pet the kitten. *Everyone loves a kitty, no one loves a cat.*

"Who are you here with?" he asked.

"My mom, her new friends, and my weird brother," she said. "You?"

"My parents are camping down the road. They have no idea I'm even here. They think my brother and I are camping overnight Boy Scout style, which technically isn't lying." He smirked. "My twin and his girlfriend,

Tess, are around here somewhere." He gave the crowd a quick glance to no avail. "My dad kept saying, 'What the hell is going on with all these hippies?' on the drive up."

"My mom told us we were going on a 'fun family adventure.' I had no idea anything like this existed. I mean, they don't even use money," Urse said.

"Right? I had a guy ask me if I had a dube for a fry bread taco," he said. "I mean, well, uh, I've been around it before and all, I—"

"I don't smoke either."

He flashed a toothy smile.

Urse spotted Johnny lounging on a plaid blanket acting like a hotshot. Like he just got off tour with Van Halen surrounded by adoring fans. One of his hands was behind his back, fingers crossed like he did when he was lying. He noticed her, stood up, turned around, wrapped his arms around himself, and pretended to make out with someone.

She cringed.

The temperature rose as the thermometer lowered and the mood of the gathering shifted. It was then that Urse saw it: a fleshy, jiggly, white, middle-aged lady dancing naked to "The Wreck of the Edmund Fitzgerald" by Gordon Lightfoot.

She didn't seem to mind that her body wasn't magazine ready, or there were people around.

"Um, Andy?" She elbowed him. "Check out the grandma at 11 o'clock."

"Eleven o—oh, man, what? Stop it—no," he said. "I mean, if that's what you want to do, yeah, that's cool."

"Oh God, her husband's undressing." Urse moved her head but her eyes fixated.

The human beer belly began stripping in the single most technically correct sexy striptease ever performed. The crowd stirred a moment then raised their red Solo cups and carried on. A handful of part-time nudists joined in. After a rendition of "No Woman No Cry," people returned to their own thing, as if gawking at naked people was now unsavory.

Urse and Andy laughed uncomfortably.

Johnny's head sprang up between them. "Did you see mom and dad's dance of love?"

"AW!" Urse screamed, jumping at the intrusion.

"I'm scared, too, Urse! Seeing your parents' junk flapping in the fresh air of Gitche Gumee *is* upsetting," Johnny said, staring at Andy.

"Idiot!"

"I'm Urse's big brother, Johnny," he said, extending his hand for a shake. When Andy offered his hand, Johnny pulled his back and pretended to smooth his own hair.

"Kidding," he said, going in for a real shake this time. "And this is my new friend, Opal." He motioned to a strawberry blonde who stood hoisting her tube top up. Urse inventoried the girl. Her top kept edging down while the bottom floated above her big boobs like in dirty magazines. Urse noticed an uneven fake tan at her neck and wrists and Kangaroo sneakers that matched her green satin shorts. Caught gawking, the blonde gave her a dimpled, friendly smile and said, "Hi. Your brother's an idiot but I like him."

Johnny put his fists in his pockets and kicked the dirt in mock shyness.

"You are correct, he's a prized idiot. And he's my younger, immature brother."

"Have you seen Ma?" Johnny asked.

"No, but here are Irv's van keys in case you do," Urse said, relieved that Johnny was now errand boy.

"Oh, nice. I'm going to walk Opal back to her ride and go grab some TP from the van. I understand that's the shit around here."

Johnny laughed at his own joke. Opal rolled her eyes.

"Seriously, though, I heard you can get tons of food with it," he said and jogged off.

Urse smirked, knowing full well they were in her Hefty bag.

Andy turned to Urse. "Do you want something to eat?"

Urse made a point to look into his eyes long enough to know his eye color. A tidbit she read in a semi-dirty magazine. "Sure."

"Do you have anything to trade with?"

"Hmm...a kitten?"

"You!"

"Okay, this is a little embarrassing, but look in the Hefty bag."

He peeped in the bag. "So, what can I buy you with your own toilet paper?"

"I'll have jumbo shrimp and a baked potato with extra sour cream," she kidded.

"Weiner water soup it is!" Andy flashed a smile and left for food.

Ma appeared.

"Urse, have you seen your brother?" she asked.

"He headed to the van with the keys."

"I'm going to go take a nap. I'm not feeling...like myself." Something about the look in her eyes made Urse's stomach lurch.

"Do you need me to go back with you?" Urse offered.

"No, I'm just...tired," she said, spaced out.

"You sure?"

"Yaw."

Ma walked slowly but steadily toward the van. *She's fine.*

Andy returned with their food: fry bread tacos, fries with vinegar packets, and two cokes. Urse covered her mouth with her hand as she ate.

She started to wonder if he would be her first kiss.

As natural light was replaced by campfire light, they decided to bring their blanket, backpacks, and Hefty bag closer to the fire for privacy. The warmth, golden colors, and slow-motion crackles of the campfire inspired romance. They inched toward one another while looking forward.

After another inaudible mumble, she leaned forward. "What? I'm sorry I couldn't hear you."

"I said you are very beautiful."

Urse had never heard such a nice sentence. Maybe she'd imagined it.

"Really?"

"Really."

With that, she leaned her head on Andy's shoulder and stared at the fire in silence. He put his arm around her and nuzzled in. A hot pinball zipped around her stomach.

Then, in an unforecasted moment, he kissed her on the lips. *Parted* lips.

Thank God the wait was over. He tasted like TJ Swan, Carmex, and a hint of bug spray. His lips were thick and wet, moving all over hers, making her body respond in unfamiliar ways. So, this is what it felt like—sort of spicy down below. Now she understood why everyone was so nuts about sexy stuff. Then, out of nowhere, his tongue squirmed in her mouth. Her eyes popped open to see if it was intentional. He looked as if he was concentrating on a project. She went for it, and met his tongue with hers.

Gooey.

He moaned.

Probably a good sign.

His hands cupped her face; she slowly leaned back to her elbows. He moaned again, and she laid flat on her back, Andy on top of her.

In a fancy move, Urse reached around and grabbed his butt. The seam of her shorts felt delicious against her throbbing crotch.

Suddenly Andy froze.

He stopped kissing her and closed his eyes. "I'm so sorry...uh...it's just that you are so cute—"

She didn't understand his embarrassment but was afraid he would bolt.

People were always leaving her.

"No, you're fine. I'm having so much fun with you."

Andy untucked his shirt over a wet spot in the front of his jeans, his eyes cast down.

Had he peed his pants a smidge?

"I feel like I ruined everything." Andy said.

"No, you didn't. I'm having the best time."

"Can we not talk about it anymore?" he whimpered.

"About what?"

At that exact moment, a blood curdling scream pierced the night air. Marshmallows stopped mid-browning; all hippies and otherwise looked around for the source. People started running in all directions.

"Get him!" someone yelled.

An anthill cluster of people swarmed a man who was screaming, "I'll kill all you sons of bitches!" Blood smeared his face as he fought.

Women gathered their belongings, kids ran for their moms, and the circle of people being thrown expanded.

It was Irv on Steering.

Andy turned to Urse. "C'mon. We gotta get going. It's getting out of hand and I don't know where my brother is."

"I need to find Johnny and my ma."

Urse squeezed his hand so hard he stopped moving. "Hey. I think the crazy guy is my mom's friend."

"Oh no—"

"Go find your brother and I'll meet you back here after," she said.

"I don't want to leave you. I know it's weird, but I think we are soulmates." His eyes were as wet as the spot on his pants.

"I think so, too, Andy."

The crowd pushed them apart.

Bloodied Irv was heading in her direction. Urse bolted for the van.

Someone screamed, "He bit off some guy's finger!"

The horde was in a tizzy.

"He's trippin'!" a guy yelled as he ran, frayed jean shorts slouching.

At the van, Urse banged at the side panel door, panic rising in her chest.

Johnny slid it open. "I'll deny it, but I'm happy to see you." She climbed inside. "What's with the flip out?"

"Is Ma here?"

Johnny's thumb pointed to the back of the van. "Yeah, but she's acting all weird. Get this, I think she's *trippin'*."

"We gotta get outta here," Urse said. "You still have the keys, right?"

"What the fuck? *Why*?"

"Mr. Hot-for-Ma is freaking balls. I think he bit off someone's finger!"

"What about the others we drove up with?"

Their mom whimpered.

"We need to go now, Johnny. If we get stuck in traffic and she goes all finger biting, we gotta get to a hospital. The people here are weird but nice. Someone will grab them."

"Okay, but I don't like it," he said.

"That's so fucking helpful right now. Really fucking helpful."

While she had driven down a dirt road twice with their father, that didn't mean she was a fluent driver.

As if reading her mind, Johnny said, "Urse, you can do this. It's not that big of a deal. Tons of dumber people than you drive all zee time."

She knew it was a vote of confidence.

Her hands shook as she fiddled with the keys.

Swallowing hard, she put the van in D, let up on the gas, and edged forward and back. They were parked behind a Toyota pickup with two bumper stickers. One read, "I brake for hallucinations" and the other, "Lizzard's Art Gallery." With one bumper out, she gained confidence and a feel for the van. Fortuitously enough, Irv had pointed the van in the direction of home in anticipation of traffic.

Two hours later, the three rolled into their trailer's driveway on fumes.

"He's not getting his van back," Johnny said.

"You know that's right." This was only the second time she'd seen Johnny's sour face. The first was when their dad had left.

Their mom threw up in the back. Urse and Johnny hauled her from the van into her own unmade bed. Urse cleaned up the sick in the van while Johnny made grilled ham and cheese sandwiches.

He squirted ketchup on his plate, mustard on hers, and slid it to Urse who had finished scrubbing her hands.

"Well, that *was* a fun family adventure," he said.

"Yeah. Dad doesn't know what he's missing."

Ma lost her mind for a day fair and square and now Opal is losing it just like Ma did.

The creepy form of a body in Opal's bed, the note on the fridge, and the insistence that her husband was away on business...maybe Opal isn't *trippin'* but she could have lost it from the stress of Oliver's death.

Pancreatic cancer, my ass. Opal needs a reset, love, and a kick in the pants.

Now, I just need to prove it before she does anything stupid.

Chapter Fourteen

Luna

Vibrant house plants contained in various hues of red and copper planters surrounded Luna at her kitchen table. One industrious vine stretched toward a window handle as if it were making a break for it.

Luna cupped her hands around her coffee mug, then pressed them to the back of her neck. Since Opal's cancer news, her eyebrows had been falling out and her neck was as stiff as a giraffe's neck brace. As if losing her wasn't bad enough, it was even worse participating in getting her lost.

I can't have anyone sniff around my past. Ruby's too rich and Urse is too, well, Urse *to go to prison. Not me. I already have one odd situation, and there's no such thing as two.*

Sure enough, when Luna was a little girl, her grandma had warned her about things like this. Grandma Ada had pointed her bony index finger to the heavens and said, "Sometimes the moon and tides and creatures of the world want to be heard. It doesn't happen often, but they will screw you up."

Luna, dogs, and the wind could recognize those odd nights her Grandma Ada had spoken of, the pre-earthquake jitteriness of it all, borderline sexy. Shuddering, she thought back to the night of the full moon—twenty years ago, now—and her big confession.

The women had lounged around Opal's gazebo in La-Z-Boy patio furniture. As Opal made more money, the furnishings had been swapped for more chic pieces, but on the tell-all night, Luna remembered the woven chairs left wicker patterns on the back of their smooth legs.

Luna had put her feet on Opal's chair, her short skirt framing her long, tanned legs. Beck's "Lost Cause" played on the house system.

Urse stood, feet wide, bucking her back in slow motion with a bottle of Caymus in her outstretched arm. "It's been a good day, ladies. Full moon time." She glugged wine from the bottle. "Come on, let's dance." She kicked off her Escada shoe; it spun heel over toe and stuck in a crevice from the force.

Luna, Opal, and Ruby cheered.

Opal went to the house and returned with a golf pencil. She drew an outline of the shoe on the gazebo wall like a dead body and handed the pencil to Urse, who pretended to lick the tip of it and sign autographs. The women clapped and nodded when she bowed.

Luna stood and slow-motion danced; Urse extended a hand to Ruby, who smiled and kidded, "I'm so good. I've been slo-mo dancing the whole time." She laughed and waved them off.

The music and barometric pressure rose, glasses emptied, and livers clocked in overtime. The full moon lit the women's faces as if they were children, blurring out freckles, dimples, and lip lines.

After three drinks, Ruby's eye wandered.

"You eyeballin' me, girl?" Opal teased.

Ruby nudged the bottom of Opal's glass as she sipped; wine spilled down the front of Opal's Metallica shirt, narrowly missing her blazer. They laughed as Opal blotted the spill with Ruby's extra sweater, which was draped over her chair.

Urse jabbed her finger at Ruby to get her attention but was laughing too hard to speak.

Luna piped up. "She's using your sweater."

Closing her eyes and throwing her head back, Ruby said, "Outplayed."

Opal was the first to get sentimental when soaked in wine. "I gotta say," she said, "you know when you are with people that love you when they"—she tried reattaching the end of her fake eyelash but it kept popping off—"are happy for you when you're on top." Her gray-blue eyes watered. "Any half-wit is happy to help when you're down and out. Hell, they feel good about it, don't they?"

Ruby nodded.

"It's to the point where I don't say anything about good stuff—hell, they have me convinced I'm bragging anytime the proversial—no, that's not right. What is it?"

"Proverbial," Urse said.

"I've heard it both ways," Opal smirked. "Proverbial windfall comes. What was I talking about? Oh, the three of you get up early to cheer one another on, and I, for one, thank and love you all for that."

Luna leaned to Opal, put her cheeks in her hands and kissed her smooth forehead. "Same," Luna said.

Urse nodded, opened the sixth bottle of wine and smelled for vinegar.

"My mom couldn't manage to fake one 'good job'—not at the first house, first hotel, or first million for that matter," Ruby said. "When that jerk sued me, for what? Thirty mil? She said, and I quote, 'You flew too close to the sun, Icarus.'"

Luna tilted her head. Ruby seldom spoke, let alone of her alcoholic mom.

"When I brought the lawsuit up on a gazebo night, I remember Urse said, 'Fuck that guy. We'll kill him before he gets that far.' Ope, you said, 'It's okay. Worse comes to worst, we remake your money.' Luna, well, I remember you looking pretty with that Parisian scarf you had on." She elbowed her, smiling.

"My own mother broke my bones and you all put it in perspective. I trust you with everything." Ruby leaned back in her chair and crossed her arms signaling the end of her thoughts.

Now, the lump in Luna's throat was less of a rock and more of an egg. It was as if she spoke her truth, it could be swallowed or moved. The full moon hoped it for her.

"As long as we are talking about hard stuff, I need to tell you something," Luna slurred. She had kept the secret for decades and wasn't sure where to begin. Her hand covered her mouth as it had kept the secret, too.

"Ooo, fun. A new story," Opal said, rubbing her hands together.

"My grandma raised me, you all know that." Luna cleared her throat. "I've never told the story about my mom and what happened."

The women quieted and feigned sobriety to concentrate on Luna. The night air held a small breeze.

"You all have to swear—" she started.

In unison, they chorused, "Swear." Opal flipped the Girl Scout sign. Ruby put her hand flat over her heart.

Luna took a deep, steadying breath as she fiddled with the end of her hair scarf. "Growing up, my mom lived on the streets, which couldn't have been great as she was schizophrenic."

Urse clasped her hands and leaned in; her seat tipped forward, and she scooted back.

"When I was sixteen, she postcarded to say she was coming for a visit. Mind you, my grandma and I begged her to live with us, invariably there would be some drama with the voices in her head and she'd ditch. I still have the postcard. There was a dried-up Luna moth Scotch-taped to it saying she'd be coming." She cracked her knuckles.

Opal poured another round of wine.

"First off, I read my mother's diary after her death. I'll give you the details according to that, then, the hard stuff. As I mentioned, my mom suffered from mental illness, she heard 'nippits.'" Luna put air quotes around the word, went for her glass of wine, and spilled it. "Prolly for the best," she mumbled, continuing.

Opal used Ruby's ruined sweater to clean up the wine.

"These nippits told her what to do, how to act, and actively screwed her up. Apparently, my mom thought the nippits could read her thoughts through the Mercury in her cavities which prompted trips to dentists in whatever city she was in at the time. I can't make this up. She walked around with one of those heavy vest thingies." Luna fidgeted with the stem of her empty wine glass as she gained courage.

"From the dentist," Opal said.

Luna nodded.

Opal, Urse, and Ruby's eyes glued on her as she spoke.

"My mom was a beautiful woman and I'm not just saying that. She looked sixteen and a prettier version of myself and grandma."

Urse mumbled, "Whoa."

"Turns out the good dentist was a pedo, so he probably figured, 'Heh, she looks young, so I can't get in trouble.' Fucking weirdo attached himself to a schizophrenic."

"My God." Urse shook her head, disgusted.

"Right? So this pervert, one Dr. Rain—yeah, can't make this up—somehow gets into my sick mom's head, gloms onto her, and boom, they are coming for a visit. Mind you, my grandma and I hadn't seen her in years when she strolls up with some peach-pit-faced motherfucker, smarmiest guy on the planet. He's hard to describe, like one of those guys who acts like his fingertips are dick ends."

Opal grimaced. "Ew."

"Don't think badly about my mom, but she put her period blood in a cocktail he drank as a love potion." Luna gulped loudly and continued. "Her diary had a bloody fingerprint and a heart drawn around it. That speaks to her mind."

"Does that work?" Urse clearly tried lightening the mood.

Luna's shoulders dipped, her posture softened, and she relaxed.

"Can we pause for a bathroom break?" Opal crossed her legs for effect.

The women stood up and made for the bathrooms. From under the table, Carol stirred and followed them into the house. Ruby dug in her purse for weed. When they returned, she lit it on Opal's gas range.

Ruby passed the joint to Urse. "Good idea," she said.

Urse offered it to Opal who shook her head. Luna took a big drag, held her expanded chest, and sank into it.

They headed back to the gazebo.

"Where'd I leave off?" Luna asked.

"Dirty dentist, period blood potion," Urse said, smelling her fingers after the weed.

"Right. She brings the creep dentist Dr. Rain to meet us. Short story long, I'm fixing after dinner coffee when I catch him putting something in my drink through the reflection in our kitchen window."

Ruby gasped, Opal covered her mouth, and Urse said, "Fuck."

The night air felt heavy.

"Exactly." Luna gulped air.

It could have been the end of the confession, but the moon egged her on.

"Turns out my mom and grandmother were drugged. I pretended to drink it to buy time. Let me back up a bit. The closest neighbor was too far to hear me scream. My grandma went to bed early, I couldn't wake her up, and my mom was conked out at the table. It took me a minute of sheer terror to concoct a plan, rapid speed."

"Oh, man—and you're such a plotter, you must've been freaking," Opal said.

"Exactly. I told him I was beat and headed to bed."

Ruby bit the skin around her nails nervously. Luna expected her to leave when conversations got rocky.

"In my mom's diary, she wrote, 'The nippits make my bedsheets squiggly with their handwriting, and they are scratchy and smell like cinnamon.' I cannot get that out of my head. In a weird way, I see how she tried making sense out of what she went through." Luna's voice cracked. "Like she needed order in the chaos. You guys, my poor mom." She fought back a sob.

Ruby's eyes welled.

"I'm sorry." Urse spoke barely a whisper.

With a shaky hand, Luna had a sip of water and drew a big breath. "I laid next to my passed-out grandma with a pair of tweezers in my hand. My mom—in her tactical vest—was out cold in the other room. I heard the dentist watching TV. I mean, was he going to Dahmer us, or what? My only plan was to wait, to see if he would try to hurt them or come after me. Then, he tested me. 'Luna, are you awake? What channel is the evening news on?' He waited and asked again. 'Luna?' But I kept quiet. He needed to think I was drugged."

She leaned forward, taking another drink of water as if it provided calm. "I heard him creep down the hall toward my room."

Opal noisily sucked in and held her breath.

"He stood by my bed. I could hear him undress in the darkness, the whole time he kept saying, 'My baby girl, are you sleeping? Are you, sleep...ing?'"

Tears rolled down Luna's cheeks as she spoke. "The saying should be *scared paralyzed* not *scared stiff.* I couldn't move an inch. When he touched my thigh, something gave, like the fear cracked away and BOOM!" She paused. "I tried counting to seven. I swear I tried, but only got to six. Then I hy-po-thet-i-cally stabbed him in the neck with the tweezers, over and over until all I could hear was gurgling." Her fingertips pressed into her eyes at the memory.

Opal's hands framed her face as if in bright sun. "Oh God."

"That's not the worst part." Luna said, eyes closed.

Urse was quiet for the first time in their friendship. Ruby had blood coming from the nailbed she chewed.

"Rube," Opal motioned to the blood. Urse handed Ruby a linen napkin.

"Go on," Urse finally said.

Luna stiffened and finished her story. "I blamed it on my mom so I could get her off the streets into a mental health facility. It worked. I mean no one, and I mean no one, believes schizophrenics."

"Holy cats," Urse said. "You wanted her somewhere safe."

"And she was. We had three awesome weeks before she, my pretty mom, she—"

"Take your time," Urse said.

"—she killed herself—resorted to suicide or whatever the hell people say these days." Tears streaked down her face.

"No. Oh God, no." Opal covered her face in her hands, regrouped quickly, and spoke. "You did the best you could, Lune. None of us could have managed as well as you did."

Ruby nodded, her dark hair hiding her rapid sign language tic.

"It's weird to say but the, well, *stabbing* wasn't as bad as having my mom believe it was my grandma who—" Her eyes searched the horizon for a better word than *killed*.

"Ended?" Opal asked.

"How about 'fucking defended yourself'?" Urse offered.

"My mom's big brown eyes looked so betrayed. She called him her 'husband' and kept repeating, 'Why would I kill him? I loved him? I love him.'" Luna's strength melted from the admission, yet the burden felt more digestible now.

After the confession, the women had swallowed portions of Luna's grief. There had been questions, of course, but they needed their brains and hearts to settle.

The full moon, tides, or whatever magic forced the secret's hiding spot, and screwed Luna up for now. But as with all things in nature, it leveled out in the end.

The truth was out and the world still spun.

Chapter Fifteen

Opal

Movement in the birdbath caught Opal's eye. Peering out her living room windows to the wooded area that butted up to her yard, she spied two birds frolicking in the heated water.

Fucking bluebirds? Are you kidding me?

The home was so quiet she couldn't tell if thoughts echoed in her mind or in the house.

We were the bluebirds of happiness. Now what? Oliver, you should be here taking care of me. My hand was supposed to be held. It's not fair. It's not fair that I have to meet with a death nurse, either.

Tess Hokanson, her new friend and unassuming heir to Opal's friendships, would be there shortly with a few questions about her medications.

Ding dong.

Opal smiled, opening the door. "Tess. Gorgeous as usual."

"You're not so bad yourself."

Tess wore a forest green blazer over an ebony jumpsuit with platform Converse sneaks and a matching bag. She took her shoes off at the entryway bench.

"You can leave your shoes on. Oliver and I put in hardwood so people could wear them. You probably don't know, but shoes are a big part of short women's outfits."

"Funny, part of my tall gal outfit is to be barefoot."

They nodded, entertaining the other's point of view.

"Come on." She motioned Tess into the kitchen. "Oat milk latte, right?"

"Good memory." Tess slid her boots off. "Opal, your home is beautiful. Your artwork is—oh." She stopped, eyeing up the nudes. "Did you paint them?"

"Thank you. Not these, no. I've been meaning to hit my painting hard, but I guess 'back burner' is 'never burn' now." She forced a smile and led Tess to the kitchen.

As Opal tapped her espresso machine, Tess settled in a chair at the kitchen island.

"We have some work to do, right?"

"I suppose we do." Tess unpacked a leather journal from her bag.

Opal handed Tess a rectangle mug with a round rim.

"Weird." She smiled, tracing her finger around its edge.

"Thanks." Opal began, "What I'd like to accomplish today are timelines, legalities, and finances."

"I hear you. I'd like to review your doctor's reports and care plan first, if you're comfortable with that."

A crafty bitch that won't be brushed over.

"Absolutely. Question, can I assume our...what are we calling it?"

"Meeting?" Tess sipped from her mug. "Holy buckets of mud, Andy, that's good coffee."

"Kind of you to say—Juan Valdez minus Juan Valdez plus locally roasted beans. I worked at a roaster for six months to figure out the secrets of good coffee. The amount of technical prowess is insane. I ended up working the front counter, mostly."

Tess's crooked tooth peeked from her broad smile. "You remind me of my brother. He had the same sense of humor and sense of adventure," she said.

"Had?"

"Yeah, he died when I was young. But every now and again, I'm reminded of how damn funny he was."

"May I ask how?" Opal asked tentatively.

"Not entirely sure. It happened in New Orleans at some festival or something. My parents and I were eating dinner, a hot wild rice dish. Still can't eat it to this day." She sipped her drink. "The phone call came in and my dad answered. He was so irritated to have our dinner interrupted he probably only heard 'police' and assumed they were asking for a donation. He barked, 'I don't pay for protection!' and hung up. A few seconds later, they called back. I heard the man on the other end of the line yell, 'Mr. Hokanson. I don't need any of your nonsense! Your son is dead.'"

Opal covered her mouth with her hand.

"Yeah. My dad started apologizing and crying, 'We're on a budget. I didn't know. I'm sorry, blah, blah.'"

"That is so horrible," Opal said.

"Right? Being on a budget *was* horrible," Tess kidded.

Opal nodded.

"The cop told my parents it was an allergic reaction. Details were murky as he was '*with-with*' a married man when it happened. Mind you, I knew he was gay—my parents didn't. Figured if he wanted them to know he would've told them. Keeping his secret made me feel closer to him."

"It's not fair," Opal said.

"You of all people know it isn't."

"I'm sorry about your brother."

"Me, too." Tess took another sip of her coffee. "Sorry, you were talking about our meeting before I got to blabbing."

"That was honesty, not blabbing, my friend." She paused. "Okay. Can our conversation be off the record?" Opal asked.

"Well—"

"I ask only because I'd like to give you a friendly amount of money to take care of my... my..." Opal's eyes lifted, searching for the word.

"Transition to the hereafter?" Tess offered.

"Death."

"I enjoy the hell out of you." Tess's dark eyes, full of compassion, didn't shy from Opal's.

"I don't need a 'friendly amount of money.' I believe in ethical end of life care. Our culture is screwed up on the natural process of dying. Hell, the same week I put my greyhound, Carol, down, my grandfather died—"

"Wait. Hawhat—what did you say your dog's name was?"

"Carol."

"Say it louder," Opal said.

"Carol!"

Opal's dog sprang out from under the table and rested her head on Tess's lap.

"You gotta be kidding me." She laughed, patting the dog's head.

"Sorry, I interrupted you with some clandestine shit. You were saying that your grandfather died?"

"Yes, he had Parkinson's. He struggled for three days with start-stop breathing and excruciating pain before he passed. Meanwhile, my Carol had a shot and was gone within thirty peaceful seconds. It did my head in. Still does, I guess. So, yeah, we can be off the record."

"I'll just ask. Are you afraid to die?"

Tess's forehead lifted. "I should say no, but you're like human sodium pentothal, so, yes, a bit."

Opal nodded, rubbing her forehead of sweat. "I don't want to miss the fun. Our wee friend group figured it out. I mean, hell, Urse lived in a single-wide with no heat, Ruby had a mom that should've raised cobras, and Luna had a schizophrenic mom that killed herself. Together, we plotted and bulldozed to get to a place with safe digits in our bank accounts," Opal said.

"And you? What's your struggle?"

The question caught Opal off guard.

"Me? Oh, I'm angry, mentally poor, and live a fear-based life."

Tess's eyebrows furrowed.

"Excuse me. It seems the bathroom calls more often than not these days."

"Are you feverish?" Tess asked.

"Maybe. I can't tell if it's in my head or not. Hell, I might just be crazy."

"I see."

Opal slid from the counter-height chair. "Help yourself to anything in the fridge. Whether you like it or not, you're family now."

When Opal returned, she knew Tess would shelve the tricky prescription questions.

"I'm having my friends procure items for the day. Death cap mushrooms, brown recluse, and heroin."

Tess put her hands up, palms out. "Whoa, whoa, whoa." She jerked back, crossing her arms tightly.

"It's not like any of us has ever tried it. We aren't druggies." Opal shrugged. "I figured, if not now, when? And what a way to go, right?"

Tess squished her mouth to one side before speaking. "This could put us all in serious trouble. I get what you're saying, but I've worked hard for my license." She paused. "What are the others' feelings on it?"

"They love me and are willing to prove it by helping," she fibbed. "Listen, if we put our heads together, there will be no problems, I can assure you."

"Forgive me for being indelicate, but you won't be able to assure me, you'll be dead."

Opal swallowed hard. "Right. The assurance comes with the acts prior."

Tess, no longer demonstrating buying signs, pushed her chair back.

"Listen, for whatever reason, you were put into our lives for a purpose,"

Opal said. "I think it's to help me die and continue on with the group of friends. I don't buy into the woo-woo, but according to Luna, you are in our group's tarot cards."

Tess rubbed her eyes. "I'm overwhelmed and feel like running."

"Me, too." Opal's eyes watered.

Tess's shoulders dropped. "I don't doubt that." She put her coffee mug in the sink and gathered her things. "Can I think on it and get back with you tomorrow?"

"Of course. Whatever you choose to do, it's fine. There are only five of us in this world, turns out you are one of us. That won't change, and I know you feel it, too."

Tess smiled through tight lips.

Opal walked her to the front door. Tess stopped halfway down the sidewalk, walked back, and hugged her.

She watched Tess's taillights shine on and off then went back into the house, Carol trailing with a stick.

She'll do it, she just needs time.

Chapter Sixteen

Ruby

It had taken five years of tedious due diligence to get to the closing table. Her friends knew the details of each offer, counter, and earnout structure, but Ruby kept the date of signing to herself. If all closed soundly, the Redstone Holding Company would soon be absorbed by a Canadian entity. By 2:01 p.m. today, her share would dribble to five percent and her new swollen bank account would be divided between HSBC and Morgan Stanley, respectively.

Ruby never prioritized money. Every birthday candle, shooting star, and penny tossed into a well was spent wishing her mom sober. *Had I used my wishes on money, it still wouldn't have been this big.*

She slid oak hangers from her closet to and fro. The closing required something professional yet chill. Her clothes, shades of charcoal and navy—with the exception of one dazzling red dress with tags attached—were used to blend in, unlike the way Opal and Urse dressed. They took it seriously. *Showy.* Opal played with color, and Urse, structural components. Nighttime Mom once said, "People that are dead inside wear L.L. Bean, for Chrissake. L.L. gol-damn Bean. Rich bastards."

Ruby smirked as she grabbed the most L.L. Bean outfit in her closet. Dark, straight-legged pants, and a simple T-shirt under a St. John blazer—one Opal insisted that she buy. Not Bean, but nothing to argue with.

Her height served her well when dealing with businessmen. *Nothing to see here.* The numbers were good, the deal, sound, but the papers weren't filed yet, and sometimes during high tension dealings, things hiccupped. *God, I'll miss the rush of a throbbing forehead vein signaling an opportunity to turn anger into gold.*

Ruby's team of attorneys arrived at the office five minutes before their slotted time. They shook hands, straightened ties and skirts, and headed to the conference room with their bulging messenger bags and briefcases.

"Excuse me while I run to the restroom," Ruby said.

Once in the stall, she heard the door next to her open. Out of habit, she peeped under the partition to see their shoes. *Large wing tips?*

"Ah..." A low sound came from the person.

She stood on the toilet seat and looked over the wall to catch a well-dressed man about to shoot heroin into his junk. Her eyes widened.

Opportunity meets preparation.

"Hey, buddy," Ruby whispered.

The man covered his crotch with his hands, looked left to right, then up meeting her eyes.

He scrambled. "Uh, excuse me. I—"

"You're in the women's restroom. I suggest you hand that over. I'll dispose of it, but no more."

"It's not what you think, I'm, I'm—"

She opened her hand and curled the tips, armpit resting on the wall. "Easy does it."

He handed her the syringe, pointy end facing out.

"I'm diabetic."

Ruby risked it. "No, you aren't. You're struggling. I get it. Try to get yourself sorted, okay?"

He scurried out of the restroom without washing his hands, the door clunking shut behind him. Ruby lowered the toilet lid with her foot and sat.

Unfuckingbelievable. Junk in his junk.

Hooow, hooow, hooow...her breath sounded like those in child birthing videos. She smiled. Her hands trembled as she wrapped the nearly full syringe in toilet paper. She found a pen cap in her purse to stabilize the needle and mummied up the whole thing. Her heart raced; this was more exciting than selling her business.

She washed her hands and headed to the boardroom to find Wingtips sitting across the table—one of the buyer's army of attorneys. After watching his Adam's apple bob nervously, she ignored him as papers slid toward her for inspection. An hour later, the deal closed.

"And to think it only took five years to make the signing this easy." Her lead attorney smiled. Hands shook, backs clapped, and smiles of the now-wealthier beamed; her team insisted on champagne. All parties drank one glass—the business version of breaking bread—and left to maintain professionalism.

Mentioning family obligations, Ruby dodged invitations and hurried to her car.

"Call Luna Low Luna Bo Beena."

"Calling Luna Low Luna Bo Beena," her car parroted.

"Hey, Rube, how's it going?"

"Glad you asked," she whispered. "I found...the stuff."

Luna matched Ruby's volume. "Get out of here! How?"

"I'll tell you later. Meet me at Signature Flight Support and bring a going out outfit, ASAP."

"Call Urse. I know she's not doing anything, and pick her up on the way."

She tapped *end* and called Opal. "Hey, how are you feeling?"

"Good, you?"

"Grab an overnight bag. We're celebrating in Montreal tonight."

"Okay. Let me find someone to watch Carol." Ruby's playlist popped into her car. Aimee Mann's sultry voice filled the air.

Ruby hit *next.*

Cage the Elephant.

Next.

"Cool, cool. I'll be at Signature waiting for you."

"Let me in on it?"

"Ruin the surprise. See you soon."

Ruby called her aviation team. She wanted to spoil her friends with the good booze and Atiki's Flight Catering for the aircraft.

I can't believe I found heroin—in the wild, nonetheless.

Ruby's playlist popped into her car—Winehouse, *next,* Salt-N-Pepa, *next—*

Dessa—*there it is.*

"Matches to Paper Dolls."

Chapter Seventeen

Urse

Scanning her wardrobe for a sexy one-night-only outfit, Urse threw her over-the-knee boots, a butt-covering blazer, and an old hotel soap into her J.W. Hulme overnight bag.

Luna would have makeup and she could wear the same outfit on the aircraft both ways. *Luna could hit up a coronation as easily as a dominatrix dungeon as prepared as she was, the anal freak.*

She called Johnny.

"Hey. What's up?" he asked.

"Am I on speaker?" Urse rolled her blazer like a cigar.

"Not anymore."

"Opal wanted me to ask if you could feed and let Carol out tonight and in the morning. She said you could crash there if you felt like it."

God, I hate packing. Heels and going out clothes. I can sleep in them if need be. She smelled the band of her La Perla lace bra and stuffed it into her shoe.

"Sure. How do I get in?"

"The code is 8008."

He laughed. "Boob."

"You're a real mental giant. Listen. I need you to snoop around her place for any medical records, medication, or signs anything's off." Urse tested her overnight bag's zipper by adding her kimono.

"Come on, Urse. What if she has cameras? Fucking awkward ask."

"There's a lot of fucking awkward asks going around. Johnny, if she's having some sort of a psychotic break or dementia or something we need to know before—"

"Okay, enough."

"I told you about the gravity blankets forming Oliver's body, right?"

"A million times. I think she misses him. It's not a psycho thing."

She paused packing to yell at her brother. "Well, did I mention she says he's away on business and is coming back?"

"Grief is tricky—"

"So is euthanizing a friend without all your facts," Urse snapped.

He sighed loudly. "Don't worry. If there's something to find, I'll find it."

She went to the hallway closet full of samples and grabbed a fresh toothbrush courtesy of her dentist.

The hotel will have toothpaste.

"Where are you nutters going, anyway?" Johnny snapped his gum.

"Ruby's taking us to Montreal for the night."

"Ruby? Tell me more. Like, what do you think she'll wear?" he asked eagerly.

"Idiot."

Johnny laughed. "Have fun. Stay out of trouble this time."

She rolled her eyes. "I gotta go. Luna's here already. Text me after."

Approaching the car, Urse waved. Luna popped her trunk. Urse smiled, noticing a dozen boxed crystals from The Crystalporium and made room for her bag.

Once in the car, Urse nodded and said, "Ready."

"You look cute today. Say, is it weird we're doing this with Opal being as sick as she is?"

Urse clicked her seatbelt scooting out from under the chest strap. "Might be what we all need. Maybe we can slow Opal down so we are all comfortable."

"Maybe we pretend Opal's fine for one night." Luna put the car in reverse and navigated out of the spot.

"What's Ruby up to, anyway?"

"She mentioned finding Opal's drug." Luna closed her eyes and shook her head.

"Where? Wait, alone? She found it *alone*?" Urse asked.

"No idea. She said she'd tell us later."

Sirens sounded.

Luna pulled her car to the side of the road and waited until an ambulance passed. They followed the emergency vehicle halfway to the private airport. At the front of the gate, Luna slid her window down and hit the intercom button.

"We are with the Redstone party."

Beep. The chain link gate slid to the right. They pulled to the door where a smiley valet took their bags and keys.

"Thank you." Unseasoned, he looked down at his tip.

The lobby smelled of fresh chocolate chip cookies, popcorn, and money. A fireplace crackled, and phones rang unobtrusively in the background. A cleaner wearing a jumpsuit-like uniform touched up the windows overlooking the runway while scruffy men in fluorescent vests walked back and forth on the tarmac with handheld lights. Two pristine red and black carpets ushered passengers to their aircraft.

A woman who could model Scandinavian sweaters for a living greeted them.

"You must be Luna and Urse. I'm Erin. May I get you coffee or tea?"

"No, thank you," Urse said as Luna shook her head, smiling.

"Your party is onboard already. Follow me." The leggy blonde matched their height, which happened so seldom, it drew attention.

They walked past the smiling customer service reps at the front desk down the short red carpet to the G650's steep staircase with polished steel handrails.

The pilot standing at the top of the staircase, in a crisp uniform and polished shoes, greeted them. "Welcome aboard."

He must not have a dog.

Urse grinned. "I'm going to need your hat for a bit. You don't need it to *foxtrot-lima-yankee,* do you?"

He handed her his still-warm hat and said, "Nope."

Urse donned his cap and chin upped him.

"He's married. Leave him be, you maniac!" Luna called out laughing.

The pilot turned and slid the door closed behind him. Preflight knobs, clicks and winding noises grew loudly as safety procedures kicked in. Urse strutted down the plush cream carpeted aisle, trimmed in glossed mahogany, and tipped her hat to each woman before taking her seat.

Erin, their flight attendant, handed them floral swag bags with beet and apple shooters, Burt's bees lip balm, French macaroons, and hangover medicine twisted in navy tissue paper. Urse took the cap off the balm and brought it to her nose. "Smells like Luna's angel food cake."

"Glad you like it. Now, drinks before drinks." Erin smiled. She offered nips in black cherry-colored cordials then whisked them away for takeoff.

Once safely at walking around altitude, Ruby motioned the women to the conference table toward the back of the aircraft. The flight attendant remained in the jump seat by the cockpit.

"You will not believe what happened today," Ruby eagerly began.

"Morrissey showed at a scheduled concert?" Opal was still salty about his no-show a month ago. "I wonder if I told him I'm almost dead he'd play."

"Sadly, no, but I did get your—" Ruby checked around for unauthorized ears. "—ask." Her pouty lips widened.

"Ha—what?" Urse cupped her hand by her ear.

"Yeah. I caught a guy shooting junk into his—"

"Oh my God. Throw us a detail or two," Urse said.

"I was in a public bathroom at an office when I saw a guy's shoes under the stall. I snuck a peek over the top and low and behold, he had a syringe."

"Holy shit," Urse said. "For a minute I thought this was at your house. Jezus, go on."

Ruby lifted her chin motioning to the flight attendant coming their way. The women settled into their seats.

"I understand that celebrating is in order?" Erin asked, pouring champagne into flutes. She set down small artisan cheese and cracker trays surrounded with edible flowers. The women turned to Ruby.

We can't be celebrating the way Opal wants to die.

"Thank you, Erin," Ruby said.

Opal craned her neck toward Ruby and raised her hands in the "what?" sign.

"I closed on my business today," Ruby smiled.

Applause erupted. Seatbelts unfastened, Luna jumped to hug Ruby and tipped over her champagne.

"You buried the lead, Rube!" Luna laughed.

Amidst the celebration, Opal began to cry. "I am so proud of you. Look what you've done, just look at you." She produced a napkin from her blazer pocket and blotted her face.

"Right place, right time," Ruby said, eyes watering.

Opal raised her glass. "Here's to, 'we all know it's more than that.'"

The women lowered their voices to mimic English barristers. "Hear, hear."

"Attention, ladies, we will be landing shortly. Buckle up, please and thank you," the pilot said over the PA.

They returned to their seats, handed Erin their empty glasses, and prepared for landing.

Fifty-four million and she's more excited about catching a guy doing drugs in a bathroom stall. This isn't a good sign. Don't fall apart now, Rube, I need your help with Opal.

Urse's cell vibrated a text.

Johnny: *Nothing but curcumin, vit D and a bunch of sex toys- looking her in the eye will be tuff going fwd*

Urse: *You looked everywhere? Freezer?*

Johnny: *Y. Carol says woof- Outta h*

Urse: *Thanks*

She put her phone in her bag and squinted at Opal. *It's too weird. She looks yellowy-gray. Even at Oliver's funeral, she looked put together—pale and daft, sure, but now, hungover Warhol in pallor. No. It can't be, Johnny would've found something proving her illness.*

Fuck.

Chapter Eighteen

Luna

Luna evened out the batter to a thin circle in the hot pan. Once it was cooled, she placed parchment paper between the crepes. *One wrinkle and the neighborhood stray cat gets a little taste of France.* She flipped a cookie sheet upside down and placed the crepes on top.

Done and smooth.

She slipped into the other room to grab her laptop.

Might as well get after it. I've procrastinated long enough.

Her laptop was cool against her bare stomach. While others capable of driving a stick shift dreaded technology, she flourished. The anticipation, the forecasting, and the patterns society left scattered over the cyber world made making money as common as the letter L. She and her friends used it to their advantage. Ruby's empire? Began from a tip from a hacked database at 3M headquarters. Opal's portfolio? Intel of passengers lists from a corporate pilot's computer. Were some of those people meeting to merge companies? Certainly. The Crystalporium? She and Johnny built it fair and square, but when it came time to go international, the *tip tap* of Luna's keyboard came in handy. Mind you, they had gazebo meetings on the morality of some of their moves, but frequently landed on the ambiguous, "Would men ask themselves this question?" Luna rationalized it as "insider guessing."

Hell, most of our information came from plain old paying attention. Not to mention the sloppy nature of the men they loved or bedded, with their unsecured lines and 4321 passwords. Luna smirked, remembering their coups, and stopped, thinking about the price she paid.

Arthur. The only shoulder I rested on while slow dancing. It was always him.

Opal's cousin and the man whose shirt she currently wore.

She wished he'd just come home.

Their last argument played in her head ad nauseam.

"Your allegiance to your friends always has me second string." He had pressed his eyes as if it could keep him steady. "Do you know how that feels? To find out your friends knew you were pregnant before I did? They know everything. I'm the last to know, and what? Are you all sitting around laughing at me? That's some trash, Lune." He'd paced, like a Rhesus monkey at a makeup lab.

"The *baby*"—she put air quotes around the word—"died two weeks after I knew we were pregnant—"

"But *they* know? You're supposed to be the master reader of all people, right? Common fucking courtesy, Luna—can't you figure that out? And the reason? Oh, yeah, you get to be queen of the broken."

"You're being mean. And, what? You're leaving me because I tried to protect you?" Luna's voice cracked.

If he knew half of everything, he'd never sleep again.

Only her friends knew about the three other "nonviable intrauterine pregnancies." The last time Opal had hugged her tightly and said, "I'm so, so, sorry. This must be really hard. You'll get the baby you're meant to get, Lune." At that moment, the words had felt comforting. Now, the same phrase sounded like *maybe I don't deserve a baby.*

"You don't get it. I don't need protection from hard things. I need it from you." Arthur had closed his eyes, picked up his overnight bag, and left.

Two months ago.

He'd really freak out if he found out the women knew about killing Dr. Rain. No chance of that slipping out. But between the murder and the barely there pregnancies, he had a point.

I'll act like I don't know Opal's sick, somehow get through it, and get him back when I need him the most. I'll start telling him everything—going forward.

Until that happened, she needed to find the stupid spiders Opal requested for her death.

Urse or Ruby can be responsible for her actual death. I'll get fakes. Then if it all hits the fan, no one will ever know.

She searched for brown recluse look-alikes online.

Even if the spiders were real, how many would she need to kill her, anyway?

When Opal first asked for the spiders, Luna had hit up her local library for assisted suicide laws. A librarian with sharp features, big boobs, and tight sweater had looked up from the front desk. Luna had done a double take then returned her eyes to her book. Since when were librarians overtly hot?

"Computers?" Luna had asked.

The librarian responded without looking up. "Back of the library, Northside."

"Thanks."

Luna swiped her library card, which allowed her access to unrestricted computer use, or until her twenty minutes were up.

Beep.

"Connie V. Lingus, welcome to the Oaks North Municipal Library. Please be mindful of those waiting behind you."

She typed: *assisted suicide laws MN.*

MN Statute 609.21 popped up. She held her breath.

Up to fifteen years in prison.

Her mouth had dropped. She'd scanned the library, envying everyone that wasn't facing prison time and a dead friend. A bookcase pervert had peeped at her and licked his lips. She'd gathered her things and, with a stomach feeling like quicksand, headed home.

Maybe Urse had a point. Opal was losing it. Now, all that crazy talk about Oliver coming back, the blanket body thing, and the note about blueberries looked bad for her mental health. Better to be safe than sorry. No use in anyone going to prison if she's just sick.

Luna needed clarity.

She hit *favorites* on her cell.

"Hey, Lune," Ruby answered.

"Busy?"

"No, what's up?"

"Emergency meeting with weed?"

"A million yesses. You at home?" Ruby asked.

"Yeah. You eat lunch already? I made crepes."

"I did but don't care. Put me down for three to start. Be there in twenty."

Curious. Ruby seldom eats, let alone three of anything other than celery sticks.

Luna texted Urse next: *Emergency mtg w lunch? I made crepes.*

Urse: *cu soon.*

Luna swiped her teak Danish dining room table with a cleaning wipe. She set three plates painted with gold hummingbirds and a vintage ashtray on the table and pulled out a bowl of freshly whipped cream.

While slicing strawberries, she remembered Urse liked powdered sugar and lemon on her crepes then deseeded the wedges so as to not annoy anyone. Forks, knives, glasses, and weed splayed out.

"Siri, play Depeche Mode then don't listen to my conversations."

"Playing Depeche Mode."

Luna unlocked the back door and waited. She sat at the dining table, put her feet on the next chair, and lit up.

Being a part of someone's plan felt a millimeter off. Normally, Luna organized and led the group in hatching a strategy. *It's not about me, though. This time, it's all about Opal.*

She glanced at the three plates and the three glasses and the three sets of silverware. *This is how our get-togethers are going to be going forward.* The three of them, sans Opal.

The backdoor opened, and a plume of smoke greeted Urse.

"Smells like fun memories," she said as she set her bag and keys on the kitchen counter. She washed her hands and turned her head to Luna, hands still dripping over the sink.

"Laundry day. There are paper towels in the bottom right drawer," Luna said.

Urse opened the drawer and froze.

Shoot. I forgot about the "Future Mayor of Hoboken" onesie. Please, Urse, pretend you didn't see it.

"Did you get more plants?" Urse asked. "Looks like a rainforest in here."

Luna handed Urse the joint. "Crepes are ready. Dig in."

Urse toked, coughed, and grabbed a fork to spear a crepe onto her plate. After squeezing a lemon wedge, she lifted a spoonful of sugar a foot over her plate, and wiggled the spoon so the sugar dusted the crepe evenly.

"I'm worried," Luna began.

"Me, too."

"Before she gets here"—she looked around—"Ruby seems more fragile than Opal. You don't think she's cutting again, do you?"

"I'm not sure she's ever stopped. Mr. I'm-Obsessed-With-Ruby thinks we should talk to her about it," Urse said.

"If it's so easy why doesn't *he* talk to her?"

A door creaked open, making Luna jump.

"Ladies, how goes it?" Ruby asked from the entryway. Her Ferragamos clunked as she kicked them off.

"These crepes are tits money," Urse said.

Luna gave Ruby a side hug, grabbed a plate, and handed it to her.

"Thanks. Day weed? You rascals." Ruby put three crepes on her plate and spiraled a beehive of canned whipped cream on top.

Luna side-eyed Urse.

"Want in?" Urse asked, holding the joint midair.

"Twist my rubber arm." Ruby tasted a bite of her crepe. "Whoa, these are fan-freaking-tastic, Lune."

Luna loaded the dishwasher with freshly cleaned plates and wiped down the table before the other two stood to help.

"Well, here we are. Might as well dive into this Opal mess," Luna began. "Ruby, what are your thoughts?"

Ruby stretched her neck. "Opal's never asked for anything." She leaned forward and relit the joint. "She's saved all her asks for this one huge thing." Holding the smoke in her lungs, she tipped her chin up and passed the weed to Urse.

Urse shook her head. "I think I'm already high."

"Me, too," Luna said. "I'll take more."

They giggled.

"What do you think?" Urse asked Luna.

"I agree with Ruby but have some concerns as to her...well...*competency.*"

"She looked gray-yellow the other day," Ruby mumbled.

Urse tucked her lips into her mouth to hold back emotion and nodded.

"Super yellow. I worry if it's real, I worry if it's not," Luna said.

"It shook me, too." Urse's voice didn't hold the same confidence it normally did. It was terrifying. The unsteadiness of the steady.

"But I can't help wonder if we are being played. That grief has made her sick. I mean not intentionally, but—you know." Urse picked up her water glass, then put it down. Luna reached for it, straightened the napkin to the right of her plate and set it back.

Ruby cast her eyes down, the tips of her fingers pushing against her forehead.

Luna noticed a new stack of opaque bracelets on Ruby's wrists. "New bracelets?"

"Huh?" She looked up. "Oh, yeah. Oldies but uglies."

"Ruby, you're okay, right? I mean, are you, well, I—" Luna hedged.

"Are you cutting again?" Urse blurted.

Ruby jerked back as if presented with an electric fence. "Are you kidding me? No. That was a lifetime ago."

Luna stood, turned in a circle—as if she was looking for some-thing—then busied herself at the kitchen sink. She listened to Urse ratio-nalize.

"It's just that, thi...this is a—" Urse stopped. "What I'm trying to say is we need you to be okay."

"I said I'm fine. Opal's sick. I'm not. I did what she asked. You two need to do the same."

"What did *I* do?" Luna yelled from the other room.

Ruby picked up her bag, slid into her shoes, and left.

Luna watched her through her kitchen window. Her head low, sign language hands moving so quickly, it seemed as if she slurred.

"She's cutting again," Luna said.

"Yep," Urse said. "I hate when she takes off. She needs to grow the fuck up, the gol-damn delicate genius." She dipped her head all the way back. "You know I'm right, Lune."

"I know, but we need her."

"We need *her?* What exactly does ole energy-sucking Ruby bring to the table?"

Luna rubbed her face. "We need her to feel better about ourselves, I guess."

Urse flinched. "Naw. We just need to fly privately."

Chapter Nineteen

Opal

Opal wandered around her house pretending to be at an estate sale. As if an outsider looking in. *Would I like me only looking at my things?*

Prized art under dusty museum glass. Roseville pottery mixed with lopsided pinch pots, the weirder the better. Kids' pots—the kind made in elementary schools, abandoned at some point or lost when the maker turned their little backs on the untraditional beauty of their pride personified. Two of the pots were so bad they had to lie on their sides because they couldn't stand up.

Oliver had teased her about them until one day at a sale, back when their knees didn't pop and their necks weren't stiff, he understood her obsession.

"This pot is a blue ribbon. Anyone know the artist?" Opal had asked loudly enough for a boy playing with a slingshot to hear. The boy had stood behind a Cloris Leachman look-alike, manning a makeshift card table serving as a checkout. Opal had found the dented metal money box funny as the lock couldn't thwart a theft from a Gerber baby.

"Why, yes, I do. Would you like to meet him? He's my grandson, Edgar." She beamed and ruffled his hair.

The boy *aw-shucked* over, hands in front pockets of his jeans, smiling.

"Did you make this?"

"Yes."

"Well, your use of color is something. I think you should think about doing more art," Opal said, holding the pot at eye level.

"What do you say?" Cloris asked the boy.

"Thank you."

"Are you sure you want to sell it to me?" Opal asked.

The boy nodded. "I put blue and green together."

"I think that's what makes it so good. How does ten dollars sound?"

His eyes bulged and his smile revealed a missing front tooth. "Okay." He stood taller.

She forked over the ten spot and asked his grandmother, "Do you think you could wrap it for me?"

Nodding, the woman grabbed a sheet of old newspaper, wrapped the pot, and put it in a grocery bag. As she handed it to Opal, she winked.

"Remember, no one can do what you do." Opal turned, almost knocking over Oliver. She jumped. "Creeper! What did you find?"

Oliver held something behind his back, his thick woolen coat stiff as he moved his arms. "Nothing." He smirked.

"I swear. If that's a battery charger, you need to look for another wife."

He pulled his hands from his back producing a rusty battery charger and laughed.

"Oliver, you've jumped one car in your entire life."

"The ole battle ax says 'no,'" he said, smiling to the checkout grandma. She wagged her finger at him, grinning.

He tucked Opal into his shoulder and headed to their car.

"I get it now. The weird pots," he kissed her on top of the head. "You know, you're pretty good with kids. It's not too late."

The memory seemed like yesterday.

She'd donate the collection to the Art Institute. Hell, they owed her for all the moola she and Oliver gave them over the years. *Anonymously—until, that is, you need over three hundred pinch pots displayed.* Getting her way in death made her giddy in the same way exasperated looks fueled her.

Memory lane would have to wait.

The if-this-then-that letters have to be written for my attorney with copies going to Snookie. And I've got to account for all possible outcomes on this end of life thing, if one or none of my friends comes through. If they value themselves over our friendship. As it stands, Luna will help if her tarot cards say, Ruby will feel indebted, Urse won't, but if I put the squeeze on her, she'll cave. It'll have to be a face-to-face. Unless Luna chickens out. All that tarot card rot sometimes gets in the way of common sense. Unless it's not rot. Four separate letters if they help, four if they don't.

She rounded Oliver's desk and the pinch pot in his dusty study, and noticed a picture in a heavy silver frame and laughed. There they were. Well, there Oliver was. Head thrown back in laughter carrying her over his shoulder at a work picnic. Basically, it was a picture of her ass.

Smiling, she settled in his heavy desk chair believing she could still smell the campfire and bergamot scent of him.

"Oliver? Where are you? I'm getting sicker by the day." She inched the chair closer and threw herself on the desk sobbing. "I know something's not right, I just know it." Carol, who had been following her of late, approached her tentatively and leaned against her thigh.

"Where is Oliver?" She stood quickly, prompting the dog. "Go get him, girl! Oliver's home, Carol, go on!"

But when Carol sat motionless staring at her...*she knew.*

Oliver was never coming home.

She screamed with the realization and smashed the blue pinch pot against a dart board across the room when something caught her eye. Among the cracked clay bits was a folded sheet of stationery.

"Stay." Carol obeyed.

Oliver's blocky handwriting on the note read: *Opal.*

Oh no. Please, Oliver, no secrets. I beg you, let our love be the truth.

Her hands shook as she unfolded the letter.

Dearest Opal,

Couldn't sleep for thinking. I wrote this poem for you, my sweet, round-bottomed love.

Slipping into bed beneath warm blankets.

I hear your reliable breathing.

Looking out the window, the moon is breathing, too.

I worry it will outlast you and I will be alone.

I will love you forever, plus a spell.

Forever yours,

Oliver

Overwhelmed yet calm, she pulled the letter to her chest and closed her eyes.

Oh my God. Urse is right. I am crazy.

Chapter Twenty

Ruby

The end of the razor blade pressed against Ruby's wrist. Slightly at first. A tease, really.

When the scratches drew blood, it focused all her pain to a pin prick, nice and clean. It hurt no one. It was contained. It had always been an escape, a tasty treat, a fresh shower after gardening.

The blade hadn't met her skin in over a week. But now she *had to,* not wanted to. At this moment, it seemed like an addiction—and that didn't sit well. It was beginning to feel out of control, which, if she were being honest, was a bad look.

The clock ticked toward her suicide. While the cutting had nothing to do with the price of corn, it would make sense to take her escapism one step further. *Not my job to teach people that they are worlds apart; they can look it up in a psychology journal on their own.*

Urse and Luna, with their busybody ways, guessed she was cutting again. She had the good manners not to mention *their* proclivities. Opal's anger, Luna's weird exhibitionist tendencies, and Urse looking like she just left a glaucoma test for the past decade. *Naw, I would never bring that up.*

As a matter of fact, she *protected* them.

Ruby had a designated spot on her wrist for Opal, Urse, and Luna. A dot scar. She poked the spot in the middle with the metal and dragged the lines out like the sun, a source of hope. Anything related to them sunk into that area, so the world's problems wouldn't touch them. She wanted them safe. *I'm a scar designer, really.*

Her other arm would be reserved for the final act; no cross contamination, so to speak.

The prerecorded message would be sent to the local medical examiner first, then forwarded to her attorney. Ruby practiced it in the mirror:

"My name is Ruby Redstone. I reside at 20 Berkshire Place. I have decided, by my own volition, to end my life. I apologize for any inconvenience this may cause. My attorney, Mr. Stallworth, will handle all forthcoming inquiries as deemed necessary. Everything I own goes to the best sister in the world, Ann Redstone, who is the only reason I lasted this long."

The plan was to be sent Rube Goldberg-style after the act.

Everything was organized except for a faint nightlight in the shady part of her mind.

Johnny.

I don't want him to think badly of me. The only man to make me feel safe, or what I think safe feels like.

Of all the boyfriends, lovers, weirdos, and men using her for status, only Johnny knew about her jacked up past. What she hadn't expected was him to wait for her to get her head out of her ass. He proved himself over and over through the years. He was a fixed rate; she, a variable.

Her mind drifted to the night their lips met.

In the fall of 2008, Ruby had decided to buy one hundred twenty-five private aircraft hours for business. A splurge only a handful of people knew about.

Her inaugural flight had left from Minneapolis to Chicago with Opal, Urse, Luna, and Johnny. They had washed down chicken crackers, aged cheddar with vermouthy martinis, and arrived at the hotel pie-eyed.

"Afternoon. Rooms under Redstone, please," she told the man in a navy blazer and gray pants at the front desk.

He seemed humorless as Urse kidded, "If I were one month younger."

She'd burned a hole in him with her eyes, his face red with the attention.

"Thank you, ma'am."

They laughed.

"I hoped he'd call me that," Urse slurred. She reached for an apple in a glass bowl on the front desk, bit into it, and put it back, teeth mark side down. "Wax."

"Urse, leave him alone." Luna winked at him though he looked down at his computer screen. "What's your name?"

"Declan."

"Of course it is. Declan, put me in a visible room, I'm going to need a nice big window if you know what I mean." She touched her nose and pointed to him with the other.

Johnny laughed.

"Come on, drunkies, we've got black coffee pots in need of emptying." He looked at Declan and smiled an apology.

"I have Asperger's," Declan said.

"Lucky," Johnny answered as he corralled the tipsy women.

"Go down the hall to the second set of elevators. Use your keys to get to the executive suites. Again, my name is Declan if you need anything to make your stay more comfortable."

Luna put her hand up to make a point when Johnny covered her mouth from behind.

"Appreciate it," Johnny said, nodding Luna's head with his hands as she laughed.

Urse pointed to Johnny. "He's like a brother to me."

Luna dropped her luggage handle in the middle of the corridor then fell attempting to pick it up. Rolling to her hip, she inched her skirt up to her thong and stretched her leg out.

Urse laughed and offered her a hand. "Get up, pervert. Let's get dressed to go out."

"It's six thirty," Johnny reasoned, trying to herd them toward the elevator.

Ruby tilted her head to Johnny, "You. You. You." She touched the end of his nose with her fingertip. "You."

His eyebrows elevated.

She smiled and stared at him, keeping her head tilted.

Their moment was interrupted by loud laughter. Opal fell. Urse lent her a hand; her heel slipped and she toppled.

"That's it." Johnny pointed to Urse. "You're making a scene. Get it together." He grabbed Opal under the armpits and hoisted her up. "Let's go—now," he said sternly.

They straightened up and headed to the elevator.

"Dad's mad," Luna said sarcastically.

Ding ding.

Urse pushed the ES button—executive suite level.

Ping.

Johnny escorted the women to their rooms. Ruby lingered at her door.

"You'll come to happy hour, right?"

"Maybe a movie night in with all you partridges would be good?" Johnny's eyes darted to the hotel corridor.

"Hmph." She turned and swiped her room card over the lock.

Beep, beep, green light, go. She pulled her luggage into her room, one wheel caught on the door sill jerking her back.

"Rube?"

She yanked her suitcase into the room, the door closed with a thick *slam.*

Click.

Ruby hoped he heard the deadbolt lock.

Once in the room, Ruby pulled the comforter off, turned the heat to seventy-eight and laid on the bed, head spinning.

Knock, knock, knock.

Ruby lifted her head from the bed, disoriented.

"Rube." Opal's voice from the hallway.

"Two seconds." She got her bearings and shuffled to the door.

"Not gonna lie. I'm a bit tipsy," Opal said as she walked in.

Ruby wiped the drool from the side of her mouth. "Not used to martinis," she said and smiled.

"Urse and Luna are already at happy hour. They are way drunker than I am. I'm starting to get sleepy."

Ruby turned on the TV, searching for music.

"I'm as ready as I'll ever get." Opal put her palm out, inching her fingertips for the remote. Ruby planted it in her hand and headed to freshen up.

"Who else will be there?" Ruby asked once in the bathroom.

"Who else *is* there?"

As Opal continued loudly, Ruby remained quiet. "Rube, you're only mysterious to the rest of the world, not to us. We know you and Johnny are dying to make babies without babies."

She popped her head out, mascara wand in hand, to find Opal fidgeting with the remote. "No, I don't. Wait, do you think he likes me? How do you know?"

"Where the hell is the music on these things?" Opal mumbled.

Ruby, not one to push or be obvious, wanted to know, but aimed for indifference.

Opal called the front desk. "Yes, excuse me, what are the music station numbers on the TV?" Pause. "Uh-huh. Okay. Very good, thank you." Opal returned the phone to its cradle.

"Are we going out after? What should I wear for happy hour?" Ruby asked.

"14080. Eh? Oh, throw on that white linen shirt and black mini, with heels—let your legs do the talkin'. We can geek it up later if we can last."

"Roger that." Ruby retreated to the bathroom.

Crack!

Something being smashed.

Crack, crack, crack!

Ruby poked her head out of the bathroom again. Opal stood over the TV, exasperated after smacking the remote on the dresser. Ruby walked over and Opal handed her the remote.

14080, enter.

The smooth sounds of Hall and Oats floated through the TV.

"Thanks," Opal said, sounding relieved. "It's a start." She scrolled through the stations landing on *Death Cab for Cutie, acoustic.* "I'm sorry, I don't mean to get insta-mad," she said, reclining in the bed and staring at the ceiling.

"I know." Ruby laid next to her, taking her hand with a squeeze.

"Do you think Johnny likes me?" Ruby edged.

Opal turned to her. "We don't know what you two are waiting for."

So, the other friends knew. She nodded, in silence, the bed spinning.

"Alright, let's go." Ruby got up pulling Opal with her.

Opal twisted her skirt so the zipper was in the back, smoothed her hair, and checked her nude gloss.

They met Urse and Luna at the executive club. Luna's arms went up to greet them.

Johnny smiled at Ruby. He looked smart in his white button down, flat paneled pants, and brown shoes with thick stitching. Simple, unassuming, as only the confident can be. She mustered up the courage to look at him longer than she ever had. A flicker of something in his eyes made her stomach corkscrew. Luna handed her an old fashioned.

The business elite had gathered at the watering hole, eager, posturing, and well-connected. As the noise level raised through the hours, the laughter and banter became playful.

A cocktail waitress with a henna-dipped high ponytail set down a tray of tequila in front of Luna. "Seems you gals have some admirers." She lifted her chin motioning to a group of stylish men. The presumed leader lifted his glass to them, nodded once, and turned around. The waitress leaned in. "This tequila is, well, let's just say, spendy." She set the shots on the bar.

The women picked them up.

"Oh, boys," Luna said across the room. "Thank you."

As custom, the women lifted the shots together. "To all of it!" they cheered, and threw the liquid over their shoulders pretending to drink. After sharing the creepy dentist story, Luna had made the women promise never to drink anything sent by strangers.

The next thing Ruby knew, Urse was challenging a suave man in a precision-seamed suit to a push-up contest. She noticed Urse trying to smell his armpit as he touched the small of her back, a hesitant ownership play in a crowd of silver-backed men hiding wedding rings.

Feeling her eye wander a hair, Ruby set her drink aside.

"Naw, naw, naw. I know I can do more than you," Urse teased. She squeezed the man's arm and laughed higher than usual.

"What do you want to bet, cheekbones?" he said with his chest stretched out.

"A hundred unmarked bills."

He put his hand out to shake. She spit in her palm before shaking his, provoking laughter from a crowd of interested onlookers.

He loosened his tie, flung his jacket, and dropped to the floor in the push-up position, struggling to hit fifty.

Ruby smiled, knowing Urse could do fifty before she brushed her teeth in the morning.

"Ladies, a lift up," Urse said to Opal and Luna.

As the bartender nervously moved glasses and bar top candles, Luna put her hands together for her to step up. Urse planked on the bar,

"It's fine," Opal told the bartender. "It'll be over in a minute." He shook his head.

Urse did fifty quick push-ups, the last with one hand behind her back like a psycho military lady. She rolled to her back and off the bar, breathing heavily.

She smiled. "Pay up."

The man's face reddened, as he tapped his wallet against his palm. "What, is this some sort of set-up?" he said, voice tight.

The crowd quieted at his serious tone, raising the stakes.

"Naw, she beat you fair and square." Ruby said playfully to avoid trouble.

It wasn't the first time Urse picked the biggest pig in the room to trifle with. "Yeah, fair and square, my ass." He flicked a hundred at Ruby; it floated to the ground. "Glad to contribute to your firewater fund."

Ruby grimaced.

In a flash, Johnny's fist landed against the man's nose, knocking him over backwards. Johnny was on him, punching so fast his fists blurred. Opal jumped up and down giddy, as Urse grabbed the back of her brother's shirt. Luna scanned the area for security.

"That's it. He's garbage, forget it!" Urse struggled to stop her brother.

"Johnny!" Ruby said firmly.

He turned to her, eyes locked, then got off the man, tucked in his shirt and faced the bartender. "I apologize, but I think we both know he had it comin'." Johnny dug into his pocket for a tip and laid a hundred on the bar. "Thanks, governor. You make a mean old-fashioned."

Urse spit on the bloody man on the way out, earning her a round of *oohs*.

Opal picked up the hundred the man had thrown at Ruby, and set it with the other one on the bar.

Luna hooked Urse's arm in hers, looked at the gaping crowd, and yelled, "Lessons."

Once at the elevator door, Ruby took Johnny's hand in hers.

The moment was theirs.

He'd smiled and planted a long, wet kiss on her while the other girls cheered.

Of all the memories, over all the years, that kiss stuck. How did things get so messed up?

Ruby heard Daytime Mom's voice. "Ann needs you around, and Johnny's a good guy. Get it together."

Screw it. I'm calling him tonight. Maybe there's one last chance.

Chapter Twenty-One

Urse

Not long after the Fitz mess, Urse took the opportunity to sex up Pierre, a fifty-seven-year-old salt-and-peppered chief financial officer from St. Paul, who had hit on her for years. Three days ago, they had a quickie at her office. Now, he was on his way to her house. He was no Andy, but he wanted her. And Pierre was as good with his tongue as only a divorced middle-aged man with high blood pressure can be—eager and capable.

Glancing at her vanity mirror she noticed a shadow on her face. *Oh no. An ear beard.* She gasped, searching for her grooming supplies. *Over-freaking-night this hair.* Scraping off the black fluff to a smooth face, she blew the fuzz off the derma plane razor into the sink and rinsed it down the drain.

She sucked in her cheeks, and turned her head, eyes still on the mirror.

You still got it.

She loosely tied her non-weird kimono and cracked open a bottle of Sancerre to breathe. As much as she spent on a bullshit Scandinavian dishwasher, her wine glasses still had soap spots. Her mind drifted as she cleaned them.

I wonder what Opal's doing.

NO.

The cool air hit her from the fridge when she moved the to-go packet bowls aside, fishing for an opened bottle of wine. *Just a tish before he gets here.* The doorbell rang. Quickly, she put the wine bottle behind freshly cut veggies stacked in blue-lidded Pyrex. Sauntering toward the door, she stopped to fluff her hair.

On the other side of the peephole was Johnny.

"Urse, open up. What's with changing the code to the door?"

She loosened her kimono, folded it over—closing the chest—and retied it tighter. She unlatched the lock and let him in.

"It's late. What are you doing here?"

"What's going on with zee Ruby?"

"Oh God, Johnny." She rolled her eyes and headed for the kitchen to get her cell. Pierre needed the *drive-around-the-block-til-I-get-rid-of-my-brother* courtesy text.

"Urse, don't be a twat. I'm serious."

She stopped, closed her eyes, breathed deeply, and said, "I'm going to pretend you didn't just call me that," and continued to the kitchen.

Johnny followed. "Urse, I *am* serious. I got a wacko call from her earlier, and now she's not picking up."

"Why do you have gobs of makeup on?" Johnny asked.

"I don't have *gobs* of makeup on!"

Johnny walked toward the two wine glasses. "Mm-hmm. Gross. Were you having a freshly released convict over?"

"Tell me about the wacko call."

Johnny was already filling the glasses. "She said, 'Johnny, I just wanted to say, you are the best person I know.'"

Urse intentionally blinked slowly. "You interrupted my night for that, psycho?"

Johnny touched his cell. Ruby's voice played, slurred nearly beyond recognition. "Johnny, I just wanted to say, well, you are the best person I know."

"You misquoted her—she had a 'well' in there. But, yeah, she sounds off. Really off, actually." She tapped her temple. "Wait. Do you two talk on the phone?"

"Once in twenty years to be exact."

She picked up her cell.

A text from Pierre. *"I want to lick..."* She swiped it away and called Ruby.

Ruby picked up, first ring. "Urse? What is going on? Is Opal okay?"

"Opal's fine. I was just checking on you." She looked at Johnny who was shaking his head and mouthing *I'm not here.*

"Why wouldn't I be?" Ruby asked.

"The crystals gave me a weird feeling, is all." Urse motioned to Johnny to hand her a glass.

"All good. Hitting the hay. 'night," Ruby said.

"'night."

"Wait—Rube, promise you'll meet me for brunch tomorrow, okay?"

An uncomfortable pause.

"I promise." Rube finally said.

"'night."

Johnny stood and asked, "She used the word 'promise,' right?"

She met his eyes and nodded. He exhaled with a *whew.*

The water softener kicked on.

"Want a grilled cheese?" Urse asked.

He nodded.

She pulled a cast iron pan from her island cabinet housing the stove top then grabbed thick sourdough slices and smirked.

"Ready for it?" she asked.

"For what?"

Urse opened her crisper of fresh veggies, moved them aside and dug out four slices of pre-wrapped American cheese.

"Childhood!" Johnny laughed.

"If you tell anyone I'll call you a liar."

"Delicious, delicious plastic."

She spread mayo over the slices of bread and put them face down in the hot pan, and unwrapped the slices.

"Speaking of childhood, I've been meaning to talk to you about something," Johnny started.

Urse slid her empty glass toward him. "Do I need to open another bottle for this?"

"No, but open one anyway."

The smell of melting cheese filled the kitchen.

"When I was snooping around the other day, I saw a piece of paper with 'Tess Hokanson' written on it."

"So?" Urse flipped the sandwich with a slotted spatula.

Johnny widened his eyes and stared at her. "So?"

Mouth opened, Urse lifted the spatula. "What?"

"Tess Hokanson is the woman who bought Irv the Finger Biter's car."

"Oh, stop it. There's got to be a million Tess Hokansons."

Urse's eyes darted across the room.

"You might want to lay off the weed for the sake of your memory." Johnny eyed the hot pan. "Watch it. I don't want mine burned."

Urse lifted the sandwiches onto a wooden cutting board. She looked at him and put her arm up diagonally.

He formed an X with his arms. She cut his sandwich as such.

"How does Opal know Tess?" Johnny asked. He bit, pulling the sandwich away from his mouth, and a string of cheese stretched a foot from his lips. "Dude, that's an award-winning grilled cheese."

"I think Opal hired her as her nurse," Urse answered.

"Pfft," Johnny said, shaking his head.

"Oh my God. Do you think Tess is behind Opal being sick? I bet she's some shyster weaseling in on Opal's money. I've watched enough true crime docuseries to know," she finished.

Johnny's arms went up, he cracked his knuckles midair and put his palms out. "Just because you think it, doesn't make it true. Jesus, Urse."

She downed the rest of her wine. "Okay, yeah, and how the hell could I forget my scariest high school memory? Man, that was some brazen shit we pulled, Johnny."

They laughed and clinked glasses.

If they were teens today, social services would have their family on speed dial. Ma's child rearing book was Joan Crawford's autobiography, and only because it had been in a clearance bin.

Once their dad had vanished, the family's focus had moved from struggle to loyalty. *Loyalty this, loyalty that*, Ma would mumble. Urse, Johnny, and Ma hadn't thought twice about hurting each other, but if anyone else so much as hinted at taking a pickle off their lunch plate, they'd end up with swollen eyes and IRS problems.

Shortly after the *fun family adventure*, Urse and Johnny plotted revenge for the Rainbow Festival finger biter and all-round dick, Irv.

Urse smiled, remembering how the whole caper went down. They had grilled cheese that night, too.

God, we were so young.

Johnny had been so excited after he showed Urse the final plan for getting back at Irv that his voice shook. While other kids were studying for the SATs, Johnny had been spying, stealing mail, and forging car titles.

Urse had been stunned. He had anticipated every freaking detail right down to the weird outfit he was going to wear. Apparently, revenge had meant something to him. She'd felt the same way when he brought home straight-A report cards. Proud and annoyed.

"The plan is great. Let's do it," Urse had said.

Once "Operation: Get the Douche" was upon them, the players in the game rehearsed their roles.

Seeing as though Opal was the only one with a driver's permit, she'd drive the van back. "I'm as nervous as a whore. Not in church—I imagine they're nervous all the time. But you wouldn't ask unless it was important, right?" Opal's voice jittered.

"I'm glad she wants to be your friend instead of my squeeze-box. Her wild side is sorta tame," Johnny said to Urse while facing Opal.

"Whatever, virgin. I'm only doing it for Urse," she said.

Urse pinched her face. "'Squeeze-box'? You are truly embarrassing."

"Okay, okay. Let's be serious." Johnny disappeared into his bedroom then returned in a postal carrier outfit with his legs apart and hands out as if accepting applause.

Opal snort laughed. "It's a bit big in the shoulders, don't you think?"

Urse couldn't keep a straight face.

"I stand before you a bona fide man, and you're concerned with haberdashery?" He pushed his chin up, nodding in mock seriousness. "If anyone has the nervous pees, go now or forever hold your peace," he said.

The three teenagers drove to Edina, a posh suburb of Minneapolis, where they parked in front of Irv's home.

Surveying the neighborhood, Urse spied crisp-edged lawns, garage doors ajar, and newspapers at the base of uniformly-painted mailboxes. None of the homes had patches of dirt as front yards. No broken trikes, cigarette butts, or cars on jacks, like in their trailer park.

All of a sudden, her clothes embarrassed her. At least Opal had a fake Fendi.

"Urse," Opal nudged her and slunk down. An ash-blonde woman left the marked house with two toddlers in tow. She buckled them up in a white Cadillac, checked her lipstick in the rearview mirror, and drove away.

The three decided to wait a few minutes as moms often forget things.

At noon, Johnny donned his postal carrier hat, picked up his folder of evidence, and headed for Irv's door.

"You got this," Urse said. "One more thing. Here's a piece of citrine for safety and luck." She tossed it high, giving him enough time to catch it.

He ripped it from the air and shoved it in his pocket.

Johnny approached the house.

Ding Dong.

Johnny tapped his foot nervously and pushed the doorbell again,

Ding Dong.

Living room curtains pulled back.

"Can I help you?" Irv asked.

"Sure can." Johnny stepped into the foyer.

Johnny pulled out a picture of what appeared to be Irv naked. "Mr. Irv, you took advantage of a woman I am acquainted with," Johnny said as if arguing at the Supreme Court.

Irv appeared rattled. "What the hell is this—"

"Here's how this is going to go," Johnny interrupted. "As you know, I already have your shit van. My acquaintance uses it to get to her many shit jobs. Now, to settle up for zee pain you've caused her, I'll need you to sell me your other car for five dollars. It won't make everything right, but it'll be more even."

Irv closed his eyes, head dropping.

"I truly loved Wanda. I just had a bad trip that led to therapy and some difficult decisions." Irv deflated, settling on a maroon bench that matched the wallpaper behind him. "I'm sorry. I really am."

Johnny hadn't anticipated the man apologetic. "Sign over the titles," he said, handing Irv the motor vehicle forms.

"How'd you get—"

"Never mind, just sign."

Ding Dong.

Johnny froze; his grin disappeared. Irv, eyes wide, smiled. "Coming! One moment!"

The power shifted.

Before Johnny could morph to the moment, Irv opened the door revealing his real postman.

"Hi, Karl, how's it going today?" Irv over-animated the greeting.

Karl looked Johnny up and down in his non-USPS-issued uniform; his eyes narrowed. "Um, I have a box for you."

Johnny shifted weight on his feet.

Irv put his hand on Karl's shoulder. It dipped an inch.

Interesting.

"Irv and I have some business we need to talk through," Johnny smiled at Karl.

Karl's fists clenched. "That's not a real postal uniform."

It wasn't a question, just a statement of fact.

Johnny changed his plan on the spot. He glanced at Irv, who smiled as if he just won a spelling bee.

"Exactly. Thank you for that. He makes me wear..." A nice gulp of theatrical air. "...*things,*" Johnny said.

Checkmate.

Karl stiffened. "I've gotta go."

Irv's smug smile was now a distant memory. He started talking quickly. "He was joshing around, I...Karl, I...he's kidding—"

Before Irv finished his guilty-sounding explanation, Karl left, the door shutting behind him.

"You're not getting the five bucks now," Johnny said. "Shut up and sign."

Using his knee as his clipboard, Irv signed the titles, pulled the key fob from his front chino pocket, and handed it to Johnny. "Tell Wanda I'm sorry I hurt her, and I think the world of her," he said.

"You were never good enough for her—know that," Johnny said. "Plus, your fly is open, loser," he added.

And with that, Irv opened the garage door and they drove away.

Urse felt comfortable in the Mercedes. She couldn't believe how smoothly Johnny's plan had played out.

"Urse, did you not see the fucking actual postman come to the house?" Johnny wiped his brow with the back of his hand.

"Well, yeah, but when Opal tried to run interference he said, 'I'll be right with you. I need to drop this package off,' and went in. It happened so fast, I didn't even have time to do my fake fainting bit."

Urse rubbed the leather on the steering wheel.

Johnny nodded. "Okay, okay."

"How'd it go down anyway?" Urse asked, checking her rearview mirror for cops.

"I karate chopped him in the dick and he handed everything over to me!" Johnny said, visibly sweaty. He tossed his postal carrier hat into the back seat.

"No, you didn't."

Johnny sighed. "He said he loved Ma and felt badly, then signed over the car." He paused. "I almost felt sorry for him until he got all smirky when the real postman came in."

Urse didn't care about Irv's guilty conscience. "What do you think this car is worth?"

"Blue Book is around twenty thousand."

"Dollars?"

"No, Urse, pierogis."

"Stop it! I swear, if you're jerking my chain—"

Urse hit the brakes accidentally, shooting them forward until their seatbelts pulled them back.

Johnny continued, "I promise it's true. We either split it or give it to Ma."

Urse gasped. "Tell her? No way."

"What do you suggest?"

"Let's sell it as soon as we can and keep it in an account to pay for things like rent, heat, or I don't know, *hot water.* We can get extra jobs and act like the money's coming from there. We should each take six thousand for ourselves. She'll never know and we'll finally be able to get ahead."

"Opal. We need to give her a piece."

"One thousand should do it. She took a drive, not a risk," Urse said as she oversteered.

"Deal?"

"Deal."

A month later, Johnny signed the title of the Mercedes to Tess Hokanson for nineteen thousand five hundred dollars.

Urse drifted back to her grilled cheese.

Who the hell is the real Tess Hokanson and what is she up to?

Chapter Twenty-Two

Luna

Luna put a pinch of saffron into a small bowl of hot water and watched the liquid turn orangey yellow.

Her grandmother would be proud of her for two things: her cooking, and her ability to sell cats and dogs and laugh at who buys them. *Surviving, I should say.* Luna had hung on the woman's words, the old wives' tales. While you probably wouldn't find the fables pinned to a bulletin board at CERN, she couldn't help but believe in them. *You won't catch me getting a manicure on a Sunday or wiping spilled water away with my foot. Bad luck comes from somewhere; it sure isn't random. No coincidence Katrina happened in my hometown after I killed Dr. Rain, after all.*

Luna poured the saffron mixture into the soup and spooned a taste. *Opal will like this batch—it'll make her feel better.* And while Ruby and Urse may dip celery in mustard and call it a buffet, Opal had never been shy about asking for seconds.

"I can practically smell your grandma's kitchen. Mind you, it's tough to eat over that dead dentist on the floor, but, you know." Opal's first joke after Luna's confession made her laugh so hard the water she was drinking shot from her mouth in a spray.

"You love me." Opal had winked at Luna and bear hugged her. "See? Nothing's so bad you can't joke about it eventually."

Now, with less than a week until her death thingy, Opal was coming for dinner. Just the two of them. *I want to be sure she's sick and not bonkers like Urse insists. If Grandma Ada were alive she would say, "Watch for the direction of their eyes. Down and to the left means they are searching for facts. Looking you straight in the eye is too much confidence. There's a fine line between trickery and honesty. Sometimes honest people will screw you up with their excitement. Study their specific patterns."*

A knock at the back door.

Luna greeted Opal with a hug. *It's like hugging a two-by-four. How did I not notice?*

"I brought you something." She handed Luna a glossy white gift bag with a tag that read: "This prized possession is second only to our friendship" in her showy cursive. Luna unwrapped a blue and green pinch pot.

Luna winced. "Opal, I can't accept this. It's one of your favorites."

"It's not coming with me."

Luna's eyelids were heavy. "Thank you."

"What's for din-din?"

"Tomato saffron soup, grilled shrimp, and mixed greens."

"You really know how to treat a gal," Opal said. Her arms crisscrossed her stomach, as she bent forward slightly.

"A glass of something?" Luna asked.

"Anything easy, my stomach is a bit sexy, if you know what I mean."

Luna eyed her with concern. "Tums and a sauv blanc?"

Opal smiled. "The minerality of the Tums pairs well with the lemon and bile notes."

Luna inched a glass of water toward Opal.

While Opal's misbuttoned shirt isn't that out of the ordinary, the chunk of chewed gum in her hair and lipstick only on her bottom lip certainly is.

"How are you holding up?" Luna asked.

"Dying."

Luna left the room and returned with a soft blanket.

"You could open a better Ritz Carlton with your hospitality." Opal spoke through the blanket. *Why is she clinging to that quilt?*

"What is going on?"

"Well," Opal said.

Luna's stomach felt how a taffy pulling machine looked.

"Oliver." She paused to gulp. "My sweet Oliver isn't coming back."

Luna reached across the table to hold her hand. She nodded. "I know, sweetie, I know."

"I wish you would've told me he's dead," Opal said.

It wasn't the time to disagree with her.

"You weren't ready."

The oven beeper sounded. They both jumped.

"I forgot. I made you popovers," Luna went into the kitchen to turn the timer off.

"Need help?" Opal called.

"I'm good." Luna put her hot pads on and turned the pan a rotation, resetting the clock for five more minutes.

A loud thud came from the dining room.

Luna threw her oven mitts and ran.

Opal lay on the floor, her skirt kicked up over her thighs, revealing black and blue marks and white, boy-short undies.

"Opal, come on, wake up!" Luna put her hand under her neck, pushing her hair from her face. "Okay, sweetie, I'll be right back. I'm going to call for some help. I'm not going anywhere, alright? You're fine." She jumped to find her phone.

"911, what's your emergency?"

"Yes, my friend passed out—she's sick."

"Is she breathing right now?" the dispatcher asked.

"Yes, I think." She shook her hand as if it were wet and paced.

"You think or know? I need you to put your—"

"I know."

"Good, I've got help coming, are you at 25 Lake Como Boulevard?"

"Yes."

"Ma'am, I need you to make sure your door is unlocked. Can you do that for us?"

"Yes." Luna unlocked the door.

She returned to Opal. "It's okay, Ope, help is on the way." Luna tried to pull the gum from Opal's hair then smoothed her colorful skirt.

"I can hear the sirens in the distance. I'll wait on the phone until the first responders arrive, okay?" the dispatcher said.

"She's sick, you know, she's really sick—"

"Yes, I understand. You mentioned that. I need you to make sure everything is out of the way for their equipment, okay?"

"Right, but we didn't believe her. I didn't believe her—"

"Ma'am, the responders are on premise. I'll let you go so you can speak with them."

Information arrived in chunks. Bits and stems.

The first responders carried what looked like a tackle box and set it down next to Opal's ear.

"What's your friend's name? Can you tell us what happened?" a portly man with a cross necklace so big it seemed unchristian, asked.

"Her name is Opal. I heard a clunk from the kitchen and found her out on the floor." Luna felt lightheaded, her stomach like the second hill on a roller coaster.

"What's your name?" The other responder untangled equipment but kept eye contact. He moved so close she could smell aftershave.

"My name?" Luna said. "My na—"

Her eyesight tunneled.

Oh, fuck.

Clah-lunk.

She fell to the ground unconscious.

Coming to, Luna mumbled, "Where's Opal?"

"Do we need to take you with us as a patient?" the blond paramedic spoke, poker faced.

"No, no, I'm fine." Luna struggled up. "I haven't eaten yet," she lied.

"Are you okay to stand?"

"I'm fine. Honestly. Can I ride with Opal?"

"Okay, let's just take it easy."

She took her time rising to give herself a minute.

Luna took a few tentative steps in search of her phone. "What hospital?"

"North View," he said.

Luna breathed deeply and texted Ruby and Urse: *Heading to North View hosp Opal passed out - think she's actually sick.*

Her balance steadied, Luna headed for the door.

"Miss? Do you mind if I shut off your stove?"

"Oh, I forgot, yeah."

As they walked out of Luna's house, the local looky-loos—smug in their driveways—lined the street, gawking at the excitement. The blond responder helped Luna climb the steep stairs and ushered her to the jump seat behind Opal.

Sirens on, monitors beeping, they sped to the hospital.

Don't let this be it. I'm not ready, don't let this be it, don't let this be it...

Chapter Twenty-Three

Opal

Opal woke to the smell of flowers. *I must be at my own funeral.*

"Honey, we're here. It's okay." A vaguely familiar voice. A metal chair slid against the floor.

Drowsy, Opal opened her eyes enough to catch her friends and a vase of lilacs then shut them quickly. *Aw, man, a hospital. The opposite of my funeral.* She imagined her friends leaning in.

"Oliver, I'm coming, the light, it's so beautiful, give me..." Opal whispered. "Give me five more minutes..." She bugged her eyes out and yelled, "Suckers!"

Urse clutched her chair arm. Luna covered her mouth with her hand, and Ruby said, "Not funny."

"All dick, all the time." Urse shook her head.

"How are you doing?" Luna asked, ignoring the joke.

"What happened, anyway? I feel pretty good now," Opal answered. Looking around the room, she noticed dried rust-colored spots on the bottom of the window's curtains. *And yet it smells like bleach in here.*

Urse said, "Your blood sugar got too low and you passed out."

"I was just about to dive into that soup Luna makes. That's all I remember." She shifted in her bed and tugged at the thin blanket over her cold legs.

Urse pulled the blanket to Opal's chest and said, "Mmm...smells nice and sanitary."

"When can I go home?"

Ruby answered, "I'll grab the nurse."

Urse dropped her head to her hands. "Opal, I'm sorry. I didn't think you were really sick..." Sobs finished her sentence.

"Told you so," Opal smiled, reaching for her hand.

"I'm a garbage friend," Urse said. She wrapped her arms around herself and rocked crying.

"It's true." Opal grinned. "Urse, come on, people live their whole lives wishing they had a friend like you. How I lucked out, I'll never know, but you've made me as good as I can get." She reached for Urse who fell into her hug.

"Oh God, now you've got me crying." Luna said. She wiped her watery eyes on her sleeve.

Ruby returned with a nurse wearing pizza-printed scrubs.

"I'm Anna." She fiddled with knobs on monitors as they beeped. "How are you feeling, Opal?"

"Good. My friends just started crying baby shoes. It's time to go home."

"No one should have to be here, including me." The nurse winked. "I'm going to take your saline out and your doctor will be right in."

Metal sliding out of vein, wrapped; nurse gone.

"Speaking of baby shoes." Luna said. Her toothy grin widened as she put her hands under her flat belly where a baby might reside.

"What?" Opal asked.

"Pregnant? Really?" Urse stood to hug her.

Luna leaned in. "It's been a few months with no rager and the only other time I've fainted was—"

"Which of the three guys is it?" Urse interrupted.

The laughter was a welcomed release. Luna pushed Urse.

Ruby embraced Luna, resting her head on her shoulder. "You will be the best mom."

"Thanks, I hope so. If anyone asks, you knew *after* Arthur," Luna said.

Opal nodded. A wave of sadness washed over her though the happiness. *I won't be able to hold her baby.*

"I've never been happier for anyone in my life," Opal said. "Now, let's get you and your baby out of here."

"But the doctor's on her way."

"Pul-eeze. What can anyone tell me?" Opal asked. She stood tentatively and noticed Urse's look of concern.

The doctor walked in reading Opal's chart from her iPad. Prada sneakers poked out from navy scrubs that matched her hair claw clip. Her cheaters slid down her nose revealing a patch of freckles.

She bit the bottom corner of her lip before speaking. "Hello, Opal, I'm Doctor Williams." She acknowledged the other women with a mortician's smile. "It's nice to see you have so many people that care about you," she continued solemnly. "Would you like to speak privately?"

Opal shook her head, embarrassed at the fuss. "No. They already know. I'll get to my oncologist as soon as I can," Opal said.

"Do you have a health care strategy?" the doctor asked.

The question struck Opal as funny. *Fighting until you die is more of a motto than a strategy.*

"Yes. I was made aware of potential hiccups like this before hospice care."

That's right. Document it on my medical records that I mentioned going into hospice. Nothing fishy going on here. We are law abiders, no question.

Ruby put her fist to her mouth as if spitting cherry pits. "Excuse me," she mumbled before scurrying from the room.

Opal motioned to Luna to follow her.

"Hospice? That's way too soon," Urse blurted.

"Urse, it's for the future, luv." Opal smiled weakly at the doctor.

"Are your medications up to date?" the doctor asked. She tapped buttons on her iPad.

"Yes," Opal said. "Thank you for everything."

The doctor gave her shoulder a small squeeze. "Take care of yourself, okay?"

Opal and Urse nodded, and she left.

"Let's go home," Urse said.

"Poor Carol needs to be fed," Opal said.

Deflated, Urse whispered, "Yeah, poor Carol."

Chapter Twenty-Four

Ruby

Ruby gripped the handicap accessible bars in the hallway of the hospital. *I could go for some wrist etching right now.* Her Lucite bracelets clinked against the stainless, while the excess saliva in her mouth signaled trouble. *You're fine. It's all in your head. Keep it together.* Last time she and Opal were in a hospital, their roles were reversed. Opal had taken care of *her.*

Now, I'm falling to shit. All the money in the world and I'm still fucking useless.

Ruby seldom thought about her past, but seeing Opal in the hospital brought back all the bad dominos—the Nighttime Mom memory and the reason for her stacks of bracelets.

Bracelets.

Her *history.*

There was a time when she only wore one and it meant friendship. Back in college—when Ruby and Opal had been hired at the same restaurant.

"Can you believe we get *paid* to hang out?" Opal had asked Ruby before their shift as they rolled silverware.

"Plus, that Michael is cute, too," Ruby said. She noticed Opal wrapping faster and sped up her pace. Smooth linen, fold in half, place silverware, tuck ends, roll, and stack.

Opal nodded. "Well, *you* get to hang out at the hostess stand, while I hoist heavy trays like a peasant."

"You get tips. I get old weird guys calling me 'young Sophia Loren' all night, doofuses that they are." Ruby rolled her eyes.

Opal went to the bar to grab their pre-shift free soda.

As Ruby finished rolling silverware, Michael slid into the booth across from her.

Michael, a busser, looked as confident as a one-hundred-thirty-five-pound teenager with muscles could, with sandy brown hair neatly trimmed at the sides and nice manners. A caricaturist would zoom in on his big, brown eyes and the thick, dark eyelashes monopolizing his face. He appeared even-tempered, though Ruby often heard their managers yell, "Michael, NOW!" She assumed that must get his blood boiling.

"Hey, Ruby. How goes it?" He stared at his hands folded on the table. They were nice hands, with big knuckles.

"I'm fine. You?" She smiled sheepishly knowing if she were quiet, she would be who he wanted.

"I've been watching you with customers."

She cocked an eyebrow.

He tipped his head back. "That sounded bad—not in a stalker way, in a friend way, I mean."

"Oo-kay?" She crossed her arms and inched back.

"People say you're stuck up because you're quiet, but you aren't. I mean, I...I don't know, I catch you doing nice stuff all the time," Michael said.

Ruby unfolded her arms and leaned in, her head barely above the table. She smiled. "Like what?"

"Like when you sent over sodas to that poor family all dressed up, who shared an appetizer and ordered water. Seems there were quite a few 'mistakes from the kitchen' that found a home on their table."

She shook her head.

He continued, "The old woman that used the men's restroom? Ruby, I heard you apologize, that you *told* her to use the men's because of a maintenance issue. All to make a confused woman feel better and her family less embarrassed."

"It's no biggie."

"I know, but it…is," Michael said.

He cleared his throat. "Okay, so, now or never. Will you go out with me this Friday? Nothing big, maybe a lake walk?" He patted the top of his hair.

"Yes. I would like that." Ruby lifted her eyes to his. He left the second she agreed.

Opal approached and wiggled her eyebrows.

"You can't say anything, but he asked me out."

"You!" Opal smiled and pretended to punch a speed bag.

"He's deeper than you'd think." She sipped from her straw.

"This is good. He's cool, seems together, and has a J, O, B."

Their manager, Bruce, a portly man with a 1920s hairstyle featuring curly bangs to one side, walked to their booth, knocked on the tabletop and said, "I'm not paying you to drink free soda all night. Let's go, doors open in five."

"Ruby, do you think one day we'll be lucky enough to marry someone exactly like Bruce?" Opal kidded.

"Opal, I doubt with your mouth anyone will marry you, period."

"Sweet talker."

Ruby daydreamed her way home after their shift as Opal drove.

"You good?" Opal's standard question before delivering her to her less-than-ideal home.

"I'm cool, thanks for the lift."

Not even Nighttime Mom would get her down. Ruby skipped up the front stairs into the house and headed for the kitchen. Her mother sat at the table with her vodka tonic and cigarette.

"Why are you so smiley?" Nighttime Mom slurred spittle at the corner of her mouth.

"A good day is all." Ruby hadn't wanted to stick around—it only meant trouble.

She sighed. "Oh, well, that's nice."

Ruby shut the opened refrigerator door and hurried past Nighttime Mom, when, out of nowhere, Nighttime Mom's foot moved out. Ruby stumbled, sliding across the floor with her hands out, slamming into the wall.

SAH-nap!

CAH-RUNCH!

Her wrists jammed in pain, her eyes bulged, and blood spurted from her arm. She tried to reconcile the damage, to assess the wounds as taught in the safety class for babysitting at the YWCA.

"A nice day. Well there you go, now you're just like the rest of us...portals. Wait—no, no." She laughed. "*Mortals,* now you're just, just like us mortals." Nighttime Mom grabbed her green glass tumbler and cigarette and walked past Ruby on the kitchen floor.

"Nightie-night, and no need to be so dramatic," Nighttime Mom said and went to bed.

Ruby lay on the floor, bleeding.

The floor felt comfortable, like home. There was no threat of anything getting worse.

She wondered why her mom didn't love her. There was no denying it anymore, no fooling herself that Daytime Mom was her real mom. It turned out Nighttime Mom was the crux of it all; *she* ran the show.

And she didn't give a damn if she bled to death on the kitchen floor.

She needed to get up to protect Ann.

Ruby got to her knees by pushing off from her elbows; twisting around, she fell on her butt.

Her sister Ann ran into the kitchen.

"Rube! What did she do to you?" Ann looked around and tilted a chair under the doorknob.

"I'm fine. It's worse than it looks, is all. Where's dad?"

Ann's bottom lip quivered. "Went out for more beer."

"I think something is wrong with my wrist—she freaking tripped me." It was hard to tell where the blood was coming from. Her arms looked like knotted, chewed up tongues.

Ann's brown eyes met hers with authority. She lifted Ruby's chin. "It's only you and me, that's all we need anyway. Now we have to get you into the ER, okay?"

Ann grabbed a clean peony-print dish towel to wrap Ruby's wrist.

Bones weren't meant to be in open air.

Ann moved swiftly and called their uncle. "Uncle Ethan, can you get here as soon as you can? Ruby needs to get into the ER," Ann said, in her *calm-during-trouble* voice. "Okay...yep...uh-huh...fell. Yep, yep...okay, see you soon."

Ann hung up the phone. "Uncle Ethan will be here in a jiff. He'll know what to do."

"Michael asked me out today," Ruby said, talking herself out of the wooziness.

"Well, he's probably daft," Ann joked.

"You are my little glass of turpentine, aren't you?" Ruby soft joked back while squeezing her eyes closed.

"Let's get you up on your feet so we're ready."

"Ann, you know I—"

"I know, I know. You can tell me how much you love me and Michael later," Ann said, trying to hoist her up without causing more damage. She hooked her forearms under Ruby's armpits and lifted, then slipped on blood and regained her footing.

"Ann, I'm sorry. You shouldn't have to deal with this."

"Why are *you* apologizing? Rube, never mind that now, Uncle Ethan will be here any minute."

Ruby heard the roar of their uncle's GTO; the back door opened.

His eyes were big, surveying his nieces.

"Hey, kiddo, you okay?" He lifted the sides of his waistband.

"I am," Ruby said before passing out.

Uncle Ethan and Ann had watched as Ruby disappeared down the corridor with the hospital staff.

A seasoned nurse with puffy arms popping out of her short-sleeved uniform tilted her head and smiled at them. "Well, I bet you two have had easier nights. Come with me, we can get started on a cup of something and paperwork," the nurse said.

"Thank you," Ann said somberly.

"Oh, and one of my favorite support people is on her way as well," the nurse added.

A young, pretty woman in a navy pantsuit approached Ann carrying a clipboard, her black hair so tidy and shiny, it looked like a wig Daytime Mom would wear.

"Ann?" the woman asked, smiling.

She looked like Ruby's age, too young to help.

"Yes." Ann shook her soft hand.

"My name is Tess Hokanson, I'm an assistant social worker. May I talk to you for a few minutes?"

"Sure." Ann looked back at Uncle Ethan as they walked to the chapel for a quiet place to talk.

"You must've had a tough night. You did a good job getting Ruby the help she needed. You are very brave. I'm here to make sure you two are safe, alright?"

The kindness she was afforded seemed patronizing.

"Ruby had an accident. She tripped. She's not a liar and neither am I. What else is there?"

Tess's eyes widened.

"Where are your parents, Ann?" Tess matched her candor. Seemed the gloves were off.

"They weren't there when we left. It happened so fast we didn't have a chance to call. They had gone out to eat."

"Interesting. Well, we called your house and your mother picked up."

Ann's stomach lurched.

They stared at one another, each comprised of walnut shells.

Tess went back to small talk. Rapport building again, playing the game Ann invented. And just like that, Tess and her navy pantsuit left the hospital lobby.

The doctor came out.

"Good news. Ruby will be fine. The surgery went well. She will have a long road to recovery with her right wrist. The left is broken but straight. We repaired the right wrist with three rods and we will need to keep her for a few days. She's been through a big injury. She'll need to sleep to heal as I say," the frosty-haired surgeon said as if in a canned presentation. "Any questions?"

"When can we see her?" Uncle Ethan asked.

"She's in recovery," the doctor said. "You can head on back."

He left, fluffing out his white coat as he turned like a TV doctor.

They pulled the door open to Ruby laying there quiet, with skin vaguely the color of canned peas under fluorescent bulbs.

"That's one way to get hospital Jell-O," Ann said.

"You okay?" Ruby asked.

"Me? Uh, yeah, I'm not the one with—"

"I've never been so scared," Uncle Ethan admitted as he kissed the top of Ruby's head.

Ruby looked down at her broken, bandaged wrists. As swollen as they were, they looked fake. "I'm fine—really. They're keeping me overnight so I can get some shut eye."

When she was released, Ruby called Opal to pick her up.

"Oh, Ruby, I'm sorry." Opal helped her from the wheelchair to her car. "Let's get you home."

She wasn't sure if *home* was the right word because they were headed to Opal's grandma's.

When the door opened, Grandma Ivy gave Ruby a hug and ushered her into the guest room. It was painted lilac, warm, and had clean but dusty pillows. Grandma Ivy had preheated a gold Sunbeam electric blanket to number six, and a cup of hot cocoa sat on the bed stand resting on a coaster that read: "respect the wood." The home smelled of freshly baked cookies, Bounce dryer sheets, and old, fancy soap.

After a week of warmth in Grandma Ivy's home, Ruby showered, thanked her hosts, and headed back to Daytime Mom.

"Got this?" Opal asked.

"Got this." She gave Opal a car hug and lifted her arm in a painful half wave.

Ruby had opened the front door, walked into Daytime Mom's open arms, and said, "It's fine."

Just like then, and in this hospital now, things were definitely not *fine.*

Leaving Opal's hospital room, Ruby threw up in the hallway on the way to the restroom.

Chapter Twenty-Five

Urse

Urse heard a kerfuffle coming from the hallway of the hospital and somewhere in it, Ruby's voice. She peeked her head out of Opal's room where she heard Ruby apologizing to a nurse.

"Oh, dear, it's okay. It happens all the time around here. Let's get you squared away." The nurse reminded Urse of a kindergarten teacher.

"Ruby? You okay?"

She turned, her index finger under her nose, thumb up. "I'm cool—overheated, is all."

Urse noticed the pool of sick on the floor and grabbed paper towels from the wall dispenser and began cleaning.

"Oh, dear, let me call someone," the nurse said.

"I already got it, thanks." Urse turned her head trying not to gag.

Don't be a little bitch, it's just barf. You run a huge corporation, enough with the gagging.

"Code orange 0005, that's code orange 0005." The calm voice alerted the staff over the loudspeaker. The nurse half-smiled and dashed off.

Urse stood with chunky, yellow soaked paper towels in her hand, looking for a garbage can.

Ruby pointed to a bin. "Sorry." Her head still down, hand flat against the wall.

Urse chucked the towels, hit the hand sanitizer and pulled a plastic chair from an empty room.

"Well, when you really screw up, you shit in your mom's mouth, am I right?" Urse asked.

Ruby smirked. "I wish."

Urse hoisted her up by the elbow crook. "Look, you can't do anything stupid, like..." She paused. "...offing yourself." Speaking through her tears, she continued. "I'm just so tired, Rube. I'm so fucking tired, is all, and I need you to be there for me. I mean, fuck, Opal's doctor talked about *hospice.* Hospice, Ruby, I...you can't leave me like..." Her voice trailed off.

Ruby held her as she cried.

"I won't go anywhere, Urse. Shh, don't cry."

Urse lifted her head from Ruby's shoulder and said, "Your hair smells nice. Plus, you know my idiot brother's in love with you, right? That should count for something."

Ruby snuck into a room and returned with a box of tissues. She tipped the box toward Urse.

"Thanks." Urse sniffed, taking a sheer tissue.

"This may come as a surprise, but I like your brother."

Urse took three more tissues, wadded them up and said, "'Like' is a funny word to use when it's love. And it sure as hell isn't a surprise."

Ruby put her head down and smiled.

The two returned to Opal's room arm in arm and found her dressed and standing by the foot of the bed.

Luna turned. "You two look like you just came from an allergy convention."

"You know ole ironsides puked in the hallway," Urse said. "Our little debutante."

"Urse cleaned it up. I think she wanted a whiff," Ruby joked.

Luna's surprise animated. "Oh, damn. Ruby's funny today."

Urse chuckled.

"Let's go," Opal whispered, her knuckles white, clenching the bed frame as she stood.

"You're coming with me, Opal," Urse said.

Luna grabbed the plastic bag filled with Opal's things.

"Meet us at Opal's?" Urse asked.

Urse's car was parked in the emergency patient spot up front, past the outdoor smoking section. *We'll beat them to Opal's house.* Her car came to life, *Limp Bizkit* spilling from the speakers. She reached for the knob when Opal said, "How can you show your face in public listening to that shit? If it's not elephants, it's pissants. My God."

"You don't think I know it's shameful?" Urse said. "Listen, I want to ask you something."

In the passenger seat, Opal looked like she was sitting on an oversized tourist chair. *When did she get so small?* Urse turned off the airbag on her side.

"What's on your mind?"

Urse fiddled with the controls. "Want your seat warmer on?" She put her visor down to shade her eyes, when a coupon for a free donut fell out and landed on Opal's lap.

"Always, thanks." She studied the coupon. "You only have three more days before it expires."

"Oh, thanks," Urse said. "Say, how exactly do you know Tess Hokanson?"

"My stylist Taylor recommended her. Why?"

Urse rolled through a stop sign. "No reason, she's familiar is all."

"Yeah, the second we met I had this weird, meant-to-be-feeling. Goosebumps, the whole thing." Opal rested her head against the window. "I'm going to sleep a bit. My head hurts."

Steering with her knees, Urse reached behind her seat, feeling for a chunk of clear quartz that had been rolling around for months. Her fingertips touched the edge of it. Her car swerved into and back from the other lane.

Inching the crystal forward, she pinched it up and swirled it in the air above Opal who slept.

Please, fix her. I'll be good, I'll do good. Charity work. I'll donate all my money. Well, not all, but I will if I knew it would work.

She looked at Opal.

Okay, fine. All.

Taking her cell from the holder, she texted Luna and Ruby.

Urse: *Deep dive on Tess Hokanson. All info you can find*

Ruby: *On it*

Luna: *Done and done. pls don't txt and drive*

Fifteen minutes later, Urse pulled up to Opal's house. Her lawn was as pristine as a golf course, with marigolds fading to make way for the last round of perennials. Had a root from a snobby oak not lifted one paver on the path to the house, it would have been perfect.

"You're home," she whispered, and gently touched Opal's shoulder.

"Will you feed Carol? I'm heading to bed."

"A cup of food?"

"Yeah." Opal moved to the side of her seat and stood on shaky legs.

Urse put Opal's arm around her waist, lifting most of her weight as she shuffled into the house. Carol ran to Opal, squiggling as she moved. Throwing herself to the ground belly up, the dog made a half-moan, half-cry in her presence.

"Oh, Boo Boo," Opal whispered and scratched behind her ear.

Getting Opal down the hall was like carrying a water balloon with the top cut off. Once safely in bed, Urse untied her shoes and tucked her in.

"Can I get you anything?" Urse whispered.

"I've always had a thing for Jeff Goldblum."

Urse sighed, relieved. "Give me three days."

"And water."

Urse headed to the kitchen.

Luna stood, facing the stove, looking concerned, arms in a self hug.

"She just needs sleep."

Luna nodded then opened the fridge, pulled out Vidalias, celery, and carrots then began making soup. Urse searched the cupboards for Opal's favorite glass, a tall crystal tumbler. She brought it to Opal, who was lying on her stomach.

"Here's some water. I'll leave you to rest," Urse said.

"I'm just spent, is all." Her finger flicked the side of the glass.

Ting.

Opal smiled and set her head back on the pillow. Urse tiptoed out and closed the handle of the door quietly.

Ruby sat at the kitchen island watching Luna chop carrots when her phone pinged an email. "The Tess Hokanson report is in."

Urse pulled up a chair and Luna stopped chopping.

"Read it out loud," Urse said.

"According to my investigator, she checks out. Three speeding tickets, a bunch of parking tickets, and a public urination a decade ago."

Luna snorted. "Could be any of us." She went back to her vegetables, lining them in tight rows.

"Addresses?" Urse pressed.

Ruby studied the email. "Blah, blah, blah…okay, here it is. Minneapolis, Duluth, and Bloomington. Occupations: assistant manager at Mars Drive in, front desk at Drive-N-Go Motel, student, assistant social worker at St. Mary's hospital, administrator at Joan of Arc Hospice, and RN in various capacities." She rubbed her temple. "*Duluth.*"

"Johnny sold that creepy Irv's car to her. That's weird, right?" Urse picked up a carrot; Luna shooed her hand away. "Take the ones that aren't cut," she said. Urse put a whole one between her incisors and crunched down.

"Yeah, that's weird, alright," Ruby said. She looked around the house and rubbed her forehead. "I need to do something productive," she continued.

Ruby grabbed supplies from the mudroom closet and began cleaning. Urse polished the windows; Luna finished the soup, organized, and threw out expired food from Opal's fridge. They worked in silence as if their sanity depended on the home's order.

Urse looked around, pleased. *Reverse nesting.*

Ruby's eyes got big; her mouth formed an *O.* "I think Tess Hokanson worked at the hospital the night of my broken wrists. I'm not positive, I'll have to ask Uncle Ethan, but I remember someone social workery named Tess."

"Super strange," Luna said. "I don't get it. I don't know her. You don't think she's a scammer, do you?"

Chapter Twenty-Six

Luna

According to the FedEx website, the brown recluse look-alikes would arrive at Luna's between 10 a.m. and noon. She had already set up a terrarium for the creatures to crash until Opal's big, ugly day.

Is she going to let them bite her? I don't get it.

In any case, Ruby and Urse mentioned getting the asks on their notes already. One or both will help ease Opal into the next life.

No one will know my spiders are nonvenomous. No sense in risking fifteen years of freedom. I need to be here for this baby.

There's work to keep my mind off it. Houseplant cleaning.

"What are you up to today?" Luna expelled extra carbon dioxide with exaggerated enunciation onto her favorite plant. She opened the cupboard for cleaning supplies, and picked up mineral oil and a green shammy. The green was reserved for Fridays, the yellow for the next week, and the blue for oiling her heels during sandal weather. Tipping the oil onto the rag, she began rubbing the leaves. The caladiums shined up the most satisfyingly; the other plants' scrub downs were merely routine. After the leaf shining ritual, she cleaned up the various red pots that the plants called home and plucked dead leaves from their beds.

Once, Arthur had asked, "Why don't you keep them there as mini mulch?"

"How would *you* like to live next to a dead body?"

His face looked so cute scrunched up.

I wonder what he's doing right now?

The wait to tell him about their baby was excruciating, but she had to follow the plan.

She went to her bedroom, pulled the bed from the wall, and pried a loose board from the floor with a screwdriver from her nightstand.

There you are, my old friends.

She blew dust off the wooden box as if in a mystery movie. After replacing the board and bed, she brought the box to the living room, sprawled a yoga mat, and sat to open the lid.

"It's been awhile hasn't it?" Luna asked the tarot cards.

She shuffled the wooden circles. The cards splayed out told the story.

First card: The Empress. *Cool.*

Second card, dodgy, but okay, third, card, prosperity, duh.

Fourth: Death. *Sigh. Opal.*

The fifth and most important card: another Death.

She laid on her back and stretched her arms and legs out.

Two Death cards in a row. No. Oh God, no—this isn't fair. I have to keep my breathing calm.

The ceiling corner had a cobweb.

One more thing I hadn't planned for.

She was out of tears, and the blandness blended into numbness, vast and heavy.

I'm at the bottom.

Flipping to her side in the fetal position felt right. The hardwood floor was unforgiving against her hip bone. She wondered if her baby mirrored her posture or if her mom had laid this way when she lived inside of her. Did her mom draw the schizophrenic card? Maybe the Death card is luckier for my baby?

These cards are never wrong. Opal will die soon; apparently my unborn baby will die. I'll need to dig deep for the positive or the dark will get the jump.

Luna pushed herself up, brushed herself off, and set off for her "icky stuff" broom with its frayed, uneven ends, clumped with old strings of hair and fluff. *It probably won't mind another cobweb.* As she swept the ceiling corner, the doorbell chimed. She hustled the broom back to its spot and yelled, "Coming!"

The spiders.

She opened the door and gasped.

"Arthur!" She jumped toward him and threw her arms around his neck. He stood stiff, mouth open.

Her head turned to rest on his chest. "I'm sorry, Arthur. I've missed you so, so much."

He softened, burying his face in her hair. "Don't you know you are my home?" His face puffy and pale as if he, too, hadn't slept much since he left their house.

NO.

Luna backed up and shoved his chest.

"You left me!" Luna's index finger pointed at his tired face. "You left *me,* Arthur. We were the one thing I counted on. Now, if I make one wrong step, it feels like an earthquake will eat me whole."

She began to sob.

Arthur gingerly wrapped his arms around her. "Oh, Lune. I may have left but I've never been gone."

She kissed him with urgency backing into the kitchen. Sex would make the Death cards, the doomed baby, and the spiders melt away, if only temporarily. They stripped off and lay on the kitchen floor naked. She opened her legs wide and reveled in the blue of his eyes until they dropped. *Oh, you do love a show.* He tugged her hair firmly. She returned her eyes to his.

"You know what I want," Luna said.

He nodded and fingered her so roughly, he broke a sweat. She was on the edge of eruption and having him stop. *Just a little longer...*

She looked down to see the stream shoot from her and smiled, face hot still wet from crying.

"Now, do your job—clean up the squirt, naughty man."

Arthur backed up, then licked the wet from her tanned thighs to her calves, paused, and continued to the kitchen floor. Once the wet on the floor was cleaned, he put his cock in her mouth and finished.

"We're good at this," she said.

Arthur rolled onto his side facing her. He folded his arm behind his head, and she did the same. They stared at one another until the pain melted into love.

"You can't leave me again," Luna whispered.

"I just needed time. You hurt me, you know? No matter what, I'm the last one standing in your corner."

Luna nodded.

It was time to tell him everything.

"You know how I clean out the dead leaves in all of the red pots?" Luna began.

Chapter Twenty-Seven

Opal

Opal dreamt her hand sifted through a bag of flour, silky but dry, then realized Carol was licking her palm hanging over the side of the bed.

"It's you." She sat up, groggy from sleep and cancer.

Oh, why not?

She patted the spot on her bed where Oliver used to sleep.

"Come on girl, up!"

Carol squinted and lowered her head.

"It's allowed. Come on."

The dog leapt onto the bed and quickly rolled over, exposing her stomach.

"Look at you, ole girl, *Breaking the law, Breaking the law,*" she said, poorly imitating Rob Halford.

Carol rolled over, the flecks of brown and gold in her eyes rimmed in black caught the sunshine from the window. Pinpricks of emotion hit Opal's nose. *How can you be so good? What if the whole freaking point of life is that look from your dog?*

I could be dead tomorrow and it doesn't matter.

Matter. What a funny word. I'm matter and carbon and a few old memories, fogginess, and bone cracks, peppered with love. Enough for others but never myself.

Opal nodded at the thought.

I wish I could squish all the worry and bad down and expand love in all forms. To squeeze it like a lime, then put it in the microwave for more. I've wasted so much time being mad. Why did I assume there would be more time?

Since her prognosis, Opal spent an unreasonable amount of time imagining what having your life flash before you might look like. Your highest and lowest actions condensed, then someone or something would judge and deem you salvageable or not. She hoped she was good, but sure the fuck hadn't given away all her money, washed a bum's feet, or taken in senior dogs. Naw, she opted for seven course meals, the newest i-whatevers, and four-hundred-dollar highlights. Shame, sure; she lived with that and the semi-crooked decisions made to advance her portfolio.

When poor, she was no stranger to bending the rules or acting bratty—not to mention how mean she had been in junior high. Sometimes those moments faded after a Habitat for Humanity day gig, a drop off at a clothing drive, or a well-timed smile to a person of below average looks. There were times she was downright heroic, taking the utmost care not to hurt people's feelings—*well*, sometimes it couldn't be helped, but generally. All the practice and patience to quell her anger, then *whammo!* Someone looked past, over, or through her, and in a flash they needed to feel how small they tried to make her feel. And she lashed out—and stung—with precision. *Then* they saw her.

Reciprocity, bitches.

Until now.

Now, on the edge of dying, she wondered if being invisible wasn't the best thing for an alpha woman in their fifties. No more trying, no more scuffles for power, no more 'best of list' shit. No more rallying. A new generation was slotted for the takeover. Who was she trying to impress, anyway? Oliver was gone and her friends loved her best they could; she had a nice life—fuck, that stupid Indignation Suppression class had made a few good points.

I mean, if my life is graded on a curve...

Urse had once mentioned, "I think death is whatever you believe it will be. If you think there's heaven and hell, there will be; if you think there's reincarnation, there will be."

Opal leaned into that thinking.

Always assumed I'd be in hell on my scabby knees, crying. Best rearrange my thinking. Plus, I need my Oliver and he's definitely somewhere beautiful.

Picking up her laptop and pillow on the way to the gazebo, her eye caught a vintage Mercedes in her driveway. *I wish someone was here to murder me.* She hid behind the dining room wall and peeped out cautiously.

Tess Hokanson.

Unannounced and appearing to be talking to herself in her car.

This can't be good.

Gathering her hair and putting two Wakasa chopsticks into the bun, she went out to see what Tess was up to. Tess looked up from her phone and smiled. Opal returned the nicety and motioned her into the house.

"I'm sorry. I normally call but was in your neighborhood," Tess said.

Doubt the gate guard agreed, but okay.

"All good. What's up?"

They moved to the front porch swing and brushed away the dried leaves from the rust-colored cushions. Opal tucked her feet under her long cover-up. Next to her, Tess stared straight ahead, gently pushing the swing with her feet. The chain creaked as the wind pushed Tess's hair back like a fan on low.

"You know I think the world of you, Opal, but I'm—"

"You're breaking up with me because of my pancreas. God, you're a jerk."

Tess laughed. "There's my brother's sense of humor again. Abner would've loved your happy ass."

"You never know, maybe I'll meet him in the hereafter or something." Opal's hair fell out of one side. She took out the sticks and redid them.

"What a lovely thought." Tess paused. "Opal, I can't do it. I'm not comfortable aiding in your suicide though I think it's the smart woman's play. I'm so sorry. I'd be happy to show up as a friend if you'll have me."

Tess's feet stopped moving as she nervously rolled the edge of the indoor-outdoor pillow.

The possibility of a "no, thanks" had always been there.

Opal bit the side of her lip. "Thank you for letting me know and not doing a no-show."

Tess's shoulders eased and she began swinging again. "How's your appetite?"

"Starving, but look," she pulled the sides of her dress taut revealing her distended stomach.

"Have you had it drained lately?"

Tess's medical background was comforting; it was too much to explain to the other women, and it seemed too gross if you weren't accustomed to the ick of disease.

"Two days ago."

"Good as you can do, right?" Tess tilted her head to look at her.

A phrase jumped out at Opal from a pamphlet she'd read at the Mayo Clinic a month ago about *meeting patients where they are.* "Burden of care, my friend, burden of care," Opal said smugly.

"You know that's right."

Opal sighed. "May I ask why you won't?" She hopped off the swing, picked a daisy from the side of the sidewalk, and returned to where she started.

Tess waited for her to get situated before she spoke.

"Yeah, it's just a feeling is all. I had a shit dream about it going sideways and woke up in a sweat." She shook her head at the recollection.

"I'm a biggie on going with your gut, well, not *my gut*, but you know." Opal plucked a petal from the daisy. "He loves me." The wind blew the petal. "He loves me a lot. He loves me—"

"Hey." Tess squeezed Opal's hand, squishing the daisy. "I mean it. I'm sorry."

"Me, too. Is there anything you can tell me to ensure everyone comes out of this on the right side of prison bars?"

"Not according to my dream."

Opal remained still, though the swing moved them.

"Tess."

"Yeah?"

The swing's chain creaked, back and forth, to and fro, as the wind blew through the pampas grass until Opal could boil her words down.

"What if I don't matter?" Opal bit the inside of her cheek in an effort not to cry.

Tess stopped the swing on the bottom of the back and forth. "I'm about to give you the story of a lifetime." She wagged her finger at her. "Ready for it?"

Opal nodded, relieved not to talk.

"I was taking care of an old guy a few years back when I worked in hospice. A huge turd—I mean it, huge. Literally. He would poo poo cake his bed on purpose to make the staff's life hell, when he wasn't hitting the call button for serious requests, such as extra ice in his water."

Opal appreciated her cheer. "Ew."

"Exactly, ew. Anyway, this son of a bitch would not die, and trust me, he was what we call in the business a real 'Marvin K. Mooney,' if you know what I mean.

Opal laughed, finishing the Dr. Seuss line. "Please go now!"

"You get it. Okay, so this nightmare of a man finally gets a visitor, a gorgeous woman about his age who rolls in on a wheelchair, hair all done up in that fluffy gray way they do. She edges to the bed and says, 'My darling, I'm so sorry I haven't been here, I was in the hospital with a small stroke and a broken hip, nothing to worry about.'

"'You look so beautiful, my pumpernickel,' he said, all soft. I kid you not, 'pumpernickel.'" Tess shook her head and continued. "I watched them from the corner of my eye pretending to fix a monitor. This despicable man was impervious to my charm. I mean, I gave him my best nurse stuff, Opal, really I did."

"You are very charming, I concede."

"Then it dawned on me." Tess paused. "He didn't matter until someone loved him."

Opal's emotions shot out of her in a guttural cry. She brought the daisy to her chest.

Tess put her arm around her shoulder and she sank into her new friend's kindness.

Now what am I going to do?

Chapter Twenty-Eight

Ruby

Ruby was meeting Urse and Luna at noon at an award-winning restaurant in downtown Minneapolis. She slid on wide-legged black jeans, a fitted white T-shirt, and a navy oversized blazer. Brushing her long black hair, she opted for an easy, slick, high pony, which at her height, swung close to six feet. She reached for the partridge feather earrings Luna had handcrafted for her fortieth birthday using real gold and plumes. Poking the end of the wire into the nearly closed holes in her earlobes, she nodded at her reflection. *Ready.*

Even though the restaurant was less than a mile from her place, Ruby's choice of footwear forced her to phone the bellman for a ride. She didn't want to haul around tenners like business commuters did in the mornings. Now that she sold the majority of her business, there would be time for leisure, to stand to the right of moving crowds—the slow lane.

Glass doors, freshly squeegeed, opened to a packed wait and a hostess who rushed forward. "Welcome Ms. Redstone. Your party is already seated. You may follow me."

Every seat in the restaurant was occupied. The sumac and cinnamon warmth of the restaurant contrasted the icy Mississippi below.

Once at the table, Urse rose to hug her. "Well, look at your hot ass."

Ruby laughed and pressed her flat hand to her chest and bowed.

"I like your earrings." Luna beamed, rising to give her a squeeze.

"Me, too."

Urse fluffed out her white linen and placed it on her lap. "Here we are, looking all good, feeling all shit," she said.

Ruby nodded. "Yep."

Urse fidgeted with her water glass. "I want to start off with a big ole clear the air apology."

Luna raised her hand. "No need. We are all—"

"No. I've been rude and mean, and you two and Johnny are all I have." Urse inched forward toward the middle of the table. Luna and Ruby parroted her. "I guess I'm ready to give Opal what she's asking for."

Luna covered her mouth.

Ruby remained stoic.

"Under one condition." Urse looked out the restaurant windows overlooking the river and turned back to her friends. "You hear me out, and we grow through this—in authenticity. No sneaky shit."

"I don't even know what that means," Ruby said.

Luna swirled her water glass.

"Well, we can start with your cutting," Urse said.

The breadbasket arrived. "Thank you," Luna said, acknowledging the server.

Ruby wanted a piece of seeded flatbread but didn't want to offer up her wrists while they discussed it.

"We love you very much, Ruby, but you can't run right now. We are bringing it up as a selfish thing—we need *you* to get *us* through this," Luna said.

Here it is, the time. I can't keep running. She bit the inside of her mouth and nodded.

"You are safe. We won't hurt you. We are all at the whim of the jacked up little kids inside of us. Your mom, my dad, Luna's fucking..." Urse trailed off as Luna picked up her butter knife and made a stabbing motion, reducing them to laughter. "...dentist."

The bison carpaccio arrived pre-plated with briny capers, just the way Ruby liked it.

"Technically, he wasn't *my* dentist," Luna corrected.

"Right, we assumed that," Ruby said. She pushed parmesan off the bison and squeezed the lemon.

"She speaks." Luna squeezed her forearm.

"So, do we want to figure out our shit before or after Opal's...thing?" Urse asked.

"What do you have to work on?" Ruby asked.

"Who, me? Let's start with three failed marriages, my unhealthy work hours, and my misplaced resentment." She looked directly at Ruby. "My husbands were trash. I knew it, the world knew it, but it was easier to blame you. I'm truly sorry."

"Don't be," Ruby said, relieved.

"Let's save the substance abuse stuff for another day," Urse offered. "We need to be realistic."

Ruby choked on her water.

Luna slapped the side of her hip. "Right?"

"Lune?" Urse asked.

"Oh, I'm good." She sucked her lips in, nodding quickly as the other two laughed.

"Hmm, well. I could—maybe, possibly, potentially—get a shrink to help with a few things, I guess. I mean there is my schizophrenic mom and..." She drifted off. "...yeah, and all the shrapnel from my dead babies."

Ruby could feel the heat of her tears rolling down her face. The server approached the table gingerly, then backed away without a word.

"I read my cards the other day." Luna straightened her place setting, the linen, and the chair. "Two Death cards. Opal and presumably, my unborn."

"No." Urse put down her fork and reached for her hand.

"The good news—Arthur and I made up. Good timing, too, with all this"—her hands moved around her stomach without touching it—"going on."

"Is your baby okay now?" Urse asked tentatively.

"I guess. But the four others started that way, too, without the Death card."

Urse shot her a quizzical look. "You told us there was no such thing as a Death card. That it means rebirth or change."

"You said, 'like when a snake sheds its skin' if I remember correctly," Ruby said.

"It does mean that. I mean, yeah. But these cards from my grandma are different, they...drat. My grandma told me these cards were only for our family and yes, it can mean rebirth, but in my case, it's actual death." She looked like split ends.

"Bill of goods," Urse said. "I bet your baby will be healthy."

The clatter of the restaurant they hadn't noticed until now took over. Ruby imagined Luna felt like a fraud having flip-flopped on the Death card. The quiet stretched in the room.

"Fine. I'll see someone about my cutting," Ruby blurted.

She would say anything to make it stop, all this pain. Seeing as though running wasn't allowed, this was the next best thing.

Urse popped up an inch from her chair excitedly, and turned to Luna, who smiled for the first time since the conversation began.

"Look at us. I don't know about you two, but can we table the serious stuff for later? Ruby looks like she's had it, Luna needs to eat, and I need a...tea, I guess—this place doesn't sell booze."

Ruby smiled and put her sign language tic under the white tablecloth.

"Why hide it? It's one of the things I love about you," Urse said.

Ruby inched her hands above the table and signed, *I love you two.*

The women had kept a few things secret. Ruby and her pending suicide,

Luna neglected to mention the venomous spiders Opal requested were nothing of the sort, and Urse figured she'd keep her secret quiet for now.

"You should tell her." Urse wiggled her eyebrows and pointed her fork at Luna.

Caught with food in her mouth, Luna spoke through her napkin. "Me?"

Ruby cringed. "Oh God, now what?"

"Well, for dessert we have invited a special guest to join you," Luna said.

She slumped her head. "You know I hate surprises. Hate," Ruby mumbled.

Johnny tapped her shoulder. "There's a fine line between love and hate."

He grabbed the chair next to Ruby as Urse and Luna left, moving apologetically. Once they were alone and settled, Johnny said, "Look, I know you're the gabby type so I'm going to do the heavy lifting." He did a double take at her half-eaten plate of food. "Are you done with your...what is it, carpaccio? I'm starving." Johnny licked his lips.

Ruby slid her plate toward him and handed him silverware, then tucked a stray hair behind her ear.

"Thanks."

All this not running is exhausting.

Johnny pushed the parmesan further from the meat as if it corrupted the dish. His bobbing knee moved the edge of the tablecloth.

"Here goes. We can agree, life is fleeting—just ask Opal. I want you to know, I worry about you, and I think about you, and...aw, geez." He sat up straighter and asked, "Can I get a small drumroll for my big reveal, please?" He rubbed his palms on his thighs.

Ruby pretended to drum, did an exaggerated imaginary toss of a drumstick, caught it then looked back to Johnny.

"I've loved you since the first day we met." His lip quivered. "So, if you aren't offended..."

Ruby grabbed his shirt, drawing him to her. His lips were plump and soft yet firm. She leaned back while he hopped his chair closer. Johnny spread his legs to fit Ruby between them.

"I knew all along you loved me back," he whispered in her ear, forcing a hot shiver down her neck.

God, he smells good, like when someone comes in from the cold.

"I've wanted this for so long."

The server arrived. "Can I get you something, sir?" Johnny handed the server the menus then rested his hand on Ruby's thigh. Ruby was keenly aware of the move, as they transitioned from abstract to tangible within moments. His hand strong on her leg felt tight and warm, like a pair of perfect jeans fresh out of the dryer.

"May I get two nettle teas and another carpaccio to go?" Johnny's eyes didn't veer from Ruby's. "No parmesan."

"Perfect." The server dipped her head and left with the menus.

He had a gulp of water. "Of course, my love requires a few things. I mean, it's not free, good woman." The restaurant's sound system played pan flute music.

"Like what?" Ruby stiffened a smidge.

He whispered, "No cutting. I need you to use your words and I promise I will make it my life's work to make you happy."

Daytime Mom's voice chirped in her ear. *"He takes care to notice you."*

She pushed her bracelets forward to cover the bad seams on her wrists.

"I'll afford you all kinds of patience—I will—but it's on you to do the work." Johnny lifted her chin.

She stared into his eyes, now welled with tears, and leaned on his chest. He wrapped his arms around her and kissed the top of her head.

I'm not even holding my breath.

The server appeared with a doggie bag, the to-go cups of tea, and the bill. Ruby looked around for the first time since his arrival; the restaurant had largely cleared out.

"No rush," their server said.

"How long did the ladies lunch before me?" Johnny asked.

She straightened her knee length apron. "Three hours."

He shook his head. "Freaking animals, these people I'm with. Don't they know you need to turn tables to make a living?" Johnny smiled.

She blushed. "No, it's my pleasure."

Johnny handed her his credit card. "You take Target store credit, right?" he joked.

She looked at his Mastercard and swiped it tableside. Johnny signed the receipt and tipped five hundred dollars.

The server glanced at the receipt. "I think you added an extra zero," she said sheepishly.

"Nope."

Ruby stood and slid her chair in.

Johnny put his arm around Ruby's shoulders.

Now I won't be alone when we kill Opal.

Chapter Twenty-Nine

Urse

It was probably not a good idea to introduce weed from a new guy to a bottle of wine.

But if not now, when?

Urse giggled to herself.

I'm going to regret this, but fuck it.

Urse's contact list blurred, as she scrolled back and forth to the entry titled, "Whatever you do—don't call."

Calling...

"Hello?"

"How's my favorite ex-husband doing?" Urse purred. She lay on her stomach at the side of her basement pool. Her free hand paddled the water.

"Give me a minute."

Urse heard doors closing in the background.

"You know you aren't supposed to be calling me. Simone would have a fit."

Urse rolled to her back. "I bet a fit is the only way to get her to move in bed." She shifted to baby talk. "Remember that time we had sex in your office on that purple chair, Daaaaddy?"

The pool heater hummed providing mugginess, always a welcome treat in Minnesota. She put her ankle to her knee and stretched her hip.

"Why do you do this?" Jeff's deep voice hadn't changed—though according to online stalking, the rest of him had. "Of course, I remember. Why do you even call? You're all talk anyway—an old-fashioned dick tease."

Urse fought to get to her feet, then wandered to the cedar-lined closet, pulling out a cheerful yellow towel. Pressing it to her face she inhaled. *Mmm.*

"You're a married man, remember?" Her voice betrayed her bitterness. She unrolled the towel, planked over the center, and clunked down.

"What do you want, Urse?" he whispered.

"Okay, okay. I need a favor, Jeff."

"One. You have one favor, make it good."

"You still an investigator?" Urse edged her wine glass closer without sitting up. Overestimating her ability to drink laying down, her glass tipped and spilled down her front. *Upfh.*

"Detective, now actually. Urse, are you drunk?"

"Are you?" She laughed. "I have serious moments of missing you, mostly when your cock isn't in me." She scooted down the towel and rolled the end for a pillow.

"I bet you say that to everyone." His voice was playful. "Seriously, though. Are you okay, Urse?"

She rolled over to her stomach and rested her chin in her palm, her face squeezed to hold a cry in. "Not really."

Jeff's voice softened to the man she once loved. "I'm sorry. I swear I am."

"I know."

She missed the idea of him.

"What can I help you with?" A children's show blared in the background.

She sighed. "Opal has befriended a woman named Tess Hokanson. I think she's a no-goodnik, a bum, a swindler, a—"

"I get it, I get it. Got a date of birth by any chance?"

"666 is all I know." She pulled a wet joint from her kimono pocket.

How'd it get soggy?

"Helpful as usual. I'll call you if I find anything." Jeff sounded like he was going to say something poignant but said, "Sweetheart, it really has been good to hear your—"

Plunk.

Her cell dropped from her hand into the pool as she fell asleep.

Chapter Thirty

Luna

"This thing gets so hot I guarantee it's against the law nowadays," Luna said as she plugged their vintage waffle maker into the tiered island's outlet. She wrapped a dish towel around the handle. *Fooled before.*

Arthur slid the heavy kitchen seat out and positioned himself by the action. "It's like your own cooking show in here. All we need is an overhead mirror."

She poured vinegar into milk in lieu of buttermilk, sifted the dry ingredients, and set the counter to eat. "Wild blueberries or plum sauce? Both from your kinfolk, Opal."

"Always blueberry. Did I ever tell you about what she pulled at Christmas when we were little?"

Luna shook her head.

"She would pick blueberries from our grandparents' cabin on the Gunflint Trail and make blueberry sauce for—get this—*two* people. She couldn't have been more than ten years old, I suppose, and awarded the jars to people that kissed her ass during the year." He shook his head. "Here's the kicker. We all wanted the sauce because it was so damn good. There were at least forty relatives at holidays clamoring for it. Crazy manipulative, now that I think about it."

Luna flipped the waffle maker upside down. Steam creeped from the edges; the kitchen filled with the smell of almond extract. "So, you never got a jar?"

Arthur shook his head. "And I tried, trust you me."

She pursed her lips. "My poor baby. I'll get a jar for you."

"Won't taste as good as earning it, plus the Christmas batches are special editions. That girl is a trip. She was—how do you say it? *Precocious.*" He chuckled. "Did she ever tell you about the time she faked her own death?"

Luna peeled the waffles off the hot iron with a freshly polished fork, ladled more batter, and flipped the waffle maker over. Once her concentration broke, Arthur's words seeped in.

"Wait, what did you just say?"

Her fork pointed up.

"Um?"

"Opal faked her own death?" Luna's stomach flipped like the waffles. She placed the first one on his plate using her fingers.

Arthur cut a bit with the edge of his fork. Luna handed him a knife, the correct tool to cut.

"Oh, yeah, when she was just a bitty thing, she planned a fake drowning at Island Lake. Our grandparents were so pissed, she got the belt, though I bet that was just rubbish. After her parents died in that accident, no one really disciplined her."

Luna played scenarios in her head. *What child fakes a death?*

"Babe, you've outdone yourself. These waffles are so damn good." He poured more sauce from the glass jar onto his plate and slid his bite in a crazy eight through the puddle.

"Oh, thanks." She sat across from Arthur and lined the butter, syrup, and plates in a tidier fashion. "So how do you fake a death when you're a kid?"

Arthur spoke around a bite. "You put your toys and bag lunch on the beach when no one is looking and chuck your favorite hat into the lake. Then, you camp in a tent in the woods for two days." His arm circled his plate protectively and paused. "Everyone walked around like zombies after her parents were killed. They worried about her so much, no one actually checked in on her."

"That is so screwed up." Luna shook her head.

"Don't you want a waffle?" Arthur asked.

"I'm good. Meeting with speak-of-the-devil Opal for lunch."

She's not smarter than me. I fucking killed someone, for Chrissake.

He cleared the dishes, stacked them in the dish drawers, and kissed Luna's cheek. "Have fun. Tell my cuz, I said hi."

"Will do."

"Heading to the gym. Gotta get fit for our bambino." He grabbed his gym bag and left.

Luna's knees wobbled. She sat at the couch and put her head between her legs and gulped air.

I'm clammy. Please, God, no one needs another dead baby right now.

Focusing on an episode of *This American Life* Arthur had left playing, she regained strength. She reached for her phone to call Opal.

"Hey, lady," Opal answered.

"How are you?" Luna asked. She fluffed the silk pillows on the couch and lined them up by color.

"Fine, you?"

Fine. She has pancreatic cancer and says "fine," so maybe it's a ruse.

"Queasy is all. Any chance you could nix the restaurant and we could lay around? I have waffles." She felt as delicate as a flour lump.

I want home court advantage. I have to hear the words from her mouth. If she tells me I'll believe her. Otherwise plans could get screwed up.

"I'll be over in twenty. Need anything?"

What Luna needed was time to straighten the house and figure out a plan to confront Opal. "Diet Sprite and crackers?"

"I have that. See you soon."

Luna grabbed a pad of Post-its and an inky pen, and wrote, "If you are lying about being sick it will kill my baby," on one, and "You are loved," on the other, folded and shoved them in her silk jammie pocket. She put her hands together and held her breath, counted to five, and let it out through her nose.

The countertops were clean with the exception of a drop of sauce where her husband usually sat. *You are such a mess, Arthur.* She rolled her eyes and grabbed the sponge to the right of the dish drawer reserved for non-dish related cleaning, sopped it up, and put it into the washer.

Grabbing a butter knife, she popped the buffet door open that held Arthur's grandmother's plates. The porcelain cobalt blue flowers faded slightly into the white of the heirloom. *I can't handle the color bleed, but Opal will like them.*

"You shouldn't leave your doors open—trash blows in."Opal set the diet Sprite and crackers on the counter and greeted Luna with a hug.

"Mr. Safety must've left it open on the way to the gym."

Opal took a seat, still wearing her long vest resembling a sleeping bag.

Luna tapped her cell app that increased the temperature to seventy-eight.

"Did I ever mention he is my favorite cousin?" Opal smiled.

Luna handed her a plate and waited for a reaction.

Opal covered her mouth. "My grandma's plates." Tears welled in her eyes.

She flipped over the plate a few times smiling. "Has the blue always seeped into the white?" She pulled it to her chest eventually handing it back.

"When I asked Arthur that same question, he said, 'Is that something I should know?'" Luna heated up a waffle in the microwave and placed a cotton napkin next to Opal's plate with flatware.

"Your ears must've been burning. Arthur was just telling me about your famous blueberry sauce," Luna said.

Opal laughed. "Arthur wanted a jar so badly."

The microwave beeped; Luna transferred the waffle onto the old plate.

"Why didn't you give him a jar?"

Opal tasted the waffle and closed her eyes. "I thought I wouldn't be able to eat today, and then you come along."

Luna tilted her head and studied her friend who may or may not be dying. *She looks gray again.*

"Well, of all the people in our family that needed the treat, he didn't. He *wanted* it, sure, but he didn't *need* it," Opal continued. "I only gave it to people who were down and out that year. Plus, he got you, the human equivalent of my blueberry sauce."

Luna should have figured. *Deep down she planned and plotted, too. I knew it.*

"You. Say, off topic, but did you talk to Urse about our Home Depot caper?" Luna asked.

"Fucking Fitz. I always knew he was shady—didn't I hate him first? I have no qualms about killing him. I'm dead anyway." Opal's arms were up; she looked winded but finished, "You'd think I'd stop with my anger, right? Lune, this little death sentence of mine has exacerbated it. I shit you not." She propped up her head with her palms, elbows on the counter.

Luna squished her lips to one side. "Opal, this is hard for me to bring up, but I have to for my own peace of mind regarding your...situation."

Opal stared at the ceiling.

Luna found strength. "No, you don't get to be mad right now. I'm simply asking you a question."

Opal dipped her chin to her chest. "You're right. Ask away." She placed her napkin over her plate covering most of the waffle, sat back, and crossed her arms.

"Arthur mentioned when you were little you faked your death."

"That's what this is about? Luna, it was no biggie, my parents died and I probably just needed attention at the time."

She's not looking me in the eye.

Choose your words carefully.

"Kids sass or pout when they're upset. They don't fake their own death," Luna continued. "Are you really dying?"

Opal began tapping her pulse points: wrist, wrist, wrist, third eye, third eye, third eye, sternum, sternum, sternum.

Luna recognized the anger management techniques. *I've seen this before, she's pissed.* She reached into her jammie pocket, pulled the paper in front out and slid it across the counter.

Opal unfolded and read the note. "Wow, kill your baby, huh? That's fucking rich, you passive-aggressive bitch." She tore the note into tiny pieces and sprinkled it everywhere, ensuring a mess on her way out.

The door is too heavy for her to—

SLAM!

Luna crossed her arms on the counter and rested her head on them. Now she had all those stupid tidbits of paper to pick up.

She sighed.

Stay calm for the doomed baby.

Opal hadn't answered the question.

Chapter Thirty-One

Opal

Opal maneuvered her car to the side of the busy interstate, opened the door, and threw up the waffle Luna had fixed her.

A car beeped that annoying *Shave and a Haircut—Two Bits* masterpiece. She spit the bile from her mouth and lifted her middle finger as the door alarm burrowed into her nerves. Without sufficient energy to freak out, she resorted to turning the car off. As she leaned back to catch her breath, the cherry light of a cop car flashed in her rearview mirror.

Of fucking course.

She started her car so the window would slide down.

I should take off. What are they going to do—take away my birthday?

From her side mirror, she could tell the trooper was about her age.

I'm in no mood to shoot for charm.

She would wait to see his attitude.

"Drivers and regist—Opal? Is that you?" The officer removed his hat.

"Naughty Sebastian? Get out of here!" Opal's laughter quickly turned as she burst into tears.

"Ah, geez, what's going on, girl?"

She couldn't speak and made a quick grab for a napkin in her glove box.

"Whoa, I'm going to need you to put your hands on the dash." His gun was out.

She turned to him and laughed hysterically. "I see the Indignation Suppression class has worked wonders on you, too." She rested her head back and closed her eyes.

"Opal, I'm sorry, but you are in a state."

He lowered his gun.

"Of Minnesota, douche." Her hands rested on the dash, which made them oily from leather conditioner. "What the fuck, psycho? It's *me*."

Beads of sweat dribbled down his cheek. "Come on back to my squad. Let's get caught up," his voice softened. She wiped her hands on her pants and followed him as traffic zoomed by. Her legs wobbled from adrenaline and throwing up.

"Had I not known your history, I'd be offended. How is—wait, don't tell me—Angie B?" Opal asked.

He opened the patrol door, pushing her head down when she got in, prompting laughter. The seat was made of hard plastic allowing for easy scooting.

"Amy B," he said. "Close though—good memory. Let's just say we aren't exactly together anymore." He sat in the front and turned to talk to her. "How's your gang of leggy delinquents? Anyone settle down? Anyone want to? And Snookie? That Bubotz character still in the detective biz?"

"She is, and the gang is giving me hell." She mustered courage. "Turns out I have some pretty ugly cancer, Sebastian."

He handed her a paper towel and a stick of peppermint gum. "Fuck. I'm sorry to hear that, Opal."

She unwrapped the gum, blotted her face, and stuffed the soggy wipe into her front pocket. "Thanks. It's okay, I don't need sympathy. I need ten thousand dollars."

"Uh, I, uh—" He began to squirm.

Her lip twitched. "Sucker. I'm kidding." She pushed his shoulder through the open barrier window and laughed.

"You dick." His shoulders eased. "Still impossible, I see."

Naughty Sebastian reached over and held Opal's hand. They sat quietly as cars rushed past, the squad lights still on.

"Listen, for what it's worth, I want you to know, you got me through a lot of b.s. back in the day. You have that rare quality of seeing good in people when they may not deserve it. Probably why you have every idiot friend you've ever made." He sighed. "What the hell, I may as well tell you. You were the reason I didn't off myself after my trouble."

"What?" Opal looked at him though he looked ahead. The squad radio squawked number codes and *Alpha, Charlie, Foxtrots.* He turned the volume down slightly.

"You said, 'for such a successful, wonderful man you sure do make a lot of—'"

"—excuses for yourself," Opal said. "I remember it well. That was right before you stripped naked and jumped into the St. Croix."

He squeezed her hand. "You were right, you know."

"I know. I still think you are wonderful—well, minus pulling a gun on me—but, thanks, I needed perspective. My old friend *rage* has been visiting more than I'd like of late."

He handed her his business card. "Let me know if I can help with anything. You know I owe you one."

She tapped it against her palm.

Oh, I will. You may come in handy for a tiny assisted suicide coming up.

He put his stiff hat back on and walked around the car to open her door.

"Hey, Ope."

"Yeah?"

He covered up his video cam and microphone.

"Keep your chin up, your tots are still banging."

He tipped his hat and smiled before pulling out.

On the drive home, she thought about Luna. *I'm ashamed of myself and owe her an apology.*

She hit her garage door opener. The gardening hose coil hung on the wall in front of her space; she thought about tidying the garage using those outlines of items on pegboards like her grandpa used at his place. His tiny garage also had a tennis ball hanging from fishing line so her grandmother would know when to stop before hitting her bumper. Opal's house had a spacious, three-stall garage and compartments for riding lawn mowers, but the tennis balls would make her smile.

I'll do it tomorrow.

She pulled her car in and texted Luna: *Your baby will be fine. I'm a jerk but really am dying. Sorry about earlier. I love you.*

Chapter Thirty-Two

Urse

Urse pushed her office intercom button.

Beep.

"Jim, get in here, I have a secret project I need you on."

The door to Urse's office opened. Jim, her executive assistant for the last decade, had his phone in one hand and their coffees in the other. Setting them down without coasters on her custom desk of crushed crystals with glass overlay, he said, "Oops," and pulled two from a hidden drawer and slid them under the drinks. His starched lilac button down didn't move with him.

"Your hair looks thicker. What did you do?" Urse asked.

He pushed in his wide, black eyeglasses.

"I hit up Opal's product guy. At first, he seemed like a snake oil salesman, then I found out it *is* actually snake oil that stimulates the scalp." He slid his fingers through the front of his light brown hair.

Urse bit the inside of her lip to keep from laughing and took a whiff of her coffee. *Italian roast.*

"I'll be damned. Actual snake oil. Well, it seems to be working. Now, onto your secret mission." She pulled Crystalporium stationery from her top drawer and centered it on her uncluttered desktop.

Jim's eyes widened. "Please tell me this project involves me going somewhere exotic to source crystals."

Urse rocked back in her chair.

I need to take him next time. Carrot. Stick. We can't afford to lose this guy—he knows a lot of secrets.

"I tell you what, you choose between Morocco and the Appalachians. Each trip is within the next six months." Urse put her pencil behind her ear.

Jim bobbed in his chair and clutched his phone. "Yes, yes, yes! Thanks, Urse." He reversed his cell, snapped a picture, and flipped it to show her. "This is me, happy."

"Okay, Mr. Thick Hair, back to why I called you in. This is of the personal nature. Johnny doesn't need to know—well, no one needs to know, actually."

He rested his ankle on his knee revealing the Hermès socks she and Johnny had bought him for an appreciation gift.

"Intrigued." He sat up taller in his chair. "Go on."

"As I'm sure you've heard, Fitz and I are no longer together."

She waited for Jim to stop tiny clapping.

"This is unrelated to my third failed marriage, I can assure you, but I need you to find someone for me."

Urse's desk phone rang. She put her index finger in the air for Jim to wait, and pressed the line from Johnny's office.

"Yep, what?"

"Well, after you two partridges left the restaurant, I made a few moves and made Ruby *me woomaan.*" Johnny hadn't sounded this excited since he heard Santa was at the mall.

Urse's smile hijacked her face. "I haven't been this happy since the pigs ate my brother." Across from her, Jim stifled a laugh with his hand.

"I'm going to give that one to you because I'm pretty damn happy," Johnny said.

Urse caught Jim's eye and wrote, *Johnny and Ruby* with a heart on the stationery and slid it toward him.

"Seriously, I'm sincerely thrilled for the two of you, and—finally. I gotta go, it's busy as hell. I'll get the details later."

Jim stood and ran a circle around the office with his hands up and down. Urse followed, and they toasted coffees before settling back in their seats.

"It's about time. Tell him if it doesn't work out, I'm there for him, if you know what I mean." His eyelids slowly lowered.

Urse touched the tip of her pointy nose and pointed at Jim. "Will do."

He dribbled coffee and laughed.

"Okay, speaking of love and your secret mission, I need you to find mine. We met once when we were young at a Rainbow Festival. I know, it sounds crazy but he's the one."

Jim stared blankly at her and sucked his lips in.

"Speak. You obviously have something to say." Urse pulled two Crystalporium-branded truffles from her bottom desk drawer and handed one to Jim. "Freely," she finished.

He plopped the candy into his mouth.

"Wouldn't you like more time to..." He paused. "...reflect?"

Urse tapped her truffle box on her desk then lifted the candy to her nose—*mmm, cayenne*—before answering him.

"No."

After taking a sip of coffee, she ate the chocolate and whisked the bite-sized boxes into the built-in recycling bin.

"Let's find this guy, then." He lifted his chin for one big nod. "Fourth time's a—"

Urse shook her head. "Don't jinx it, and we need to source a special rose quartz for love—a new one—but that's for when we find him."

Jim tapped his iPad with the ease of a court stenographer as she detailed what she knew about the mystery of which was Andy.

"Hire a private investigator if you need the help. Let's meet next week for an update."

He stood. "And I pick Morocco—not even a choice." He smiled and closed the door behind him.

Urse checked her phone for any Opal emergencies. The only fresh social media was a posting that Jim was going to Morocco for work. *God, he's fast.* And a video text from Luna. She tapped play.

Oh no.

Luna had made a meme of her kicking Fitz's bathroom stall in with an accompanying text that read, "Icon, you look sexy af, hope all is good on your end."

Urse's heart didn't hurt from the betrayal; it was proverbial scar tissue in her stomach, as now it simultaneously wilted and ached.

I need someone to keep me grounded when Opal's gone.

Chapter Thirty-Three

Luna

Luna popped three antacids and washed the chalky taste down with her morning coffee. She sat at the kitchen island, feet resting on the bottom bar of a chair. Arthur kissed the top of her head, saying, "Have a happy day, honey," before the door closed behind him and the lock clicked from the outside.

I probably shouldn't. But a break from Opal's Death card could do me some good.

Her eyebrow raised in thought. She finished the last sip of coffee, rinsed her mug, and placed it in the glassware section of her dishwasher, then sauntered to the bathroom and flipped the showerhead faucet to hot. Waiting for the water to warm, she went into her walk-in closet and grabbed a thin leather tie from her jewelry box. Foraging around the bottom drawer, she found the delicate metal flower and slid the leather through the back loop; now, it resembled the famous necklace.

Luna's first memory of Manet's masterpiece was from her Introduction to Art class in college. The image had all but slapped her in the face. Olympia, she figured, wasn't aroused by being nude; her power came from observing others' *reaction* to her nudity.

She gets me.

Now, Luna sought out reactions. The bulging eyes, double takes, and uncomfortable, darting looks made it satisfying. Sex wasn't the goal, especially with the onlookers—never them. They were mostly ugly, anyway.

It was the shock she was gunning for, the uncertainty and bossiness of it. Today, she'd settle on a response from a retired dog walker or someone working to get their knees strong again—easy picking. The bike and walking path around the lake in front of their home was littered with doctors' orders exercisers.

She hit the shower, threw detangler into her long tresses, and shaved her legs while the products sunk in. She lined her razors up in order of use. Legs, pits, and crotch had separate edges—the thought of a crotch hair stuck on her leg razor made her shudder.

Once out, she dried with a fluffy navy bath sheet and wrapped her hair in a towel. The towel was important. If anyone got weird and complained, she would rearrange logic and accuse them of being a Peeping Tom. *I mean, come on, I was clearly just out of the shower.* Luna had recited the scenario a million times in her head. How she would look indignant and flirt her way out of the trouble, all while being slightly turned on.

She hung the bath sheet up after using it to dry the shower glass and turned the ceiling fan off. Adjusting the leather necklace so the flower was a smidge to the right, Luna studied herself. Still hot, though perhaps a bit crepey at the knees. "Better than ninety-five percent of the models out there," her favorite photographer mentioned on her last photoshoot.

She pinched her nipples and headed into the living room, opened the curtains, and brazenly looked for someone to notice her. The path was empty. She dragged a chair to the window, grabbed another coffee and a copy of *Minnesota Monthly* before taking her seat. She crossed her legs, rested her feet on the windowsill above waist level, and opened the magazine. Her freshly shaven crotch peeked out from her crossed legs facing the lake.

A movement from the path. There it was—a double take. Luna contained a grin. From the corner of her eye, she spotted a construction worker presumably off to work, pretending not to look in her direction.

Well, well, aren't you naughty.

Luna rolled slightly on her left hip giving him more of a view. She waited for him to commit to the gawk before meeting his gaze.

One, one thousand. Two, one thousand…

Her eyes lifted to meet his. He jumped. She remained fixed on him, challenging the intrusion.

Sadly, he didn't look back.

Chicken.

Luna turned a page in the magazine when two familiar faces smiled at her: a picture of Urse and Johnny.

The article read, "Brother-Sister Duo Corners Exotic Rock Market." Urse straddled a backwards chair and looked directly at the camera. Legs taut, she appeared bottomless as the chair back obstructed the reader's view of her skirt. Johnny stood behind her wearing an impeccable suit and crooked smile. Urse probably bulldozed the art director as the picture conveyed ease and professionalism with a hint of playfulness—it had her branding all over it. Luna skimmed the article:

"'We grew up by humble means. We hunted for our own quartz on the banks of the Mississippi not far from our childhood home. I suppose the underprivileged kids in us never really go away. We understand our crystals could be construed as luxury. We empathize with folks not fortunate enough for alternative wellness items, and for that reason, Johnny and I started FoundNation Foundation to serve our community at large.' The CEO and founder continued, 'Johnny and I have allocated five hundred thousand dollars this fiscal year to get the fund rolling. We encourage other business owners to join with us in our efforts.'"

If the world only knew how messy Urse was, how messy our group is, really. Overachieving, overreaching, and about to euthanize a friend.

A barrel shaped man in a green tracksuit rounded the walking path; he stopped to tie his white sneaker, his head remained down but eyes scoured the area before glancing at Luna in her leather flower necklace. She arched her back slightly. The bearded man did a quick scan of the surrounding area and slid his hand into the waistband of his sweats.

Luna's feelings knotted. The white line on the side of the man's tracksuit straightened as he slid the elastic band down and flopped out his cock. The size of it was threatening, more of an instrument of violence than sexy.

This isn't how it's supposed to go.

Luna gasped and jumped to shut the curtains.

Shockingly aggressive. And the way he looked straight at me—unbelievable.

She rushed to make sure the doors were locked. On the way back to the living room, she peeked out the side of the curtain an eye's width. Her breathing rapid, more scared than turned on. No sight of him.

There was a knock at the door.

Luna jumped.

Knock, knock, knock!

She fumbled for her phone.

The knocking grew louder.

Nine, one...her finger hovered over the last digit. She was listening so hard, her ears rang.

Bam, bam, bam!

"Open up, perv, I know you're in there," a woman's voice called out.

Luna spun in a nervous circle before remembering the secret junk room.

"I said, open up, pervert!" the woman's voice boomed once more. The nasally voice seemed vaguely familiar but there was no way Luna was going to answer the door. She slipped behind her trick wall into a room painted dark crimson.

Hee-hee, try to find me now.

Arthur hadn't ventured into the secret room since storing the green Christmas tree there, after she had found a vintage white one, five years ago. The pretty tree would head to the basement after the holidays, but the green one went to the secret room with sentimental things they couldn't toss but didn't want to see.

Luna figured she'd be safe there with the four empty baby books, tents, and a dusty sewing machine. Oh, and the fake brown recluse residing in a cumbersome terrarium for Opal's euthanasia.

Holy hell, it's only a few days away. Best ask Urse for help getting the heavy tank to Opal's; Arthur can't know.

A faint, "Open up!"

Who is this psycho knocking?

Luna waited for the woman to leave and peeked out the side of the window. Gone. That was a close call. She edged into the kitchen.

With shaky handwriting she scribbled a note to Arthur that read:

Left to hang with the girls. Promise I'll be good.

Love you, Luna

As she opened the door on her way to grab the ladies, a business card fell to the floor.

Snookie Bubotz

Private Investigator

Luna laughed and put the card in her pocket. *I* knew *I knew that voice.*

Snookie Bubotz. Opal's anger management classmate who Opal had dragged back to the gazebo after one of their group meetings. A wild night which had ended with sore arms and axes stuck in the side of Opal's garage. Luna smiled. Snookie, the memory foam of people, stood eye to eye with Opal, but was thin with a round face. With all the disguises, she kept her mink-colored hair in a short pixie, frequently covering it with scarves, hats, and wigs. The women used her as character reference, often parroting her words and wishes, as she frequently led them out of trouble.

Even though the women loved and trusted Snookie, she remained the only unreadable person Luna had ever met.

Chapter Thirty-Four

Opal

*D*eath is scratching at my door.

Opal's legs quivered, buckled, and gave out on the way to the bathroom. Carol ran from the other room, paws sliding on the hardwood floors as she circled and whined.

"It's okay, girl," Opal lied.

She tried to get up. Her legs couldn't support her.

Fuck, my phone is on the kitchen charger. Normally she'd figure out a dozen ways out of a squirmish, but her body had never failed before.

Legs.

The word reminded her of Oliver. All the memories, painful in their strength, willful in their randomness, yet oddly comforting. Years ago, she griped, "Pool tables have better legs," as she flexed and pointed her toes toward their bedroom ceiling.

"I love your legs. They are strong, hard, and damn sexy. If they were toothpicks, you wouldn't be able to wrap them around me and draw me in. If the legs go, I go." Oliver had slid out of bed and kissed her chubby kneecaps.

Of all the things you remember.

Carol barked, pulling her out of the memory.

"Come here, girl, keep me warm. It's so chilly." Opal patted the floor next to her, the dog tugged at her pajama top trying to pull her. "Carol, no. Come on."

The dog barked faster, left, returned and stared at her, whimpering.

The bed sat ten feet from where she fell, the kitchen, a good thirty. *I can inch over and pull a blanket from the bed, or go the other way and scream for my phone's voice recognition app. One way I have heat, the other potential help.*

"Argh!" It felt like hot sticks poked through her stomach from behind her belly button. Her breath came in short bursts. Curling up moved the pain to a more manageable source—her side.

I need a blanket.

Her head spun right before she lost her bowels.

She sobbed.

No, no, no. Why can't I be hit by a car like a normal person?

Carol tugged her collar, this time, harder. The dog edged her for the next hour, Opal offered an occasional heel push but with the sewage beneath her, movement was sporadic.

After a good hour of inched movement, she heard a persistent knocking at the door.

Barking wildly, Carol raced toward the front of the house.

Just as Opal yelled, "Help!" Carol's barking fit drowned out her voice.

The knocking stopped.

Probably for the best. When the neighbors ask, she'd answer, "What am I up to? Oh, just lying in my own filth is all, yeah, it's something I've gotten good at, oh, and you? You have your whole life ahead of you and you're older than I am? I see, you and your husband, your *living* husband, are both fit as a fiddle. Huh, how about that?" She laughed at the ugliness of the situation.

The pain jabbed at her left side.

The dog returned to tug. Opal would be near a wall in a foot or so, maybe she could sit against it.

I don't want to die in my own sick. I have to wrap up a few things. Please,

God, not like this.

Opal's ears rang as everything went black.

Shawn, Opal's mailman, knew the sounds of his neighborhood like the bend of his dick. He fought for the highly coveted route and threatened to quit unless the Postal Service made it permanent, which they had over a decade ago. The affluent homes were spaced so sparsely, his letter bag barely weighed his shoulder down.

A disciplined man of routine, Shawn had tortured himself over how to respond to the passing of Opal's husband six months prior. He had liked Oliver. He had manners to match his level of chitchat and left big holiday tips in envelopes addressed with the correct spelling of "Shawn."

It had taken the mailman forty-eight hours to pen the sympathy card that read:

On behalf of Shawn, your postal carrier, I am sorry to hear about the loss of your husband. He was a kind man.

Sincerely,

Shawn Wentworth.

Today, however, the widow's dog lost her manners when he approached the house. He knew the dog. She never barked.

He'd taken it upon himself to keep watch of Opal when letters from various medical facilities started arriving. It wasn't lost on him. Letter carriers see it all the time, a family practice bill, then an oncology bill and, finally, the local funeral home bill.

Shawn rushed to the back windows of the sprawling mid-century rambler and peeked in. "Anyone home?" He switched windows, well, window *walls*, actually. "Opal?"

He put his hands around his eyes on the window glass to see better. The kitchen appeared as he imagined, spotless, with arty bowls of fruit on a large counter surrounded by highfalutin art. He smiled at how she filled the oranges in the orange bowl, the lemons in the lemon bowl, the apples were in...blue, well, that part made little sense.

Carol lunged at him from inside the house, running in circles; she took off in one direction then returned barking.

"What is it, ole girl?"

The rambler's floor-to-ceiling windows proved helpful once his gut feeling committed to the search. Shawn followed the direction Carol moved until he stood looking into the en suite bedroom. The furnishings looked as if Picasso himself built them, with their blocky triangles and uneven wood. A nude painting of Opal stopped him in his tracks. *I'd fuck that.* Shawn shook his head guiltily when, out of the corner of his eye, he spied the bottom of a woman's foot.

He banged on the window. "Opal! Are you okay?"

The dog sounded hoarse.

"Opal, help is on the way. I won't leave you, just give me a minute."

Not wanting his undelivered mail to blow away, he noticed a BBQ, emptied the letters onto the grill, and shut the lid. He wrapped his right hand in the crusty mailbag and headed for the plate glass window.

Shawn knocked at the window. "Carol, go! Git!" The dog refused to move.

He couldn't wait. Stiffening his fist, he drew back and punched the window chest level.

Pain shot through his knuckles. He backed up and shook his hand holding his wrist. The window remained unharmed. He ran to his mail truck, grabbed a tire iron, and headed back to the window. This time it cracked, wobbled and crashed to the bedroom floor, half in, half out of the house. The level of the loud breaking sound was oddly satisfying.

He gingerly stepped through the glass; the crunchy floor already had dried leaves blowing in when a foul smell forced his elbow over his nose. The dog cowered at the noise and barked less.

Shawn crouched to Opal, assessing the situation. Her breathing shallow. *Should I call for help or is she just drunk*? He had witnessed Opal and her friends get rowdy in the gazebo every now and again.

He shook her shoulder gently, "Opal? It's Shawn, your postal carrier. Do you need an ambulance?"

She moved slightly.

"I'll be right back, don't worry about a thing."

He'd hoped to be in her bedroom someday but never like this. Once he found the bathroom, he squirted soap and water on a bath towel and headed back to clean the mess trailing toward her. He sopped up her accident, put the towel in the garbage, and grabbed a fresh one for her legs. *I'll give her five minutes; if she doesn't wake up, I'll call 911.*

Opal attempted to sit up, moved an inch, and rolled to her side. "Wha?" With her eyes open wide, she tried to figure out what had happened. "Shawn?" She closed her eyes and remembered the mess. "Oh, no. I'm sorry, I'm so embarrassed, I'm a mess, I—"

Fuck me, my mailman is cleaning filth from my leg. She grimaced.

The loyal postman had frown lines. "I'm worried about you."

"Naw, I'm always like this." She laughed self-consciously. "Could you grab the comforter off of my bed?"

He jumped at the directive and covered her with a National Parks wool blanket.

She put her hand out. "I could use help up."

He ignored her hand and lifted under her armpits from the back. Her legs acted like cooked spaghetti.

Once up, he carried her like a child to bed.

"Thank you, Shawn. I've run into a bit of cancer. No need to say anything, actually, I prefer not talking about it. Is there a chance I could have you grab my phone from the kitchen?"

He nodded.

"Do you want a ride to the hospital?"

"Definitely not. Thank you, I have an on-call nurse. I'll have her come out and check my numbers." Opal's face was the color of blanched almonds.

"I'm sorry about your window."

The window. *Ugh, what a mess. The door was unlocked for Chrissakes.*

"I hated that window anyway. You did me a favor." Opal made an air check mark.

He shook his head. "Ah, geez. Point me to your kitchen."

"Down the hall hang a left and a right. Phone's on the charger on the counter. And, Shawn?"

He turned.

Everything is such a disaster. Oh, Oliver, I'm so alone my blood aches.

"Before you do that, is there any chance you'd be willing to lay next to me so I can pretend you're Oliver?" Her gray eyes pleaded for an inch of calm, for the world and hurt to stop. She wanted the spinning, the ringing, and the shit to pause so she could regroup. *To grab a little perspective.*

He pulled at his bottom lip hesitantly, then crawled in facing the ceiling on top of the covers. Opal poked her hand out of her blanket cocoon and met Shawn's. Their fingers entwined as the world slowed just enough for them to feel quiet.

Chapter Thirty-Five

Ruby

Ruby stopped at MNail on Hennepin Avenue to check if they had time for a walk-in mani-pedi. She also had to get in for a wax and buy new undies for the exciting event: finally sleeping with Johnny.

On their phone call last night, in a lower than normal voice, Johnny said, "Grease up those thighs, beautiful. I'll be at your place at seven."

Ruby knew there would be a certain amount of sharing Johnny with the world as his sense of humor and capable manner drew people to him. As quiet as she was, having him around alleviated social pressure. He encouraged her; she calmed him.

Now, let's see what he has under the hood. She smirked.

"For you, yes. Pick a color, Miss Ruby." Darlene, her favorite nail technician, gestured to the wall lined with bottles of polish. She wanted a color that matched the one red dress reserved for a special occasion.

Ruby's eyes scoured the selection. *It would be easier if there were a color called, "First Time Sex with Johnny."*

She lifted a red with blue undertones, landing on *"Varoom"* then searched for another for her fingers. *"Midnight." Oooh, perfect.*

Shoes and socks off, she placed her feet at the edge of the machine and waited for the water to heat. Bubbles filled the basin. Darlene turned the massaging seat on which loosened the tension in her lower back. Leaning back and closing her eyes, Ruby gave in to the pampering.

Darlene's calf tap prompted her feet into the hot water.

Relaxing in public was easy. Falling asleep, however, all but impossible. Nighttime Mom had once warned her and Ann of the practice. "Never let your guard down or they'll spit on you."

She had us worry about hits to the temples and spits when I could've used a chapter on killing a friend.

Ruby's memory was interrupted by a nail salon customer's voice from a few chairs down. "One of my clients is getting to me."

Why people insisted on talking in quiet salons Ruby would never understand.

"They are such pains in the ass," her friend added.

The massage chair stopped, Ruby felt for the remote's buttons, pushing until it moved.

"No, not like that, like *getting* getting to me. Like, I feel like she is me in a weird way. I like her. It's to the point where I can't accept her money."

"Don't you dare. It is a job, not charity. Wait, is she…" The woman lowered her voice. "…poor?"

A hush revealed the hum of massage chairs and phone ringers on low.

"Why are you whispering the word 'poor?' And no, she is definitely not poor, but that's not the point."

The sounds of filing acrylics and door chimes filled the air.

"I can't stop thinking about her. I went to her house the other day and we gabbed on her porch swing. It's like I've known her forever. She talked about her dead husband while she plucked at a daisy and said, 'He loves me, he loves *me a lot*.' It did me in."

The woman began to cry.

Ruby's eyes popped open and closed quickly.

She's talking about our Opal.

"Shh, it's okay. Nursing is a tough damn job, and you aren't a robot. If you didn't have these experiences, then I'd worry," the other woman said.

The door chimed again. "Can you come back in an hour?" Darlene stopped cutting Ruby's toe cuticles.

"Sure," a husky voice said.

The cuticle tug resumed.

That nurse has got to be Tess Hokanson.

Ruby kept her eyes closed, pretending to sleep. Their conversation switched after one of their nail techs said, "Only pedicures today?"

"Yes, thank you," the second woman said.

Ruby concentrated on their voices, trying to memorize the sounds of who she believed was Tess. She didn't sound like a fraud; she seemed heartfelt. The sounds of jackets and purses zipping and snapping.

Do you want a receipt? Oh no, no thank you, save your paper. Do you want to book for another appointment? No, I'm not sure of my schedule, ha ha, chitchat.

The door sounded and the salon was quiet once again.

Ruby opened her eyes to catch a glimpse of the women. Squinting she made out an old Mercedes and a dark-haired woman with her head turned backing out of the parking lot.

"Miss Ruby?" Darlene massaged her calves.

"Yes?"

"Do you like your color? First time red for you, no?"

Her toenails looked like stained glass, smooth and bright against the dry clean towel.

"They look beautiful. Thanks, Darlene."

Once Ruby's nails sparkled, she paid in cash and texted Luna and Urse from her car before heading to the waxing studio.

Ruby: *I thk I overheard Tess H talk about Ope at the nail sal. She cool.*

"Call from Urse," her car speaker sounded.

Ruby tapped: *Answer.*

"Are you kidding me?" Urse began.

Ruby turned down Lyndale Ave heading north toward the Wax On,

Wax Off Studio. The city street, littered with potholes, made for a bumpy ride until the freshly paved parking lot. She parked with fifteen minutes to spare near an out of place Lamborghini and Land Rover.

"I didn't want to look all eavesdroppy at the nail place, so I kept my eyes closed but she said one of her clients was 'getting to her.'" Ruby paraphrased what she overheard.

Urse crunched something. "Sorry, eating carrots," she said. "Could be anyone."

Ruby rolled her eyes. "She mentioned a porch swing and the woman that 'got to her' said, 'he loves me, he loves—"

The crunching stopped. "—me a lot."

She could practically feel Urse thinking.

"Jezus, that's Opal's saying alright," Urse said. "Comes from being raised by old people."

Ruby's stomach wobbled. "Right? Listen, I have to go. I'm heading into an appointment."

She checked her mirrors for parking lot creepers, then gathered her bag and put a fresh piece of spearmint gum in her mouth.

"Appointment for what?" Urse asked.

Bratty Urse.

"Routine mole check," she fibbed.

"Gross."

Probably less gross than what I'm about to do to your hot brother.

"Let's noodle on the Tess thing and talk later. I'll text Jeff—he should have some info."

Jeff? Ex-husband blast from the past? I thought there was a restraining order somewhere in there.

"Sounds good, talk soon."

Ruby hit her key fob lock and headed in.

Bzzt.

She leaned into the intercom. "Ruby Redstone, I have an appointment at eleven."

"Come on in, Ms. Redstone," a friendly voice said.

Ruby pulled her sleeve over her hand and yanked the door open. The waiting room, now painted a calming blue, had changed since her last visit. The furniture in the waiting area was also new. Cozy.

"Can I get you something to drink? Coffee? Tea?" The youthful receptionist wearing a tie-around black smock asked.

"I'm good, thanks."

"Perfect." The receptionist tossed her frizzy red hair over her shoulder. "Ginger will be with you shortly. She's setting up her station. You're the first client of the day."

11 a.m. and I'm the first?

"It looks nice in here with the new paint and chairs," Ruby offered.

"Thanks. The new owners did that about six months ago."

Ruby smiled politely and picked up *Minnesota Monthly* from the magazine pile. She flipped the page when an article caught her eye: "Brother-Sister Duo Corners Exotic Rock Market"

My Johnny and his crooked smile.

"Ruby? Is there a Ruby here?" a freckle-faced woman with inwardly set eyes asked.

I'm the only one here.

"That's me." She towered over the young woman with a clipboard.

"Hi, Ruby, I'm Ginger. I'll be taking care of you today. Did you fill out your paperwork already?"

"We are out of the forms," the receptionist said. "And the Wi-Fi is down for the electronic version." She shrugged her shoulders.

"Oh, great, just what we need," Ginger mumbled then rearranged her attitude real time and winked at Ruby. "Sorry, 'bout that. Let's get you cleaned up."

Ruby's confidence in the business began hiccupping. Her last appointment had taken an extra hundred bucks to weasel in. Now, you could throw machetes in the lobby and not hit anyone.

Once in the procedure room fortified with nature pictures and cream-colored furnishings, Ginger asked, "What are you looking to accomplish today?"

Ruby bit her lip to keep from laughing. "I'd like the hair off my…" She paused, wanting to be anywhere else but here, explaining this. "…bum and sides."

"So, you want a sort of Brazilian?"

Ruby's shoulders lifted. "I guess? It's been a while since I've been in. Not sure if styles have changed."

Ginger patted the maroon-cushioned plastic table. "Styles haven't, names have. I'll step out. Undress from the waist down. Make sure your feet are at this end." She closed the door softly behind her as Adele piped through the sound system.

Ruby stripped off her baggy jeans, stuffed her undies in the pocket, and folded them on the spare chair. She caught a glimpse of her naked bottom half in the mirror and hopped onto the waxing bed.

A soft knock at the door. "Ready?"

"Yes."

Ginger stepped into the room.

"I'm going to work fast. The quicker the tug, the better the procedure." She placed a hand on her shoulder and squeezed softly.

I wish she wouldn't with the forced pleasantries.

"Okay, scoot up a bit."

Ruby edged her bum closer to Ginger.

The room temperature increased.

"You are going to feel my fingers, don't worry, I'm only feeling for skin elasticity."

It's tight, trust me.

Ginger pulled gently at her labia, her fingers warm and gentle.

"You'll feel a little heat and we'll give it a second to cool and get to work."

The wax temperature was so high, Ruby jerked back. "It's really hot!" She gripped the edge of the bed.

"Push through. It'll only take a second."

The sensation felt acidic and burned, far hotter than any other appointments.

Ginger put material over the area and ripped.

"Arggh!" Ruby yelped.

Ginger's eyes bulged and she jerked back slightly. "Two seconds." Then ripped from a different angle.

"Oh, God. Uncle. I'm crying uncle."

Ruby hopped off the table and pulled her jeans on, no time for undies.

"You still have to pay for your service, you know," Ginger said.

Ginger's crossed a line.

As Ruby slipped into her shoes, her eye caught a reflection in the mirror that read as movement. She stopped, leaned back and squinted.

Sure enough—a two-way mirror. Someone is watching. I need to get out of here.

After pretending to fix her hair, Ruby opened her purse and placed eighty bucks on the table.

"Here you go," Ruby said.

Ginger started backtracking.

"Can I get you a water? You'll need to stay hydrated after your treatment—"

Water? More like a skin graft. Ruby brushed past Ginger and high stepped it out of the studio without answering the receptionist's, "Have a beautiful day."

Once in her car, she snapped pictures of the expensive car's license plates and made her way toward the local police department.

What am I going to say? Some weirdos are getting their rocks off watching quasi-genital mutilation?

She leaned into her steering wheel. "Call Opal."

Her car answered, "Calling Opal, Diamonds, and Pearls."

"Ope, you won't believe what just happened." Ruby pulled over, too agitated to drive and talk, and hit a jarring pothole.

"You okay?"

"Yeah, what are you up to right now?"

Ruby needed help with wording on what she would tell the police. Opal was good at this type of stuff, and was no stranger to oddball events.

"What happened?" Opal asked.

Ruby told her the creepy two-way mirror story.

Opal sounded distant, not her usual *I'll be right there.*

It dawned on Ruby that she hadn't asked how Opal was feeling. Embarrassment boiled up, hit her hands, and the sign language kicked in.

"I'm sorry. I'm blathering on about the stupidest stuff. How are you doing, Opal?"

The blood from the rip squished in her pants. She emptied a Target bag with ponytail holders onto the passenger seat and slid it under her butt. *Johnny is going to think my crotch looks like raw hamburger. Fucking great.*

"Rube." Her voice sounded how faint cursive looked.

"Yeah."

"I think I'm going to die soon."

Ruby's head spun.

"No. Oh no, no, no. Where are you right now? At home? I'm coming to get you." Ruby pulled into traffic without her turn signal cutting off a US Food truck. Adrenaline replaced embarrassment—she needed to run *to* the problem for once.

"Rube?"

Tears spilled hot down Ruby's face.

"Yes, sweetie."

"Why is my bra still on?"

Chapter Thirty-Six

Urse

Since Opal's news, Urse had stuffed her days with work. The Crystalporium's balance sheet reflected the extra hours, with productivity up, contracts finessed, and margins high, yet none of the numbers mirrored her spirits. If pressed, she'd say her bones were slowly corkscrewing, and her booze-marinated heart decided to skip notes of late.

Just get it over with—head up to Opal's and face it.

"I'm taking the afternoon off," she announced to Jim. Leaning on his desk, she whispered, "Tomorrow on the other thing, right?" Her hair spilled over her shoulder, and she tossed it back staring at him a foot from his face.

"That's the plan," he whispered.

Urse knocked on his desk. "Good. You don't know where I am unless your name is Opal, Luna, or Ruby."

Beep.

The intercom sounded. Jim pushed the button. "Yes?"

"Did someone mention Ruby?" Johnny echoed through the speakerphone.

Urse put her finger up to her lips like a librarian and tiptoed out of the building.

By the time it took to finish her liter water bottle, Urse pulled into Opal's driveway to find Ruby's car, empty with the driver's side door open.

With a shaky, water-filled stomach, she unbuckled her seatbelt before stopping the car, slid it in park and hurried to the front entrance. The strength in her legs faltered.

"Opal?" she yelled. The house was sour; it certainly didn't smell like its usual cedar and line-dried laundry.

Ruby jumped and spread her palm over her chest. "My God, you scared me."

"What's going on? Why are you here?" Urse asked.

"No idea. I just got here. Opal said she was fine, but there's no way."

The women began creeping toward Opal's bedroom. *Please let her be alive. Please. I'm not ready.* Ruby held out her hand which Urse gave a scared squeeze.

"Opal?" Urse boomed.

"I'm in here." A pipsqueak of a voice.

Urse closed her eyes and sighed. Ruby shrugged her shoulders.

The women stared at the scene astonished. Wind gusted through what once was a glass wall; a pair of black squirrels ran through the bedroom. Opal laid swaddled in a blanket like a cartoon character rolled in a rug with their head sticking out. Ruby pushed Urse toward the skittish animals and backed up.

"My kingdom for a slingshot," Opal said.

"What the actual—? Are you okay? No one is in the house, are they?" Urse kicked her heels off ready to fight despite the glass.

Ruby picked up a shard of glass from a heap on the floor next to a full dustpan.

"It's fine. I passed out for a minute and Shawn the mailman broke the glass to make sure I wasn't in trouble."

Urse shook her head. "What is that smell?"

"I think Shawn el poop-o-ed his pants-o-ed."

Ruby inched toward the door.

"Oh, no you don't!" Urse snapped at her.

"I'm getting a better broom and turning up the heat, not leaving. Sheesh."

Urse put her hands on the back of her head.

Fucking hell, this is really happening.

"Doesn't anyone call for ambulances anymore?"

Opal sat up in clunky movements. "Are you crazy? It'll be like fifty thousand dollars. How many people do you know call ambulances for themselves?"

Urse gave up and hugged the fragile version of her friend. Her blanket felt thicker than she did.

The squirrels sprinted down the hallway.

"I think it might be time for all of us to move in," Urse whispered into her ear. Surprised by Opal's lingering embrace, Urse couldn't help but wonder if it was really the mailman that stunk up the place.

"Okay, I give."

Opal will never be the hugger again.

Ruby returned with a push broom and large garbage bin from the garage. She pushed work gloves into Urse's chest. "You already got to say hi. Get to work." Ruby jabbed her thumb at the mess.

"Will do. I'll be right back," Urse put her shoes back on and left for the kitchen.

Opal stared at Ruby who perched at the edge of her bed. After a quiet moment, Ruby put her hands on Opal's cheeks.

"It's bad, right?" Ruby stiffened, bracing for the answer.

Opal's face pinched and she nodded.

Instinctively, Ruby's hug turned into gentle rocking as Opal began to weep.

Once the crying jags petered out, Ruby grabbed a Kleenex box from the nightstand and tilted it toward her friend.

Turning away from Ruby, Opal blew her nose when Urse returned to the bedroom, pencil behind her ear, cell in hand. "My window guy is on his way, soup's on, and Luna's headed over. I was going to write a thank-you note to the mailman, but wasn't sure I could forge your serial killer handwriting."

"Wow, you're fast," Ruby said.

"I figure we can handle the squirrels on our own. Might be fun." Urse faced Opal. "Now, are you okay to walk?"

Opal nodded. *I thought I had more time before my body gave out.*

Rummaging through Opal's dresser drawer for fresh socks and jammies, Ruby realized Carol wasn't around.

"I'll be right back." Ruby went into the other bathroom to fill the tub with hot water then slipped outside.

"Carol, here girl. Come on. Where are you? Carol!"

The wind whistled through the big oak trees lining the property, and dried leaves circled against the wraparound porch. She walked the perimeter of the house to find the dog hiding under the BBQ's shelf.

"Oh, Boo Boo, you've had a bad day, too, haven't you?" She crouched down and put her arms around the quivering dog. Carol buried her head in her lap, curling into Ruby.

"You are quiet and fierce, too, right?"

Once inside, she put Carol in a spare bedroom with a fresh dish of water and whispered, "I'll be back. We don't want you cutting up your paws. I'm the only cutter here."

"Let's get your core heated up," Urse said to Opal.

She and Ruby led Opal in for a bath.

"I don't want anyone to see me like this," Opal argued.

"Since when are we *anyone*?" Ruby asked. She pulled a pony from her wrist and pulled her hair back. "Plus, you let the postman get an eyeful. Why not us?" She opened a fresh towel and shook it in front of Opal. "Hurry up."

As Urse shut the bath water off and moved the shampoo from a high shelf to the rim of the bathtub, Ruby carefully tugged at Opal's sleeves and undid her pale pink bra with copper hooks. Undressed, Opal sat at the edge of the spa tub naked and shivering.

The women had changed clothes, lovers, and opinions in front of one another over the years, but never like this. Opal's beauty had shifted to honesty. The honesty prompted unexpected shockwaves that spilled like the water from the tub.

Ruby averted her eyes.

Urse's hands trembled to see Opal's sickly posture, back hunched and boney with tiny barnacle-like spots overtaking her once smooth skin. Broken capillaries appeared to reach upward like the tips of distant trees, and the once soft-edged woman looked knobby.

How did I miss the transformation? Don't you dare cry.

With lowered eyes, Opal sat motionless. The furnace kicked in, breaking the silence.

Snapping her fingers, Ruby said, "Okay, fine. I'm about to show you something that will make you feel better." She shook her head, looked to the ceiling, and dropped her pants.

"God, I hope you have a dick," Urse said, laughing.

Ruby's jeans landed in a circle around her ankles, the inside bloody. She scooted around and bent forward to show them what damage had been done.

Opal gasped and covered her mouth.

Urse put her hand to her forehead. "It looks like an autopsy!"

"I won't ask why you know that," Ruby said.

"There it is, alright. I feel how Ruby's snatch looks," Opal said.

The three women's laughter filled the muggy bathroom before Urse dipped a washcloth in the bath water and handed it to Ruby with a wink.

Johnny needs to marry this girl.

The front door creaked open.

"Must be Luna," Ruby said.

"Alright, up." Urse put her arms out to Opal. "Can you step over the tub's edge?"

"Not overly confident."

Ruby dabbed her crotch with the washcloth and pulled her jeans up.

Urse and Ruby lowered her into the tub. The warm water sloshed over the edge, getting their feet wet.

"I'll be good as new in fifteen minutes," Opal said. "Go eat that soup. I'm fine."

Urse left the door open an inch, and she and Ruby went to the kitchen to find Luna stirring the chicken noodle.

"I didn't want to make anything worse," Luna said.

Urse gave her forearm a squeeze.

A knock at the door. Urse furrowed her brow.

"The mailman?" Ruby offered. Luna raised her shoulders.

Urse inched the door open. A tall woman with a slight frame and a sleek black bob stared back at her.

"Hi. Opal texted me. I'm Tess." Her broad smile revealed a crooked tooth in a good set.

Urse smiled. She was too tired to be suspicious. *Tess, whoever that may be, is here to help Opal. I'll reserve judgment.*

"Of course, come on in. She's in the bathtub right now," Urse said.

Tess bent over to take her boots off when Urse said, "It's a shoe friendly house. Feel free to keep them on."

"Are you Ursula?"

Urse softened her stance. "You can call me Urse. How'd you know?"

"Opal mentioned you have an intimidating beauty about you," Tess said.

"Well, she's right." Her head shook *no* as she laughed.

Urse took Tess's soft, full-length coat. She peeped at the inside label before hanging it up. *Size 4, tall.* She wished Luna would read the newcomer.

"I'll introduce you to Luna and Ruby quickly before you head in to see Opal."

The four women stood in a circle that included Carol, who sat next to Tess and looked up at them as they spoke. Urse watched as Luna's eyes scanned Tess.

Then, in a surprising move, Ruby hugged her. "Thank you for helping our Opal."

Tess didn't appear surprised by the gesture and put her hand on the back of Ruby's head as she sank into her.

Luna caught Urse's eyes and winked.

"Our girl is back here." Urse motioned Tess to follow her, then knocked at Opal's bathroom.

"Hon, Tess is here."

Water sloshing noises.

"Oh, Tess, come on in." Urse noticed the pep in Opal's voice at her arrival.

"If you need anything we'll be in the kitchen."

Tess nodded and mouthed, *thank you* to Urse.

Damn it. Opal found her for us as her replacement I bet.

The kitchen chatter stopped when Urse walked in.

Luna licked a piece of nori and shook salt over it. "It's okay. She's cool, has gobs of money, humble beginnings, a flair for connection but worries to a fault," she whispered.

Urse smiled. "Fast read Lune. Speaking of relief, you're still pregnant, right?" She clapped with no sound then clasped her hands to her chest and raised her shoulders.

"No jinxing," Ruby offered.

Urse nodded, taking a seat.

"On a darker note, I suppose we should talk about the whole damn Opal thing," Urse whispered.

The plan morphed like a baby caterpillar to a glorious adult caterpillar.

I'll take Tuesday, Wednesday, Thursday, oh, good, I'll cook and freeze meals, yeah, that'll be good, are you sure, Friday I have a meeting I can't get out of, okay and yes and no and of course and self-care and tapping out and doctors and Tess, I don't know, best we can, yeah, we'll cross that bridge when we get to it, perfect, it's a plan, done and done.

After it was settled, Ruby left to check on Opal and Tess. She returned to the kitchen and said, "Tess wants to stay tonight to make sure Opal's numbers are stable. I told Opal about our schedule. She seemed way better."

Luna sucked her teeth and agreed.

"Cool," Urse said. "Now, for your weird bloody coot coot," she added with a laugh.

"Don't make me gag my seaweed." Luna covered her mouth pretending to retch into it.

Ruby crossed her arms over her chest.

Urse tip tapped her blush pink nails on the counter as she thought. "I need a pencil and paper."

Luna rummaged through Opal's junk drawer and handed Urse an old envelope and a pencil. She grabbed them and turned her back to Luna and Ruby as she wrote.

"You two are idiots," Ruby said as she sipped a San Pellegrino.

Urse lifted her head and rubbed her chin in mock thought. After thirty seconds of *uh-huhs* and *yeses* to herself, she spun around and presented the paper.

Ruby and Luna leaned into the scribbles of triangles, arrows, and doo-dads meant to look like a war plan. On top of the diagram, capital letters spelled out "NOT ON OUR WATCH" with a cartoon of a beaver giving the peace sign.

Ruby threw herself on the counter covering her head.

"I'll drive to the wax place, but I have to be in the background with my pregnancy, okay?" Luna's eyes brimmed with mischief.

Ruby's thumb sprang up like a kid during a *Heads Up 7 Up* game.

Urse pushed it down and said, "Let's break some glass, ladies."

The women invited any excuse for violence as the truth of Opal's illness was becoming more apparent. They couldn't blame Tess for their pain; they needed a shit bird to pay for every woe, every slight, every fucked-up thing they had ever gone through.

"Tomorrow," Urse's said.

They wanted to avenge Opal's disappearing future.

They'd heal after.

Chapter Thirty-Seven

Luna

Since the collapse and rebuild of the 35 W bridge in Minneapolis, Luna flew over it going eighty then exhaled once at the other side. Today was no exception.

She sped for safety and to make up time.

Once Ruby and Urse settled in her car and clicked their seatbelts, Luna mentioned her visitor. "You will never guess who left a card at my door."

"Jack Kevorkian?" Ruby asked.

Urse piped up, her long strands of hair staticky against her jacket. "I wish. He's dead."

"Solid guess, but better. Ready? One Snookie Bubotz."

"Whoa, there's a blast from the past." Ruby smiled broadly.

Urse clapped her hands. "I think I may have been in love with her at one time."

"Same," Ruby said.

"The very one," Luna said.

"What did she say?" Ruby asked.

"Dunno," Luna replied. "She just left a business card."

Urse shifted in her seat. "Timing's weird. Do you think she knows about Opal?"

Luna shrugged her shoulders and the women continued in relative quiet.

Merging onto 94 West, Luna asked, "Should we go over the plan again?"

Urse pointed to Luna and said, "No."

Their laughter broke up the revenge jitters.

Once at the Wax On Wax Off studio, the plan was afoot.

Luna parked her car facing north toward Lyndale Avenue. She had already wrapped her license plates with Ace bandages from an old carpal tunnel surgery and had the bananas. Ruby held the can of spray paint and Urse cradled a hammer under her jacket.

Urse pulled on her ski mask she used for winter hiking and handed Ruby the other one. "See the camera?"

"*Sí*," Luna said.

Ruby smiled. "Let's do it." She pulled her mask down but struggled to line up the eye holes.

Urse tapped her shoulder and adjusted the face covering so Ruby could see. The doors opened, and Urse and Ruby sprang from the car and walked purposefully toward the studio. The spray can's mixing balls clinked as Ruby shook it. Once at the camera, she sprayed, but a gust of wind took the first batch. She steadied herself and tried again, covering most of the security lens in Montana Black.

Urse pressed the intercom button. "Delivery."

Ruby glanced around with her head down and away from the traffic on Lyndale.

Bzzt.

The door opened.

Luna watched the women disappear into the salon.

The owner of the Lamborghini was parked in the same spot as when Ruby's trouble went down. Pretending to tie her shoe, Luna stuffed the bananas deep into the mufflers and returned to her car to wait for Ruby and Urse. *Good thing I looked up the diameter on the exhaust, one banana wouldn't have done the trick.*

As Luna munched on the remaining banana and seaweed, Ruby approached the front desk gal, who jumped and put her hands above her head.

"Don't worry, we aren't here for you, but we know who you are." Ruby motioned toward the door with her cell. The receptionist grabbed her messenger bag and ducked as she ran.

Urse followed Ruby into the backroom where Ruby's crotch had been interfered with and waited for the signal.

Ruby tapped *record* on her phone and panned the room slowly, ending on the window. Still rolling, she pointed to Urse, who produced the hammer and lifted it to the camera. Ruby tugged at her facemask, backed up with arms outstretched and cell in hand, and began recording.

Urse stretched her neck for the big move, wound up her hammer like a hockey stick, and *cah-racked* it into the mirror, shattering it into noisy shards on the first hit. Once the glass stopped falling, Urse and Ruby inched to the secret room.

Two overstuffed leather chairs with drink holders faced the front of the window overlooking the procedure table. Behind the chairs, professional video equipment sat on tripods. No one was in sight.

"Hey." Ruby shut her phone off and shoved it in her pocket. "Let's just take them."

Urse nodded agreement and stuffed the hook of the hammer into the zipper of her down-filled jacket.

They grabbed the cameras off the tripods and headed for the car when they both stopped in their tracks.

Sirens.

Sinking into her seat, Luna spotted Urse and Ruby running from the building lugging armfuls of camera equipment.

Fudge, baby's first arrest.

Luna pushed a button left of the steering wheel.

The hood made a thick clunk.

Dammit.

The metal from the cameras crunched into the trunk and closed. Ruby got in first, mask off, Urse trailed, when a squad car pulled up behind them.

The cops.

"This isn't in the gol-damn plan," Luna said.

"Let me do the talking." Urse bent down and pushed her mask under her seat. She stepped from the car to greet the officers. Luna slid her window down a tish to hear; Ruby sat still facing forward fingers wildly going over the sign language alphabet.

A gray-haired cop with a medium build wiggled his bushy eyebrows upon seeing Urse. His partner, a woman in her twenties and no more than five feet with freckled skin and slicked back bun, followed.

Luna held her breath to listen better.

"Urse? As I live and breathe. I haven't seen you since that ex-husband of yours gave every ugly cop in Minneapolis hope," the officer said.

Urse flipped her hair and outstretched her arms for a hug. "You were my first choice, Sid. The good ones truly won't fool around."

He gave her a brief dad hug.

"I'm glad you got my 911 call," Urse fibbed.

"Oh, that was you, huh?" Sid grinned. "Calling in to report someone covering up your license plates?"

"Yep. My friend was the target of a crime at this creepy business. We have the cameras in our trunk. Saves us a trip to the station. Jeff said not to do anything but...well, you know him, he has to be the star in charge, and we couldn't wait."

The corner of Luna's mouth raised slightly.

Sid rolled his eyes. "Detectives. I didn't know you two were still friendly."

"We aren't. Ran into him getting coffee at The House Spy the other day."

Urse shifted on her foot, a chunk of glass lodged under her shoelace.

"I know it's a lot to ask, but my friend Luna is pregnant and a bit queasy. Can we head out? You know where to find me if you have any questions."

Nice, the assumptive close. Good work, Urse.

This time, Luna popped the trunk revealing the cameras and equipment.

Sid and his partner's eyes widened.

"These creeps have been secretly videoing ladies getting their..." Urse paused. "...swimsuit areas freshened, if you know what I mean." She wrinkled her nose and gave a down thumb.

"Holy crap. Yeah, we'll take care of it." Sid motioned his partner toward the trunk.

His hands rested on his hips. "Woman, you are a gem, but aren't you getting too—"

"If you say 'old,' I'll burn my hoop skirt," Urse said.

Sid put his hands up, chuckling. "I was going to say 'wealthy' for this stuff."

Urse smiled and gave him a peck on the cheek. "Get to retirement in one piece okay, Sid?"

His eyebrows raised then he winked. "Will do."

Urse got in the car and Luna slowly pulled out of the lot to head home.

"I need a drink. Absinthe or grain liquor should do the trick—I want to ease in." Urse buckled her seatbelt and glanced back at the squad in the side mirror.

"That was a bad idea. I thought it would've been more fun," Luna said.

She drove under the speed limit and came to complete stops at stop signs.

"Why don't I feel better?" Ruby mumbled.

Urse spoke as if to herself. "Because Opal's still sick."

Chapter Thirty-Eight

Opal

Sometimes Opal could fool herself into thinking Oliver was still there. She'd mess up his closet, move his slippers, or put his clean clothes in the laundry so she could fold them. A pile of his neatly stacked clothes sitting on the couch felt normal in an ungrounded year.

The thought of donating Oliver's things made Opal wobbly.

Maybe when I'm gone, some of our love will attach to our possessions and find a new host who needs it.

She went to Oliver's silverware drawer and pulled out one of his bigger-than-normal butter knives for a peanut butter and raspberry jam sandwich. Smiling, she thought about the stupid amount of time she spent annoyed with his insistence of the larger flatware. The pair had finally settled on two different drawers: Oliver's organized in a wire divider; Opal's strewn in a drawer together in a hodgepodge.

Oliver had said, "Look at my gorgeous drawer, smartly fashioned in their own compartments, with no fear of an accidental cut."

Irritated, Opal had lifted the dishwasher basket that held flatware, opened her drawer, tipped the utensils into it willy-nilly, and slammed it shut. Rubbing her hands together, she said, "Time savings over a lifetime, at least a year."

Little did she know back then how badly her amortization had been off.

Oliver was dead and she would be the day after tomorrow.

Opal winced.

Fucking dark.

There was one thing left to do; she had to face it.

Opal sat in front of the fireplace with a pen and paper when Carol circled and laid between her legs commanding attention. The top of her head was as soft as a rose petal but smelled of sleepy dog and fresh hay.

She texted Ruby, Luna, and Urse: *Darlings, it's time. See you Friday. I feel pretty good, no need for my friend-sitters tonight.*

Swallowing hard, Opal pushed herself from the floor to inspect her new window wall in the bedroom. Carol followed behind her and stopped at a noise. Only Carol's eyes moved, trying to suss out the sound.

Ding dong.

Opal peeked from behind the curtains. *Tess Hokanson.* She sighed and opened the door.

"Sorry to drop in unannounced." Tess's crooked tooth peeped out from her smile. Her dark bob swung at the collar of a white button down tucked at her minuscule waist with a belt buckle of a cowboy on a bucking bronco holding a hat above his head.

Tess wrinkled her nose.

"I always have time for you." Opal's eyes drifted out the window. "Well, maybe not all the time in the world—"

"You have the entire lifespan of a dragonfly. I'd say that's something," Tess offered. Again with the nose flinch. "Opal, something smells...funny."

"Yeah. I think it's a dead squirrel."

"If I had a nickel." Tess smiled.

"Oat milk latte?" Opal offered and ushered Tess into the kitchen, shoes still on.

"Perfect," Tess said.

She sat at the same seat as her last visit, placing her bulky messenger bag on the kitchen counter next to a brass salt grinder as Opal fixed her coffee.

I wonder what's in the bag.

After the beans were ground, Opal touched the digital picture of a coffee cup with a swirl on the machine face.

"What's on your mind, Tess?" She slid the latte across the counter.

"Thanks. I'm not sure how to start."

That got Opal's attention. Right up there with *I think it's black mold.*

"I want you to know I have no ulterior motives or such, but I think I'm involved in one capacity or another with your friends." Tess's face scrunched.

Opal fought back a smile.

I hoped they'd figure it out after I died, but here we are.

"What do you mean?"

Tess wrapped her long fingers through the mug's handle, her index finger's gold ring tinged and she sipped her coffee. Her eyes shut momentarily.

"Well, here goes. I think I bought my car from Urse's brother Johnny in the late eighties." She pointed up for *one.* "Second, I was at the hospital in Duluth when Ruby's wrists were broken." Fingers flashed *two.* "As far as Luna goes, I'm not sure of the connection other than my brother Abner died in New Orleans where Luna was from. I'm starting to feel weird about it, like I'm being set up or something. I just don't get it." Tess's hands quivered as she lifted her drink. She set it down and placed her hands flat on the countertop. "Am I losing it?"

"Yes, you are losing it." Opal mocked seriousness before smiling and put her cold hands over Tess's damp ones. "In all honesty, I thought you would all figure out the connections after I was dirt-napping it."

Sitting back, Tess tapped her crooked tooth, appearing to be thinking.

"There's no explanation—no nefarious reason, it's just serendipity. You are supposed to be my replacement when I'm gone. As for Luna, I think there's a connection." Opal softened. "Luna once told me a story from her grandmother's fire walking show, of a sweet man dying in front of her when she was little. I have a sinking feeling that man may have been your brother."

Tess covered her mouth with her hand and spoke. "I'm freaked out. Why would you do this?"

Flinching, Opal said, "That's the point, no one *did* anything. It's just the way the world put us together."

"Are you looking for money?" Tess blurted.

Opal jerked back, spread her hands wide, and looked around. "What? Oh, come on. If anything, your net worth is probably nowhere near where we all are. Jezus, Tess, take your time, but be careful. I have exactly two feelings left."

"My net worth is just fine, thank you, and it really, really smells in here." She crossed her arms over her chest stiffly.

She pinched the bridge of her nose. "Okay, let's slow down. I'm not feeling great and had no idea you wouldn't find all of this an intentional gift from the freaking universe or some shit."

With widening eyes, Tess said, "Oh, right, as if my dead-brother-Luna-connection is a big, fat gift from the universe. Not to mention the legal ramifications of an assisted suicide. Are you out to get me? Just say it."

Dammit. She had promised herself the anger wouldn't resurface before she died.

But.

"Yeah, Tess. You're on to me. You are so fucking important, my friends and I devised a big plan to steal all your money. For what? Oh, haven't thought ahead on that? Did I mention I received a six-million-dollar settlement when my parents died? Faulty brake pads and my dead parents hooked me up for life, Tess, so, yeah, poor fucking you and your piddly 401K."

Her bottom lip began to quiver and she burst into tears.

"Boo fucking hoo, Tess. Did I also mention the car accident was all my fault? Yeah, all my fault and I've kept that secret my whole life. That and the six million of course, so there's an added layer of guilt. But what now? I'm after your piddly nursing money? Be realistic." Opal's voice raised to alarm Carol who stood next to her.

"I'm sorry, I'm sorry…" Tess covered her ears and began to rock back and forth.

Opal shoved Carol. "Go!" she screamed at the dog. Turning her head, she threw up and slid to the floor next to the sick, rumpled.

As hard as I try, I can't control this rage. This is what giving up looks like.

The hum of the refrigerator coated them.

With a watercolor mascara line seeping into the white fabric of her sleeve, Tess found two dish towels and ran them under warm water then handed one to Opal.

"*Sorry* isn't the right word, but it's also the only word," Tess said.

The cream towel turned yellowy green as Tess sopped up the mess.

Speaking through the damp towel, Opal balanced her elbows on her lifted knees.

"The only one who should be sorry is me." The towel's warmth blended with the heat from her tears. "The truth is, I'm mean and selfish and deserve to die."

"Oh, Opal, you can't believe that—it's not framed in reality," Tess said. She put her arm around her, their backs pressed against the kitchen wall. Carol sniffed at the towel with the barf. They laughed as Opal rubbed under her collar.

"Sorry, pup." Carol clunked down next to Opal.

"What happened with your parents?" Tess asked. "Wait, let me get my latte. Want water?"

Opal nodded.

Tess filled a gold-rimmed tumbler, grabbed her own drink, and passed them to Opal. She went to the sectional and dragged a blanket and couch pillows back to their spot on the floor.

"Thank you."

"Now," she said, smoothing the blanket to rid it of lumps and wrinkles. "Your parents?"

Opal couldn't bear to look at Tess, but knew it was time to come clean. She put her hand on Carol's back for steadiness and began.

This is all that's left.

"I was walking home from first grade, all happy that my artwork won a contest to be on the Christmas program cover. My family and I lived in a small red house on a hill with a dirt road circling our property so you could see through the woods when someone would drive up. If you dashed a shortcut, you could jump in front of cars and scare them." Opal paused though her heartbeat sped up.

You can do it. Don't stop now.

"My mom and dad told me not to throw things at cars. I had gotten in so much trouble terrifying the neighbors. It was hilarious at the time. But I had my winning drawing in my backpack and couldn't wait to show them, so I sprinted through the shortcut with just enough time to form a few snowballs. I remember being giddy right before I aimed for my mom and dad's car. I figured if I hit the middle of the windshield, they'd still be able to see."

Her hands shook as she sipped the water. Carol rested her chin on Opal's blanketed leg.

"When my snowball hit the car, it did a fishtail, reminding me of those red paper fish that squiggled in our palms as kids."

In Opal's peripheral vision, she saw Tess nodding.

"Their car skidded on an ice patch and flipped twice when a tire caught a patch of dirt. I bolted toward them. No one wore seatbelts in the '70s. Why didn't we all just fucking wear seatbelts?" Tears spilled down her tired face. "My mom's head was squished; blood trickled from her eyes and nose. She looked like my Nixon Halloween mask I had forgotten on the radiator in my room." Opal tried to lighten the mood. "I mean her hair was better, but you know."

Tess didn't laugh.

Opal sipped her glass of water as if it provided courage.

"My dad was still alive. I remember him as a little quirky, he always had a dumb joke at the ready but he wasn't being funny. I knew it was well past bad. He said, 'Opal, honey, you throw like your old man, I'm proud...you.'

"I said, 'Dad, Dad, Dad, I'm sorry...'

"I could hear distant sirens growing louder and he said, 'No time for that.' Blood gurgled and then he said, 'Aim big, go for love...*aim...*'

"My ear was right by his mouth to hear—he smelled like a bucket of old nails. He whispered, 'Love you, Ope.'"

Tess bit her bottom lip and shook her head.

"Then he died. They just up and died, leaving me there alone. They're stuck in that spot forever in my mind, cold and bloody and melty. They say memories fade, but it's a filthy lie. They didn't want to go. They left too early, just like I will."

Tess squeezed her shoulder. "Children aren't equipped to see that. No one is, really."

"When the police arrived, I had already crawled into the back seat. They assumed I was in the car the whole time. But because I'm selfish and didn't want to get in trouble, I lied. I've been lying ever since. Truth be told, I've been angry at having to lie."

There it was, how could she have missed the square root of her life's anger?

Opal leaned her head against the wall.

"The only one who noticed anything was my Grandpa Henry. He asked about my footprints in the snow. He was no dummy. I just handed him my school drawing. He carried me home through the snow and smelled like cold wool, birch trees, and aftershave—funny what sticks out. Anyway, it turned out their brake pads were garbage and it went to court. I know the truth, though. It was my fucking snowball that did them in. My grandpa told me to keep it all secret."

A floor vent expelled warm air, puffing Carol's fur up.

"Opal, no," Tess started. "Feelings aren't facts. How about another truth? You were a kid, and kids do crazy shit. I highly doubt you wanted it to turn out that way. So, the ramifications didn't match the intention of what happened. It's that simple. It's horrific and unfair, but remember what your dad said—aim for love. Well, I bet he was talking about yourself, too.'"

"Wow," Opal said, eyes up.

"Yeah, wow."

"No, look." Opal pointed into her pewter cooking hood.

Tess's eyes followed her finger. The dead squirrel slumped over a metal bar above the range, all patchy fur and stiff curves with surprised, dead eyes.

"It's rotten."

"It certainly is."

Chapter Thirty-Nine

Ruby

Pulling her tangled bed sheets to her chin as she rolled over, Ruby's phone fell to her pillow. "Oops, Johnny? Still there?" she asked.

"No getting rid of me now—or ever. Listen, it's 4 a.m. Let's get married and have a bunch of stubborn kids that look like you," Johnny said.

Caffeinated butterflies filled Ruby's stomach.

"Don't you think we should fool around first?" she asked playfully.

Johnny's deep voice cracked. "Right, we should have sex on the way to get our marriage certificate tomorrow. I'll put rose petals in the back of my car for top tier romance. I like how you think."

"Johnny?"

"Ruby?"

She didn't want to ruin the mood but had to address it.

"You know about Opal, don't you?" She held her breath. Ruby couldn't imagine Urse keeping a secret of that magnitude from him.

A few painful moments passed.

"Yeah, I know, but don't," he said.

Ruby wiped tears on her silk pillowcase that Daytime Mom swore prevented wrinkles and flat hair.

"I need to help her without you, alright?" Ruby said.

"But—"

"I know you're a pain eraser, but I have to feel this fully." She turned her electric blanket down to a seven. "Without making a break for it or...anything else."

The phone went quiet.

"Johnny?"

"It's getting late, I better let you go," Johnny said.

"'night?" Ruby's hands moved the sign alphabet.

"'night."

The call ended.

What did I do to piss him off? The only time she had seen Johnny mad was in Chicago, when he rearranged a guy's features who said something to offend her.

That was as sexy as a guy who only notices you.

Ruby dragged her covers from the bed, wrapped them around her like a cape, and opened the curtains as far as they would go. The drapes acted as a stage curtain revealing the full moon in its entirety. Silvery light filled the room. She spun the oversized bedroom chair to face the cityscape, sorted the duvet, and put her feet on the oval ottoman.

Ruby hadn't cut since the day Johnny said he loved her; she was too tired to enjoy it, anyway. *This,* this *is the tough stuff I'm supposed to fix.* She pressed the edge of a bad hangnail to feel it hurt: teeny pain, only tiny satisfaction.

"Hey, Mr. Moon," Ruby said. "What's the play? What, am I supposed to just feel miserable with no release and nothing to look forward to? Do I have to kill my best friend and navigate Johnny eventually leaving me—of everyone leaving?"

All without cutting?

She couldn't bring herself to speak about that to the moon; it seemed disrespectful to the beauty of nature.

"Hey, Siri, give me a sign."

Her home system's robotic voice came to life. "A stop sign is a regulatory sign: a traffic control device that warns drivers to slow down and prepare to stop.”

Ruby tilted her head at the moon and laughed.

She went back to bed, decided to *stop worrying,* and fell asleep.

The next morning—after three hours of sleep—her phone buzzed.

“Hello?”

“Open up,” Johnny said.

With breath smelling like the bottom of a birdcage, Ruby rubbed tooth-paste on her tongue and rushed to open the door.

Johnny wore gray sweatpants, a fitted T-shirt, and a sweater, like the guy in that cult movie with the Polish last name.

“What’s your position on morning sex so we can get married?”

She wrapped her arms around his neck. “I was worried you were mad at me.”

“Why? What did you do to me?”

He tilted her chin up to look at her. “You are my favorite person. I can’t believe I get to be with you, Ruby, so just stop and feel good.”

Just stop.

Ruby smiled. “I’m pro morning sex. But I have to show you something.”

“Welly, well, well.” He wiggled his eyebrows. “Seeing as though you are begging me, how can I say no?”

Ruby opened her bathrobe; it slid from her shoulders to the floor re-vealing her nude. Her eyes normally low, lifted to meet his, and she edged her chin up. One leg crossed over hiding her crotch.

Johnny clutched his chest. “If I don’t have a heart attack now, I never will.”

He threw her over his shoulder and headed to the bedroom, she squealed in laughter when he pinched her butt. Once on the bed, he peppered her face with teensy kisses. She closed her eyes, memorizing the moment.

The decades old fantasy about bedding Johnny was off track. Her hor-mones had gotten the best of her and she needed to slow down and use her words.

"Johnny, something horrible happened when I went in to get a Brazilian," she began.

He smirked. "Did they shave off the 'J' on Johnny?"

"Forget it." She scrunched up her face. "Let's just wait until it heals."

"Let me see. It can't be that bad. It's your glorious clam." He made a clam movement with his hands wiggling the tips of his fingers.

She couldn't help but laugh then covered her face and opened her legs to him.

He stiffened.

"Exactly as I imagined," he said, straight-faced.

She pulled her knees to her chest and pulled the covers up laughing as he tickled her. The laughter turned into a hug. He brushed her hair back from her face.

"You and I have a lifetime of weird crotch stuff heading our way. I love you and no vagina leprosy will change that." He kissed her full on the lips as she giggled. "Now, you stay here. That gorgeous mess needs my soft lips."

He was tender and moved slowly, a wait-for-it-hunger that made her body tingle impatiently.

"I want you to cum first," Johnny whispered. The hair on her neck rose like her nipples. "From now on."

And she did.

Johnny inched back to the top of the bed and pretended to smoke.

"I wish we could stay here forever," Ruby whispered.

Johnny pushed her sweaty hair from her cheek. She nuzzled into his neck breathing him in.

"Well, we have the 'forever' down pat," he said.

"Forever." She basked in the word. *Forever.* Which reminded her. "Hey, what exactly do you know about Opal's 'ask'?"

He put down his fake cigarette and lifted the sheet. "Are you wearing a wire?"

She pushed him and wrapped her smooth leg around his hairy one.

"I'm serious."

"I know Opal is really sick and wants her friends to help her..."

Ruby frowned.

"...to the next adventure," he finished. Johnny smoothed his bushy blond eyebrows.

"How is Urse doing?"

"Oh, you know her," Johnny said.

"That's why I'm asking."

Johnny sat up. "Between you, Luna, and I, Urse will get through it. Now that her latest scrub husband is gone, she stands a chance at happiness."

Ruby fiddled with the friendship bracelet she wore every day for over forty years.

"Do we have enough time to get married before Opal..." He trailed off staring at the ceiling.

"We could try, but..." She gulped hard. "...we meet in a few days."

Johnny's arms tightened around her, and she kissed his fingers.

Worry ushered them to sleep.

Chapter Forty

Urse

After the excitement of the Wax On Wax Off studio caper the day before, Urse's thoughts drifted, as they often did, to Andy. Today was the day. Jim should have information about him.

I hope I don't ruin my one memory of love.

She clicked her remote to a morning news show. "Up next: do you see yourself as others do? Deep dive into thought distortion after our commercial break," the anchor said.

Urse pulled her hair into a high, sloppy bun, and cleaned up the mascara smudges under her puffy eyes. She hadn't intended on finishing the bottle of Malbec last night. Now, her dry skin and digestive system were getting their say on the decision.

I need to reel in my drinking.

She washed an Adderall down with her lukewarm coffee and headed into the office.

Once at work, Urse headed up the stairs of her office building, pausing to admire the hand-blown glass railing. Somewhere along the way, she stopped gloating about the design everyone told her was impossible to pull off. It was her idea to surround it in resin and use hidden titanium screws so the art glass wasn't compromised. Big-brained people were always telling her and Johnny, "no." It annoyed Urse more than Johnny, who would shrug his shoulders and say, "Who cares if they think you're dumb? We are spending *their* dream moola."

At the top of the grand stairs, the sight of Jim in his seemingly starched button down interrupted her thoughts.

"Morning."

He looked up from his computer, smiling at first, then said, "What happened? You look like wet cheese."

Urse pinched the bridge of her nose. "Schedule a time for me to fire you."

Leaning across his desk, "Can we have our..." He looked both ways to make sure no one was around, and whispered, "...secret meeting early?"

Urse handed him her coat. "Coffee?"

"Already on your desk."

"I better get something to eat—"

"You're killing me. Your banana is next to your coffee, the fireplace is on, and all scheduled appointments are slotted." He tapped quickly. "And I just took the liberty of booking you a facial at the Face Founderie after noticing your limp skin. You're welcome. Once they get you fixed up, we'll get you into the Hive on Snelling and Selby. They'll find you a new house after..." He trailed off. "Well, let's just say fresh starts are the new crying in the shower."

Urse bit her bottom lip, slightly uncomfortable with the kindness. *Fresh starts.*

Jim clutched his computer to his chest and sat at his usual spot across from Urse in her office.

She twisted her skirt so the zipper lined up before sitting down and rolled her chair in as far as it could go. "Okay, give it to me straight."

"Such an ugly word. I feel a hostile work environment complaint coming on," Jim teased.

Even in jest she despised those words. She rolled her index finger for him to get on with it.

"Andy lives in Wayzata, is straight, and in 1999, published an ad in the

City Pages' 'Missed Connections' section looking for—are you ready?" Jim put his open hand in front of his face like a drunk mime and said, "Urse from the Chewed Finger Festival," then produced an old newspaper clipping. He read, "Urse, if you're out there, we have unfinished business. Please, call me, I can't stop thinking about you."

Jim's phone beeped, interrupting her racing thoughts.

"Are you recording?" Urse shook her head and pointed him out the door. "Shut that thing off, and thank…" She could barely speak. "…you, thank you."

He smiled broadly, as she pushed his bony back out the door.

Her knees wobbled as she entered her office bathroom. Flipping the water spigot afforded her cover so she could cry. A bottom of a sob. Or maybe it was the Adderall. Nonetheless, Andy had tried looking for her, something not even her dad had done.

Dabbing her face with a warm washcloth that smelled faintly of rosewater, Urse returned to her desk and opened the dossier. Attached to the inside cover was a picture of a portly man smiling in a Norwegian sweater with silver hooks across the chest. She put her cheaters on. There was a thick scar traversing his chin and crinkles at the corners of his eyes. He had a good head shape for baldness and looked as if he would laugh at any given time.

That's my Andy.

She read the file; it appeared he worked as a business consultant for a large operation in downtown Minneapolis. He specialized in transitioning companies through acquisitions and new corporate regimes. All good on paper. On the back page of the folder was her assistant's printing, which read, "Jim approved. What are you waiting for?" and an email address.

She did a double take to the photo.

Was Andy wearing lipstick?

With a swirling stomach she opened her laptop.

Here goes nothing.

Dear Andy,

Fuck it.

I drink too much, swear too much, and work too much. I love the wrong men and can be bossy. I love to-go condiments though I have money and usually get my way through sheer stubbornness. I want to be a better person but don't know how. I've failed miserably at love largely, I suspect, because I compare them to you. BUT I love hard and am loyal. I know it's crazy, but if you are half the man I met in the woods so many years ago, well, let's go for it.

Gulp.

P.S. If this is too insane of an email, I'll deny I wrote it.

Click. Send.

Urse sat down, putting her hands over her eyes, and laughed.

What have I done? That was a straight up crazy bitch email. But if he can't handle the bluntness, he won't want me anyway. Plus, I don't want another guy who will try to break my spirit and then hate me when I'm broken.

Refresh, refresh, refresh...

No response. With each passing hour and irrelevant email, her embarrassment grew.

I should've known better. The world only wants strong women when the chips are down, when messes need cleaning, when things need righting. Until then, they erode our confidence and focus on taking us down a notch.

Baloop.

Never mind.

An email from Andy.

Chapter Forty-One

Luna

The smell of banana bread filled Luna's kitchen. It was the scent of a loving home. She had used half the recipe's sugar, pumped up the almond extract, and added oats for a sort of healthy breakfast.

As Luna sat with legs crossed at the kitchen island, Arthur shuffled toward her, rubbing the sleep from his eyes, and kissed her cheek. "Morning, Mr. America," she said.

Moving to the French press, he looked up. "Want a top off?"

"No, I'm good. I've already had two cups, did yoga, and dusted the plants. I'm ready for the day."

Arthur pressed the coffee plunger. Grounds floated to the top.

"You pressed too fast." Luna removed the lid and started over. She poured coffee into his favorite green mug and said, "Here you go, Boo Boo."

He smiled.

It was time to tell him the bare minimum about Opal. Enough to satisfy his need for her to share while not breaking the promise to Opal to keep the friendly murder quiet.

"Remember that time you wanted me to tell you everything?" She folded the linen into an origami rose, pressed down the edges and set it by his mug.

She moved slightly so her dark gray silk bathrobe opened to allow him a peep.

Arthur eyed her suspiciously. "Oh, I know what you're doing. Put that nip back in your robe until after I hear what you're up to."

Smirking, Luna tightened her robe and lifted a shoulder. "Who me? I'd never."

She plated a piece of banana bread and slid it toward him. It was his favorite, but he didn't budge.

Luna scooted her chair closer and began, "You know I've never broken a promise, right?"

He nodded and bit the corner of his lip.

She spoke softly. "First off, there's nothing to be done—"

"Is our baby okay?" he whispered.

He doesn't need to know about the tarot card death forecast.

"So far, so good."

Arthur's posture softened.

Luna pushed the banana bread forward again. "Eat."

He shook his head. "Just say it, Lune."

"You can't say anything to anyone. Promise?"

"I don't like this. Tell me already."

The conversation was too pressurized; she had to be blunt.

"Opal is really sick. You can't tell your family, either."

His eyes scanned her face. "She fakes shit all the time—"

"No, like pancreatic-cancer sick."

Arthur sat back in his chair, palm on forehead.

"Bloody hell. Wait. Why is it a big secret? We can all help in some way or another."

Luna steadied herself for the lie. With her elbow on the counter, she spoke through her fingers. "I guess she doesn't want anyone feeling sorry for her."

He narrowed his eyes. "Naw." He searched her face. "You aren't being honest—you always cover your mouth before a fib."

Luna reached for his hand. He jerked it back.

"I'm telling you everything I can. You have no right pressing me when I'm already blurring the lines ethically. I am only telling you because it means something to you. If it were up to me, I'd handle it, and then tell you."

"Handle *what*?" Arthur's forehead vein popped out.

I had to marry a smart guy.

Luna sighed. "The news."

He squeezed her hand. "Okay. Thank you for telling me as much as you did. I need to go for a run, okay?" Arthur kissed her and left with the car keys, dressed in sweats and slides. No coat, water bottle, or running shoes.

That can't be good. He's not acting like Opal's faking it.

She lifted her phone from the kitchen charger, and texted Ruby for listening, Urse for courage.

Luna: *Lunch later?*

Ruby: *Sounds good, where and when?*

Urse: *Luna's at 1130, I'll grab poke bowls*

She texted Arthur: *Thought you should know Urse invited herself and Ruby over for lunch.*

Luna washed her coffee mug, dried the sink, and noticed Arthur's banana bread. She wrapped Arthur's plate in a beeswax cover and jumped into the shower. She broke out the earth-friendly foundation for light fair skin, and mascara named, creatively, "Noir." She harrumphed.

It had been ages since applying her own makeup. At photoshoots, the makeup artists photographed her for their own social media afterwards. When her face was dressed up, the guilt kicked in, as if it were somehow bragging. Other than on shoots, the only time she felt comfortable in her looks were with her friends and Arthur. She slipped on an emerald green dress, forgiving in the midsection for a baby. It was too early to show, but she wanted to inspire her body to last longer during this pregnancy.

Setting the table with big bowls and chopsticks, she put linen napkins in their correct place and filled water glasses.

Ding dong.

Urse and Ruby hurried in.

"I can't contain myself," Urse said.

Luna's eyebrows raised and she dipped her head, intrigued.

"Me, too, but you go first," Ruby said. The women slid off their shoes, lined them up by the mat, and hurried to the kitchen.

Luna took the cardboard-colored bags with their food from Urse and unwrapped the bowls. She put a plate over the top, flipped it, then once more, landing the poke in prettier bowls with the top layer intact.

"Nice work," Urse said.

Ruby and Luna exchanged quizzical looks.

"Let's eat and talk," Ruby said.

Urse lifted up a bowl. "New?"

"Out with it," Luna said. "You are seldom so saccharine."

Ruby offered Luna her hand and they slid fingers in agreement, smiling.

"Okay, okay. I found Andy."

Luna jumped from her seat. "You didn't!"

"I did. Want to see a pic?" Urse asked.

"Right now!" Ruby said.

Luna grabbed it from Urse and they huddled over it. She started, "He's good looking, thank—"

"Is he wearing lipstick?" Ruby interrupted.

Luna pulled the photo closer to her eyes and looked at Urse, trying not to laugh.

"Fuck. I was hoping it was just my interpretation," Urse said.

"I *interpret* he's wearing Chanel Rouge Coco," Ruby said.

They began to laugh.

"Seems confident anyway. That shade really plays up his beard," Ruby said.

More laughter, until they settled.

"If you can eek out any love in this world, Ms. Urse, go for it. The lipstick only matters if he isn't good to you," Luna offered.

Urse smiled. "I know. I already emailed him."

"Killing me! She buried the lead. What did you say?" Luna motioned her to talk.

Urse picked up an edamame bean with her chopsticks and circled it midair toward Luna.

"It is a pretty great start," Urse teased.

Ruby laughed. "What happened?"

Urse put her chopsticks down and cracked her knuckles. "We meet at Baldamar Steakhouse next week."

"That is so exciting! Nice choice, too. Great lighting. Get the chimichurri shrimp. Wait, no, a ribeye, and the gelato—"

"Still pregnant, I see," Ruby beamed.

"I can't wait to tell Opal. I called earlier but she was too sleepy to talk." She sighed. "Now, Ruby. What's your news?" Urse dug into her bowl, moving the pickled ginger to the side.

Luna eyed her lunch. "Chicken? That's weird."

"Babies don't love ahi from what I understand," Urse said.

"Who are you? My God, I'm not used to how nice you're being," Luna said.

"She's more 'behind the scenes' nice," Ruby said. "Now, without further ado, I'm pleased to announce, Johnny and I have sealed the deal, so to say."

Urse frowned, put a hand to her chest, and fake gagged.

"Go on," Luna said. "Never mind her."

Ruby looked at Urse. "I kiss and tell normally, but, well, telling his sister is gross even to me. So, I'll rate him a 9.8."

"He's so hot," Luna confessed.

"Someone change the subject," Urse said. She pushed her food away.

"How's this for changing the subject? I told Arthur that Opal was sick. Nothing else, just that she has cancer and it's serious."

Urse nodded.

"You had to, simple as that," Ruby said. "He doesn't know about the spiders, et cetera, does he?"

"Oh God, no. Reminds me. Will you two sneak the spiders to Opal's for me? I'm not supposed to lift heavy things and Arthur's unaware of our *hidden guests.*"

Luna had covered the terrarium in red material so as to not see the spiders. While she had worked through her fear of them in counseling sessions, she remained scared enough to avoid them.

"Sure. Let's do it now while Arthur's not here," Ruby said.

Urse stood and smoothed her crepe pants. "Let's do it."

Luna enjoyed watching people of the same height lift things. It made more sense than one poor bastard struggling while the other was frustrated. Ruby and Urse lifted, moved, and finessed corners in harmony.

"Let me get the door." Luna ran ahead of the moving terrarium and propped open the door turning to watch the women work.

"Uh, Luna," Urse said in a hushed voice.

She turned to see Arthur standing behind her.

Chapter Forty-Two

Opal

The Minnesota day smelled of old dirty leaves and cold mud. The frigid air wheezed through Opal's taxed lungs, making them feel rigid.

She threw on her favorite cashmere leggings and cream woolen sweater, and zipped up her floor length down vest that she assumed made her look like a russet. Her size six wide feet slid into her boots with ease—no laces, tongues, or tension to grapple with—and headed for the gazebo. Carol chased squirrels to the property edge.

Once Opal confessed the details of her parents' death, the world turned softer. The harsh twisting stomach pain lessened and the emotional yoke disappeared.

She would be dead on Friday, and for the first time in her life, Opal wasn't pissed off.

Why it took me this long to forgive myself, I will never know.

Her newfound self-acceptance sunk in and expanded, forcing the anger and self-loathing to find another sucker to trifle with.

The door to the gazebo was stuck. She kicked the base to jostle it open, so Carol and she could sit where decades worth of truths, tears, and cackles were shared. The fear of the last happy hour had evaporated. Now, it was just a wooden building with screens, cobwebs, and a dining set. She pulled the edge of the table to roll her chair in when her fingers felt the message Snookie Bubotz had taped under the edge.

"Don't do it. There's still time. Let me be there."

She sighed. *There is no more time.* Opal flipped the note over.

Bubotz had written: "Stubborn! You never listen."

The note continued:

"Your requested info: Ruby hasn't cut in weeks. Urse has an Adderall problem but her life-long obsession, Andy, is a good lipstick-wearing dude. Luna's still pregnant and the blueberry sauce you made for Arthur is ready for shipment. I delivered the mail Shawn left in your BBQ and his Christmas card has an unnaturally large tip ready for the holidays. Taylor has enough money to open her own salon, and Naughty Sebastian is onboard with any legalities that may arise. As for Tess Hokanson, she is a good egg. I'll see to it the group doesn't ostracize her—nothing to worry about. The other donations and gifts will be handled. As for me, I can't express how much your endowment means. It is going to change a lot of lives, Opal. I am proud to call you my friend. If this is the last time I hear from you, know you are loved and I will search you out in the afterlife."

She sat with the note in her lap swallowing hard at the sentiment.

They are better than when I found them.

Only one thing left.

Dying.

It's over. Testing them is ugly, anyway.

Chapter Forty-Three

Luna

"What's up, ladies?" Arthur's voice called out behind Luna.

Luna jumped. "You scared me. I thought you'd be back later."

The terrarium—filled with brown recluse—hung precariously between Ruby and Urse.

Arthur glanced at the women suspiciously. "Okay, what's going on?"

He looked crumpled. His one big complaint had been realized. He stood, the odd man out, always the last to know.

I can't keep this up.

"Arthur, have a seat while I call your cousin," Luna said.

Ruby shot Urse a look, and they set the terrarium on the floor. "We can come back," Ruby said.

"No. We need to stick together," Luna said.

"You're making me nervous. Did I do something?" Arthur asked.

Luna squeezed his arm. "No, honey. You've been nothing but great."

Urse, Ruby, and Arthur followed Luna into the kitchen where she put a tea kettle on and pulled out her fancy cups with gold rims. Her phone sat face up on the counter island.

"Hello?" Opal answered.

"Hey, Ope, I've got you on speaker. Urse, Ruby, and Arthur are all here."

A pause.

"Okayyy."

"Please tell your cousin what's going on. I'm not comfortable keeping it from him any longer."

"Arthur, pick up the phone. I want to talk to you privately."

Time to fess up.

He reached for the phone, took it off speaker, and went into the living room, leaving the women in silence.

The tea kettle whistled. Luna pulled out a log of cookie dough from the freezer, sliced even chunks, and popped a batch of the cayenne shortbread into the oven. Urse put her ear to the door.

"Get back here. We're in enough trouble," Ruby scolded Urse.

She raised her shoulders sheepishly. "Wanted to get the jump on what we are in for."

Luna poured hot water into the contraption filled with loose leaf jasmine tea to steep. After rotating the cookie sheet, she set the tea over their cups and filled them, debris free. A timer beeped, and Luna pulled the brown-edged cookies from the oven and slid them onto a cooling rack.

"What do you think Opal is telling him?" Urse asked.

Luna cradled her head in her oven mitts. "I'm so tired of thinking about it, part of me wishes she would just, you know, *fade out* on her own before this...this..."

Urse grimaced but nodded. Ruby stopped stirring her tea as Arthur walked in.

He popped a shortbread into his mouth and pulled up a seat.

"I wish I didn't know."

Ruby went back to stirring her tea without making a noise with the spoon.

Luna started to laugh in a way that people laugh at a funeral. *Uncomfortable, unstable. All the "un" words.*

Ruby poured Arthur a cup of tea and slid it toward him as Urse nibbled at a cookie.

He exhaled, scratched his scruff, and said, "Pop your trunk, I'll get that thing moved for you."

Urse grabbed her car keys and pointed the fob toward the window.

Bahleep bleep.

The trunk glided open. Arthur moved the terrarium and returned to the women.

"I hope you all know what you are doing. The possibility of imprisonment isn't theoretical, you know? Your charm after bad behavior won't get you out of assisted suicide charges, ladies, and this would be a lose-everything situation." He squished his face and rubbed his eyes and hugged Luna. "I love you, but *think*."

The door closed behind him leaving them alone to be scared.

The heat kicked on noisily.

"He's right, but it's something I have to do," Ruby said.

Luna refilled their empty teacups.

Urse warmed her hands on the china and smelled the tea for the fourth time. "It's less hypothetical now. I've thought about it ten ways 'til Sunday. I'll do my part." She ran her fingers over an embroidered purple flower on her napkin.

I bet these violets aren't worried about dead babies and jail time.

"Right," Luna said. "Stay as long as you want. I'm a bit queasy and need to lie down. I'll see you at Opal's on Friday."

Urse and Ruby washed the teacups and cookie sheets and wiped down the counter making sure there weren't any crumbs.

Chapter Forty-Four

Ruby

Ruby held the door for a wrinkled woman with a stoop approaching the donut hut.

The woman smiled her thanks and tilted her head. "Should I know you?" she asked with a creaky voice reserved for nursing homes.

Ruby squinted, eyeing the face under the floral scarf tied under her chin. She stomped her foot on the carpet of the bakery. "Snookie Bubotz! You gorgeous lunatic."

The women clung to one another, Ruby's chin on the top of Snookie's head. A man behind them said, "Beep, beep" and they moved in tiny steps to the side, still embracing.

Ruby tapped her back. "Come on, let me buy you one of those eggy French donuts you like."

"After all these years, you know your real beauty comes from those small remembrances."

"Next," the fluffy counter girl with an angelic face squawked.

"May I get a dozen assorted? Make sure there's a few of these guys in the box," Ruby's finger hovered around the ones Snookie liked. "And two black teas, please."

They commandeered a table near the window overlooking the strip mall parking lot. The women's smiles faded into a sentimental knowing.

"So...Opal?" Snookie began.

Ruby nodded and squished her lips to the side of her face, figuring if she spoke, the tears would surface.

"I'm not supposed to say, but she asked me to make sure you will all be okay after she's..." Snookie trailed off.

"Unrealistic." Ruby poured a stevia into her tea and stirred without sound.

Snookie tipped a black lidded sugar container from the table into her tea and stirred loudly with her spoon. "Are you ready for the..." She looked around. "...act?"

The bakery, smelling of sugar and warmth, suddenly turned quiet. Only the wall of kid's donut drawings seemed noisy.

"Yes."

"Please don't mention our visit to Ope. I want you, Urse, and Luna to know, I'm with all of you, though I need to be behind the scenes to help because the situation is...sticky."

"That makes me feel a bit safer."

Snookie polished off her donut and leaned back. "So, Johnny, huh?"

"Weird, right?"

Squishing the crumbs on the table into her napkin, Snookie said, "Hell, no. I asked him a decade ago what was taking him so long, and he said, 'What's the rush? I'm in love with her.'"

Ruby's smile broadened. "He did?"

"I think he was afraid of you hurting yourself."

She frowned. "I don't do that anymore."

"Oh, I know, sweet friend. Sadly, I'm familiar with the attraction of the act. But cold turkey is just that—a bland, dry, offering that no one likes."

"Oh, I get it. Opal wants to make sure I stop."

"Something like that."

Ruby tapped her cell to her calendar and faced it toward Snookie.

It read: *10 a.m. Thursday Cut and Burn Class* alongside a note that said: "Freaking goodie."

Snookie laughed. "Cool. If anything goes wrong on Opal's big Friday, make sure you and the others deny everything. No matter what anyone says, deny, deny, and what?" Snookie put her hand out palm up.

"Deny."

"Good looking *and* smart." Snookie began cleaning up their table.

"I assume it'll be a while before we see you again?"

Snookie untied her scarf and tied it tighter, presumably over a wig. "Not necessarily. If it goes as planned, I'll see you soon. I'm excited to get to know Tess Hokanson."

"Me, too, I guess. Though you, Urse and Luna are all the friends I need."

"While that may be true, Opal has confided in her something she has yet to tell anyone else."

No way. She tells me everything.

Before Ruby could respond, Snookie stood up, hunched over, and shuffled out of the bakery with her cane.

On the table was a note on a white napkin.

Love you and deny.

Chapter Forty-Five

Urse

Urse moved her outfit for Opal's funeral to the end of the closet and slid the clothes back and forth on the rack. Three dresses fell off their hangers to the floor. Irritated, she rehung them and continued grumbling about not having anything to wear. Johnny had once said to her, "Between the trailer we came from and your foul mouth, people expect you to dress like a Grand Marais hooker. It unnerves people when you show up looking all respectable. You, my freakish sister, are a dangerous dresser."

"Does Grand Marais have hookers?" Urse had asked.

Johnny had rolled his eyes. "You are *so* naive."

Now, she'd have to rely on her "respectable" closet.

But where's the outfit for coffee with the man you met when you were sixteen and pined for your whole life? She paused. *Good thing I don't have a wedding dress.*

There was one lady to call who would know what to wear for this occasion, she had an in with the stars, tarot, and weird stuff. Can't hurt.

Luna picked up on the first ring. "What's up?"

"Hey, Lune, I need help on what the fuck I'm supposed to wear when I meet Andy."

"Velcro stripper pants?"

"Yuck, you-are-so-funny yuck. Did I tell you the weird thing that happened when Andy's email popped up?"

"I love strange. Go on."

"Well, my office fireplace spontaneously lit. Jim started freaking out because the flames had cast a light on a heart shaped rose quartz."

"I've got the chills. It's the ultimate symbol of love." Sounds of pots clanked in the background.

Urse waited.

"Or anal." Luna laughed.

"You're all sorts of funny today. Seriously though, stay on the phone with me while I read you our conversation."

"I'm making fennel chicken meatballs. I've got time."

She read, "'Urse, I'm nervous but happy to report I've fantasized about meeting for years. You tell me where and when.'"

She hit print. *I'll need this for our wedding.*

"Oh my God, I'm dying. Urse, this is really happening. I need to read your tarot right now. It may even give me a direction on what color you should wear." Her cell clunked down, abandoned, her voice faint in the background. "Just a sec."

Urse blinked hard and stood up to shake her hands like pro swimmers did pre-race. For a second, fainting seemed plausible.

"I'm back," Luna said, breathless.

"I'm getting hives on my eyelids." Urse sat and put her head between her legs.

"Probably that American cheese you eat."

"Huh? One piece in three years—wait, how do you know? Ew, Johnny, no doubt."

"Shh, the cards are telling me something."

Urse reread Andy's email while she waited for the mystic art of tarot to blab.

I'm a bit iffy on his use of the word 'fantasized.'

"Are you ready? I only read three cards, but for today that's enough."

Urse gulped. "I'm ready."

"Seems you have undoubtedly met your person."

"Go on."

She could imagine Luna walking around naked with her curtains open lifting the cards to the light among all her plants.

"He has a kid and—and a, well, twin soul thingy."

"You are pulling my gorgeous leg," Urse said. "There's no way tarot cards would say that."

"They did. Now it's your job to let him be good to you. And if he's boring, that's perfect, it means love can grow without threat. The cards are saying to wear a hopeful goldfinch color."

"Is it bad that I'm pretending Opal's day isn't happening?"

The pots and pans noise ceased. "You're helping her, right?"

"I am. Wait, you are, too, right?" Nerves rose to her throat.

"Yeah, yeah, of course," Luna said a little too quickly.

"Whew, okay. Thanks for everything, talk soon."

Lying ass. I know her, she's not going to do it.

Chapter Forty-Six

Opal

The day of the euthanasia was upon them.

The stylish women filtered in through Opal's front door one by one, each with their hands full of bottles, flowers, and bags with twine handles.

Ruby wore a black leather dress with fringe from mid-thigh to knee, black ankle booties with pointed toes, and silver metal heels. Adorned in vintage Taxco jewelry that Opal had given her over the years, she smelled faintly of Lily of the Valley.

She looks as striking as she did in college.

Ruby went to the kitchen to unload. A bottle of Pomerol, a large fruit tartlet, and an unmarked cardboard box—the size used to house gold neck-laces.

"How are you holding up, Ope?" she whispered.

"As pristine as cracked glass." Opal smiled, revealing teeth whitening strips.

"Ope, are you...whitening your teeth?" Ruby asked incredulously.

"Maybe?" She peeled them off, saliva strings stretching. "I don't know why, but I wanted to look nice for today."

"You do, Opal."

She smiled.

Carol approached Ruby, leaning into her leg. Ruby petted her absent-mindedly.

Opal had small realizations since her grim diagnosis. The last time she would pet Carol, the unopened bottles of expensive wine by the pool table, the unanswered mail. How it didn't matter what she ate or if she flossed.

No "Cancer Diagnosis, Now What?" website had the tiniest of indications on how to deal with your beautiful pictures, art, and cookbooks going to seed. That everything would go on without you. Your friend's grocery lists still grow and New Year's Eves would continue. That nothing you own belongs to you, that you belong to your possessions. That our things are *using us* until the next fool takes them in. Those rotten bastards. *And to think I worked so hard for them. Unbelievable.*

The door opened again. Urse strolled in, wearing a black boatneck dress with a tight shift and attached sash—untied—in sturdy cotton. She sported textured black tights and Rick Owens platforms.

"Hi, how are we fe...fe...feeling?" Urse stuttered.

"Couldn't be better," Opal said. "Drink?"

"Yes, please." Urse watched her pour a thick cabernet into Fostoria glasses. The wine glugged into the glass.

After smelling the wine, Urse looked across the living room through the large windows to the forest. "I swear the scenery is equivalent to clear quartz," she said.

The door opened once more to reveal Luna in a short black dress and navy calfskin boots with her hair done and down. The women set down their bags, boxes, and cell phones before settling in on regular gossip.

They've dressed up for me as if to get in good with death.

A creaky, jerky, stop-and-start air hung in the room, as if they were self-conscious for the first time in their lives. They weren't making eye contact.

"Hey, this isn't about sadness, okay? It's about celebrating our friendship," Opal said.

The room fell hushed.

"Let's get this party rolling," Opal said. "Alexa, play Carol's Mix."

"Playing Carol's Mix." The AI played *Nasty Girl* by Vanity 6 through the home system. The women laughed at the choice. The song reminded Opal of the time Urse yelled, "Hey, music man, your fly is down," to a purple musician in Minneapolis. When he checked his fly, she called out, "Made you look." A week later a surprise bouquet arrived at her door with a note that read, "You fly."

Happy memories kept popping up, the tough all evaporated.

"We don't know what to expect tonight, Ope," Luna piped up.

"Business as usual, please. I'd like us all to be...the way it always has been."

"Don't need to tell me twice." Urse grabbed an expensive bottle of wine and took an exaggerated pull from the bottle.

The warmness of the alcohol loosened the crowd and blurred why they were there, to celebrate one of their own. The reminiscing, the funny stories relived, the good and bad lover reminders, the giddiness. Her circle hadn't fallen apart; they gave her what she needed—a night filled with laughter and loyalty. No one was going to be the weak gazelle, get philosophical, or start reading poems. They all knew how to read a room.

They never cease to impress.

"Let's make a toast," Opal said.

"Here's to looking up your old address," Luna chimed.

"To those who have seen us at our best and seen us at our worst and can't tell the difference." Ruby turned her eyes down, her hand on her heart, and smirked.

"Ichi-go ichi-e," Opal said. *May this specific moment in time be cherished, never to be replicated.*

The toast was almost too poignant—Opal wanted to keep it as light as a death party could be. "You know I love a good contest. How about one last game for the title, 'Ruler of the World'?"

Urse rolled up her sleeves. "Please tell me it's thumb wrestling."

Ruby stretched out her hammies and Luna followed suit, hands to hips, leaning side to side.

"Shoe kicking contest, if, that is, you ain't chicken," Opal chided.

A round of *oohs* echoed.

They grabbed their drinks and headed to the sprawling yard. The steadiness of the mature oaks grounded them.

"Alexa, play 'Chariots of Fire,'" Opal instructed.

The women lined up by a lilac tree. Ruby's tongue was off to the side in concentration. Urse balanced the top of her shoe with her big toe.

"Ready…set…kick!"

Shoes flew everywhere; Luna's landed in the tomato vines, but Ruby's went the furthest.

Ruby ran around in slow motion to the music pumping her arms toward the sky. The other women laughed.

"She has an unfair advantage with the size of her feet. I've seen her use them as skis," Luna kidded.

"I have it on good authority that she's the keynote speaker at the Foot Fetish Convention in Vegas," Urse said.

They laughed and sprawled out on the lawn.

"Alexa, play The Replacements' 'Achin' To Be.'"

They watched the sky fill in powder blues and orangey-pinks before it settled in for the night and—as expected—they were drunk enough to forget Opal's end game. Fun, the star of the show, sadness its understudy, would have to wait for a quiet Tuesday without distraction.

The last of them fell asleep around 2 a.m. camped out in the living room, long legs and arms everywhere. Opal covered them with blankets, mindful not to wake them. It was too much to bear, their sleeping faces.

Carol slept at Ruby's feet. *There's my answer.* The dog was sweet enough to choose. It's like she already knew. Tears filled her eyes at the scene. "I'll tell Oliver you're a good girl, Carol."

Opal dipped into the bathroom, grabbed a Kleenex, and headed for her spare bedroom closet where she had her travel bag.

The note she wrote for the women placed on the counter read:

Thank you all for loving me. After listening to my once angry heart, I've decided to take all your burdens and aches with me. They will be dropped off where you won't be able to find them.

Now flourish.

Love, Opal

Carol stirred and moved toward Opal, her tail wagged sleepily. The dog shadowed her like something was wrong. *I wonder if she can smell my pancreas? Dogs are so smart.*

She set her bag aside, sat on the floor, and made a v with her legs. The dog circled between her legs before she laid down. Opal hugged her as she sobbed into her soft fur. Carol didn't move, absorbing the tears and defeat now stuck to her. "I'm so sorry, my love. Ruby will take care of you, I promise." She put her mouth on her head and kissed her breathing out hot air, one last time.

"Alexa, play Mavis Staples, *You Are Not Alone*. Decrease volume three levels," she whispered.

Pushing herself off the floor, she grabbed the requested items and travel bag, and hit the garage door opener.

Opal quietly closed the car door behind her and turned the music off. Her head twisted to navigate the long driveway and she headed north. On her passenger's seat rested a jar wrapped in magenta fabric tied with a brown velvet ribbon, mushrooms with a quartz in a pouch, and a box with a syringe napping on cotton.

To see what Carol has coming up, feel free to visit www.Kristenwas.com

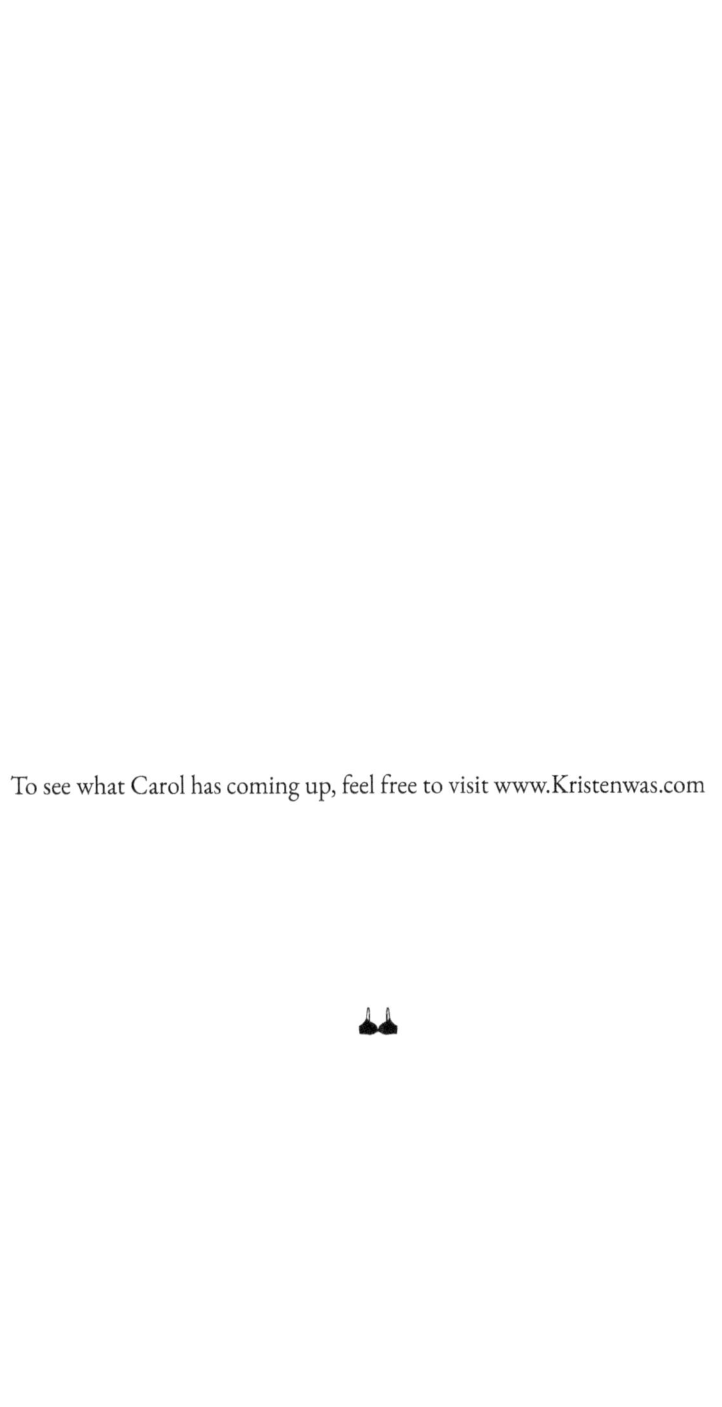

www.ingramcontent.com/pod-product-compliance
Lightning Source LLC
Chambersburg PA
CBHW071359300726
48976CB00006B/1931